THE CRYING MACHINE

Greg Chivers is a writer and television producer. For twenty years he has been making documentaries about science and history, including *What on Earth?*, Science Channel's most successful series of all time, and *NASA's Unexplained Files*, which made global news headlines. Greg is a graduate of the Curtis Brown creative writing course and the Faber Academy. *The Crying Machine* is his first novel.

THE CRYING MACHINE

MACHINE

GREG CHIVERS

HARPER
Voyager

Harper*Voyager*
An imprint of HarperCollins*Publishers* Ltd
1 London Bridge Street
London SE1 9GF

www.harpercollins.co.uk

First published by HarperCollins*Publishers* 2019
This paperback edition 2019
1

Copyright © Greg Chivers 2019

Greg Chivers asserts the moral right to
be identified as the author of this work

A catalogue record for this book is available from the British Library

ISBN: 978-0-00-830881-0

This novel is entirely a work of fiction.
The names, characters and incidents portrayed in it are
the work of the author's imagination. Any resemblance to
actual persons, living or dead, events or localities is
entirely coincidental.

Set in Minion by Palimpsest Book Production Limited,
Falkirk, Stirlingshire

Printed and bound in the UK by CPI Group (UK) Ltd, Croydon CR0 4YY

All rights reserved. No part of this publication may be
reproduced, stored in a retrieval system, or transmitted,
in any form or by any means, electronic, mechanical,
photocopying, recording or otherwise, without the prior
permission of the publishers.

MIX
Paper from
responsible sources
FSC™ C007454

This book is produced from independently certified FSC™ paper to ensure
responsible forest management.

For more information visit: www.harpercollins.co.uk/green

For Bea, Lucas and Charlotte

Nothing like this instrument is preserved elsewhere. Nothing comparable to it is known from any ancient scientific text or literary allusion. On the contrary, from all that we know of science and technology in the Hellenistic Age we should have felt that such a device could not exist.

Derek de Solla Price, 'Gears from the Greeks: The Antikythera Mechanism', *Transactions of the American Philosophical Society*

1.

Clementine

Men stare from shadowed doorways. She is too obviously alien here, even with the paleness of her skin concealed behind high collars and a tinted visor. The women are invisible in this part of the city. Two sparsely bearded teenagers in baggy *sherwal* and *thawb* unashamedly follow her. It does not occur to them she might feel threatened, that they should exercise any kind of restraint. A trapped bird of fear flutters in her chest. All the tacit understandings of gender from home, with all the protections they give, are absent here, replaced by a new labyrinth of unwritten rules she flouts with every step. She is the transgressor in this place.

The address she was given by the trafficker in Marseille should be somewhere close, but the streets are unmarked, the buildings unnumbered save for intermittent brass plaques which seem to follow no recognizable order. She shoves the paper under the nose of a fat man selling leafed oranges from crates. His eyes narrow as he takes in the curling lines of script, then his face relaxes and he stares into the middle distance, pretending not to see her. All the eyes here play the same game, following the pornography of her movement intently, becoming blind the moment she approaches.

A corner leads her into an alley that ends suddenly in a wall topped with curves of broken glass. The two stubbled faces lurch into view when she turns around. They're close enough to smell – turmeric and teenage boy beneath the faint tang of Jerusalem's dust. It's hard to tell the ages; the Arab boys grow hair younger. Their short, compact bodies warn of muscle beneath the loose fabric of their clothes. One looks away instantly in flawless imitation of his elders, but the other smiles nervously before dropping his gaze. Perhaps he has sisters.

The shorter one touches her. His hand on her cheek is damp with sweat. Her stillness should be a warning, but he is too enraptured with the discovery of blond hairs to notice. Without meeting her eyes, he fingers the stray strands behind her neck where they've come loose. Her teeth clench as she suppresses the urge to bite or kick. Violence brings attention.

'Leave me alone.' She hears her own voice struggling around the Arabic sounds, too high, too frightened. A mistake here could ruin the city for her. There are only so many places left to run.

The boy's eyes show he understands the words, but a hiss of excited breath is the only response as his eyes travel down her body. As he moves around her, something metal glints behind his ear, a flat circle barely bigger than an earring. A tiny filigree of dark lines betrays the presence of circuitry within. She raises a hand with fingers curled to touch him. He pulls back, wary, but stays still just long enough for her to brush against the thing. The burst of code that passes through her fingertip is benign, a harmless interrogative. It identifies the ear stud as a simple communication device, capable only of voice or lo-fi sub-vocalizations. It requires user authorization to accept incoming signals, but the firewall is laughably primitive.

A moment later he screams. His hand comes to his ear, fingers clawing uselessly at the lobe and cartilage. The pain comes from inside; a continuous pulse of ultra-high frequency bursts at the edge of human hearing, but still capable of stimulating the aural nerves. It will stop soon. The damage will heal quickly and leave no lasting mark that could betray her presence here.

The other one stares in confusion as his friend falls to his knees. She tries to mirror the surprise on his face, a second too late to be convincing, but he isn't looking at her, eyes fixed on the twitching figure on the floor. She presses the paper with the address into his hand.

'Where is this? Can you show me?'

A trembling hand points back down the street towards a doorway behind the orange-seller.

The fat man ignores her as she walks past. She resists the urge to brush past him or topple his crates, forcing an acknowledgement of her existence. She feels the presence of others in the room before her eyes adjust to the gloom. Faintly apple-scented shisha smoke glows in slatted light where the sun penetrates wooden shutters warped with age. Four male faces examine her, but the inspection is more human than the ruthless dissections she endured outside. Her transgression is muted within the confines of these walls. Three leather-skinned old men pass the hookah pipe between them without taking their gaze off her. The bald-headed man behind the bar is younger, on the cusp of middle age with a heavy, muscular frame only slightly turned to fat. He acknowledges her with a raise of the chin.

'I'm looking for Levi.'

He turns away and utters a stream of Arabic too fast for her to catch the syllables. A stool scrapes on the stone floor and movement reveals another figure hunched over a small circular table in the corner covered with trinkets of some kind. Hooded eyes squint to see her and she realizes she must be standing silhouetted in the light of the door. The watcher's face has the same look of indeterminate age as the teenagers who followed her, but his eyes are older, half-hidden by thick-skinned lids with heavy lashes. A too-big leather jacket fails to hide his youthful skinniness.

'Are you Levi? Can we talk here?'

'I don't know you. This is not how I do business. Maybe I don't want to talk to you.'

She uncurls the paper with the address and holds it out. He doesn't look. 'Farouz Mubarrak told me to come here. He said you could help me.' She watches for a flicker of recognition at the name but Levi's face shows nothing. 'Farouz Mubarrak . . . from Marseille?'

'I don't know anyone in Marseille. He must have heard my name from someone.'

The barman's cough doesn't quite conceal a barked laugh. For a moment, hopelessness threatens to overwhelm Clementine. The trafficker in Marseille had promised to make her disappear. The names were part of the plan. Everything was paid for. 'Can you help me? I can get money.' The lie feels obvious. If she can change the dirhams in her belt she might have enough for two nights in a hostel and a few days of street food.

'Sorry, sweetheart. In my experience, money doesn't come in off the street like a bum looking for a free lunch.'

'But . . .'

'You're pretty but I don't need a girlfriend right now. You want help? Go to the Mission. I hope you like to pray.' He bends over the table, dismissing her with silence, busy fingers teasing the tangled chains of the trinkets apart.

The barman coughs again and she realizes she's been standing, staring, paralysed by hopelessness.

'I don't know what you're looking for, but Levi . . . he's maybe not the right one to help you. He's right about the Mission though. It's full of crazies but it's safe. A woman like you can't be alone here. You understand?'

For a moment, the sudden, unexpected kindness unleashes the despair she's been holding back. She nods a silent acknowledgement to avoid saying words that might become a sob and covers her eyes with her hand before stepping outside. The orange-seller curses at the impact of her shoulder before realizing who bumped him. He's still off-balance, looking down, when she plucks a ripe fruit from the top crate and shifts it between hands quickly so her body blocks his eyeline. By the time he looks up she's got a five-metre head start if it comes to a chase, but the fat man grimaces in indignant silence, unaware of the theft, pretending not to watch Clementine walk away.

2.

Silas

The device defies explanation, like all the best toys. The report compiled by the senior curator ended with those killer words 'possible religious significance' – still the internationally recognized archaeologist's code for 'we don't know'. The ignorance was a blessing really – theories beget enthusiasm, and public interest in the artefact would complicate its theft unduly.

When Silas first got the job, it was understood the title 'Minister of Antiquities' served as a licence to divert a certain proportion of the city's excessive historical wealth into private hands. Now, the new breed of officials – curators, law enforcement – they weren't looking for the money he could bring them. Something was changing in the city. After more than a century of cold turkey, Jerusalem was getting hooked on religion again, and it was bad for business.

To keep things tidy, this device would have to disappear in a way that didn't connect to him. Today's inspection would lay the ground-work. The strangely hirsute curator fiddles with the keys to the glass case, droning on about some peculiarity in the engravings on the pottery recovered from the seabed near this Antikythera thing. The device itself bears a few scratches which could be interpreted as a kind of cuneiform similar to Sanskrit, but the pottery is marked with what looks like words in a largely incomprehensible ancient script called Linear B. Despite the discrepancy, the curators have convinced themselves both items (and other less notable finds) were cargo from the same wrecked ship. The slightly flimsy reasoning for this conclusion is that one of the pottery tablets bears what could be the latter half of the word 'Antikythera' as rendered in Linear B.

Silas lets the words wash over him. Knowing about these objects is how the curators define themselves – denying them these little moments of superiority would cause pointless upset. This one, Boutros, can be touchy about 'his' things, which makes today's performance all the more necessary. As the dreary monologue ends, the case opens and Silas pounces, hefting the device from where it rests on a little rectangle of cheap black velvet, producing an audible gasp from the beard next to him. Waggling the fingers of his free hand silences the protest on the keeper's lips. The mandatory white gloves prevent supposedly catastrophic contamination by grease or microbes.

It doesn't look like much, a lump of greyish-green rock that you might pick up in a construction site or the ruins of an old factory, but that 'rock' was two millennia of accretions from the seabed. You could see the outline of a cross-spoked circle, marked with illegible ancient symbols. Patches of vivid aquamarine glitter in the stone like little pools of the sea this thing had come from. The finely worked metal parts within are invisible, but their existence has been inferred from traces of oxidization on the rock-like exterior. Analysis of a tiny sample seemed to show the device was cast from an alloy mankind would not learn to work until centuries after this thing was made. Therein lay the true mystery of the Antikythera Mechanism, but mysteries concern Silas less than the price they fetch.

His buyers had done their own research on it and decided it met their needs. They didn't tell him what they'd found out, but he didn't need to know. The only thing Silas needed to know was how badly they wanted it, which, as it turned out, was very badly indeed. The profit from this job would be enough to check out of the game for good, but quitting while you're ahead is the coward's choice. No, this money was going to be the start of something far greater. In Jerusalem's broken democracy, it would be enough to buy power.

The curator's silent glare warns him he's allowed the Antikythera Mechanism to stray into contact with a patch of microbe-ridden skin, distracted by the daydream. The money has to come first, which means engaging with the here and now. Silas adjusts his face to assume the air of mock solemnity the museum staff deem appropriate for handling relics. The man seizes the Mechanism from his hands with visible relief and lays it on its velvet cushion in a peculiar motion of obeisance. He's twiddling through several chained key rings, preparing to seal the transparent security case when Silas holds up a single finger. 'I want you to put the replica on display . . .' He forestalls the inevitable objection before it can be uttered. 'Nobody will know or care, and I've had a warning of an attempt to steal the Antikythera Mechanism, so I want it out of public view and moved into category B storage.' The curator emits a barely intelligible syllable before Silas speaks over him. 'Category A storage is an obvious target; it would be effectively less secure than public display. In these circumstances Category B offers the best balance of security and concealment.' Silas's stare invites the man to challenge his statement, but makes it silently clear any discussion will be neither pleasant nor profitable.

The full heat of the noon sun hits the instant he steps out of the museum's discreet side entrance. The flash of blindness inflicted by its sudden light brings with it a moment of instinctive terror that subsides only as his vision adjusts. For pragmatic reasons, Silas sticks to the tenebrous edges of alleys split in two by the sun as he walks. A human eye adjusted to the dark can still perceive what passes in the light.

A water-seller nods imperceptibly as he passes. One of the perks of office was the ability to employ others to cover his tracks. If he is observed, he will know. Even so, he takes an apparently haphazard route to the Old City, taking in the sights – the ersatz, misplaced carbuncles vanishing numbers of true believers refer to as the Dome of the Rock and the Holy Sepulchre. They were crap. Everything that mattered in Jerusalem had been reduced to glass and rubble more than a century ago, but the tourists still came for the stories, and if they wanted a sniff of something real they came to the museum.

The only place you can still feel the history is in the deep Old City, but the sightseers seldom stray down here. In the last war, this walled warren of streets served as its own citadel; the buildings around its perimeter shielded the ones within from the wave of pressurized air that levelled the proud temples of the old faiths. Now, the dust-caked ruins at the edges stand as a slowly crumbling bulwark against the post-war contagion of grim utilitarian box-buildings spreading through the rest of Jerusalem.

Inside, the sun doesn't reach the streets for most of the year. The stench of refuse ripening tells you it still belongs to the Arabs and the poor. The faces change; you can see flashes of pale skin on the European hookers plying their trade, but poverty always stinks. A fat fruit-seller smiles obsequiously as Silas passes, a cheap, occasionally useful informant who's always keen to impress. That is the truly marvellous thing about the poor; tiny sums of money suffice to purchase so much goodwill.

A rainbow-beaded curtain in a doorway offers an entrance to his destination. The strands brush the sides of his face and sway noisily as he passes. This place is a dump, but it serves a purpose. This is where to find the skinny Jew boy who likes to hide among the Arabs, as if that wasn't the most obvious thing in the world. Silas waits, presumably being subjected to some form of scrutiny, before the bulky man behind the bar nods him over to a dark corner where he can just now discern movement.

Levi Peres strikes a match and holds it to the tip of a thin, straggly cigarette. The flash of orange match-light reveals a man of no more than twenty-one with a scant beard that lends its wearer none of the intended gravitas. The shadowed figure leans back in its seat with exaggerated ease. Bravado is a wonderful thing – so useful.

'You know who I am. Can we talk somewhere privately?'

Levi gestures around expansively. 'This is my office. We can talk here.'

One of the trio of old men sitting on leather pouffes at the other end of the room takes a deep drag on the shisha pipe and coughs. The bulky barman stands silent, unashamedly listening.

'All right, that's up to you. The thing you have to understand is that listening to this job description connotes acceptance. There are obligations and liabilities that go with that and they'll apply to your hefty friend if he's in.'

The youngster gives a little jerk of the head and the big man purses his lips, then shrugs and drifts to the other side of the bar, out of earshot.

'Yusuf's a good guy. If he's not around I get nervous. Tell me a big number to make me feel better.'

'Fifty thousand shekels. One fifth now to cover expenses and make life more enjoyable. The rest on completion.' Silas watches for a reaction but this Levi character has at least got front. Fifty thousand would be maybe two and a half years' labour for an honest working man. It represents a little under half a per cent of what Silas ultimately stands to make on this deal.

Levi plucks a fibre of unburnt tobacco from his tongue. 'Two hundred thousand. Forty up front. If I don't know what I'm getting into, I need to know it's worth it.'

Small-time. A few seconds feigned agonizing serves to avoid making the victory look too easy. 'OK, two hundred, but twenty's as much as I can do up front.' Any more than that and young Levi Peres will disappear from Jerusalem for good. So would anyone.

The youngster performs his own little act of silent mental arithmetic before nodding. 'There is an artefact I wish to have removed from the city. I have a buyer, but the item is sufficiently high profile that its loss will be noticed sooner or later. Later is better. It is currently in the museum's storage facility. I have taken steps to withdraw it from public view and reduce the security surrounding it, but you will have to effect its removal.'

Levi's expression darkens and his hands spread in denial. 'No way. You want a break-in, you find yourself a thief. Who do you think I am?'

He smells the trap, but he can't see it. 'I know exactly who you are, Levi Peres. I know who you owe money to, how much, and what they'll do to you if you don't pay, and I know you're just about smart enough to pull this off. Besides . . .' His voice softens; no need to puncture that useful bravado yet. 'You're not a foot soldier on this job. There's enough in that pot for you to get help.'

The thin cigarette in Levi's hand twitches and half-burnt ash tumbles onto his loose-checked keffiyeh. 'You should have said up front if you wanted a crew.'

Too late for remorse, boy, and you know it. 'The money told you that. Or were we not having the same conversation?' Silas's fingers glide against the silk of his European-style jacket, pull out two solid blocks of pre-counted money and slide them across the table. He stands with slightly stagey formality. 'One of my people will be in touch with details.'

Habit, more than any genuine fear of being followed, steers him through a skewed dogleg route back to his office. A light breeze carries the odour of the Old City away to the east. There is always a sense of relief that comes with the moment of putting a plan into action, as if the ideas had carried weight from the moment of their conception. Not that there's any guarantee of success, not at all, but the omens are good. Levi Peres is perfect. Of course, there are better smugglers and better thieves in Jerusalem, but the best ones have a certain traction in the city – they could make things difficult if they chose. No, he didn't need the best. Levi Peres was good enough, and entirely disposable.

3.

Levi

'Shouldn't you be working on your masterplan?'

Yusuf turns a chair around the wrong way and sits. The curved wicker frame creaks under the weight of those bear arms folded across the backrest. He leans in too close, like a man who wants to hear a secret.

'I'm thinking. You should try it sometime.'

He watches me for a few seconds. He doesn't care that I'm not looking at him.

'It's the woman, isn't it? You thinking maybe you should've helped her out?'

'Sure, like I've got time to burn on every *ghreeb* who wanders in off the street.'

'Come on! You got to be curious! She comes in here, from Marseille, asking for you by name? And you don't want to know what her deal is?'

A knot of a hundred tiny metal chains chinks between my fingers. He won't drop this thing about the girl. He never does. It's kind of an unwritten agreement between Yusuf and me that I bring excitement into his life in exchange for him letting me run the business from his place. The problem with unwritten contracts is they're subject to interpretation. 'Forget her. I'm working on a plan. That's all you need to know. Right now, I have other work to do.'

'Yeah, looks important. What is that shit?'

'Religious souvenirs, for the tourists. I got a variety box of a thousand from China for nothing, but they got tangled in transit, and selling crucifixes to Muslims is a quick way to go out of business.'

'What business? There's no tourists.'

'Because you're so busy with all these customers you can waste time talking to me.' That shuts him up for a second. Nobody's making any money since Europe blew up again and the tourists stopped coming to Jerusalem, but nobody wants to let on they're hurting; it's a little bit about pride, and a lot about not letting the sharks see you bleed. Another smoker's cough from one of the old geezers at the back breaks the silence of the empty bar.

'You're an idiot, you know that?' Yusuf plucks a peanut from the bowl on his bar, leans back and flicks it into the air with his thumbnail. It bounces off his lip and falls onto the floor. He looks at it a second before deciding not to pick it up. 'You should know better than to mess with Silas Mizrachi.'

'And that's your professional assessment as what? A bartender?' He always does this; he can't help himself. Telling me I'm wrong is like a nervous tic for him.

'It's my professional assessment as someone who knows how to add up – professionally. A job like this takes money. He gives you the change in his back pocket, and suddenly you're a gangster. You're not a gangster, Levi. If Silas came to you, it's because he wants someone he can screw. Take the money and get out of town – Gaza or something. Silas is nothing outside of Jerusalem.'

'Yeah, that's a fun idea, but it's not going to work. The money's not enough.'

'Enough for what?'

'You heard what he said about me owing someone.'

'Yeah, that was news to me. Who do you owe?'

'Maurice Safar.'

Yusuf's face goes tight at the name. In the wider landscape of Jerusalem, Safar doesn't even figure, he's a neighbourhood guy, but he's connected everywhere. Skipping town is not an option. 'Eesh! How much?'

'Does it matter? More than Silas just put on the table.'

'*Wallahi*, Levi! Did they not teach arithmetic at Jew school? You people are supposed to be all about the money!'

He always panics. That's why I can't tell him everything. I've got nine days until Maurice Safar breaks the thigh bone of my left leg. Yesterday he showed me a metal bar he got from his father. It's the one part of the job he always does himself. Violence is only an effective motivator when it's sincere. People have to know you mean it, and Maurice Safar always means to hurt you.

'All I need is someone to do the legwork and stay out of sight . . .'

'You mean a thief – someone who has actual skills.'

'I have skills.'

'All right, skills other than bullshitting and buying cheap tobacco.' Yusuf counts something imaginary on his fingers like a kid doing maths.

'OK, OK, you made your point. I need a thief, a cheap one.'

'So ask your girlfriend. She needed money.'

'I honestly cannot tell whether that's a serious suggestion. Seriously, I don't know.'

He holds his hands out, palms up, and gives me this look like I'm breaking his heart. I know for a fact he doesn't have one. 'She did a number on fat Saul outside – swiped one of his oranges faster than you can blink.'

'I love you, man, but sometimes you can be a schmo. This – this is one of those times. Tell you what, if I need someone to steal fruit, I'll give her a call.'

Yusuf reaches under the bar and picks up a glass from a shelf I can't see, stares at some imaginary dirt at the bottom, shakes his head slowly from side to side. This whole Mr Reasonable schtick is bullshit. He only says these things to get a rise out of me. Other people don't see that.

'Excuse me for trying to help.' The snake muscles of his forearm flex as he twists the pint jar around a towel.

'Don't be like that . . .' If it was actually possible to hurt Yusuf's feelings, I might put more effort into making nice. Or I might not; it's kind of hard to imagine how things could be different from how they are. Maybe it is a little messed up.

The sound of leathery laughter from somewhere near the door jerks me around. It's just the old guys at the shisha pipe laughing at something dumb. Sometimes I still make the mistake of trying to listen to their conversations. I swear they do not speak in actual words; every now and then you might get a sentence, but it is never, ever funny.

The door curtain rattles behind me. Outside, shopkeepers disappear like cockroaches in the fading afternoon light that creeps through the gaps between rooftops. Everything closes for 'quiet time' in the Old City. The only people still looking for business at this time are the tech cult preachers offering to solve all your problems by putting a computer in your head. A pair of them stand behind a stall like they're going to be there all night. Somebody told me they don't sleep after they get the procedure done, but I've watched them: they do shifts; they just all have the same haircut and the same smile, like they're in on a secret.

In three hours every door and every shutter on this street will be wide open again, covered with racks of carpets and leather stuff and birds in cages – all shit that nobody on the planet actually needs. Like there's some unwritten law of the souk that says no one's allowed just to sell you a loaf of bread. I still have to go to the Mahane Yehuda for real food, which always carries a risk of running into family. Right now it's the wrong time for shopping, but the kind of work I have to do is easier with empty streets. I need to see bad people, and they get busy later.

Leo's restaurant is in the Armenian Quarter. Depending on who you ask, we've got anywhere from three to five quarters – that's just Jerusalem arithmetic. Any other year I'd detour to avoid the crowds around Temple Mount, but the tourist flow dried up as soon as the insurrection in Europe started again. The one thing you can never avoid is the Haredim doing their business at the Wailing Wall, crying about a building that got knocked down two thousand years ago, and was probably somewhere else. If you think about it, it's impressive how they keep up the motivation.

It takes fifteen minutes to walk to Ararat Street. You know someone's going to be watching you from the minute you cross the invisible boundary that runs down the middle of the Cardo archways, so there's no point trying to be sneaky. When I get there, Leo's standing outside his joint, smoking a Russian import cigarillo. The old guy clocks me as soon as I turn the corner. Still sharp.

'Shalom! Well, if it isn't the Old City's very own yid prodigy! I'm sorry, kid, I'm all good for plastic replicas of the Dome of the Rock. What can I say? Tourist business isn't what it used to be. It's this damn war.'

A couple of years ago I would have laughed at the shitty joke and taken the hit, backed out of the big boys' game. I can't afford that now; opportunities to earn real money are too thin on the ground. 'I need to talk business with Shant.'

The old man's smile vanishes. 'What kind of business do you need to talk about with Shant, kid?'

'With the greatest respect, the answer to that question is Shant's kind of business, Leo.'

Leo gives me that old gangster stare. He's not playing. He can still bury me if he thinks I'm jerking his chain. 'OK, kid, I know you. Shant can listen to what you have to say, but you better not

17

be wasting his time. He's my nephew. I look after him. I hold you responsible for anything that comes out of this. You get me?'

'I get you, Leo.'

'Give me a minute. I think he's doing his yogilates.'

'I'm sorry, what?'

'Yogilates. It's a mix of . . . Doesn't matter. Sit tight. I'll get him.'

Everything is shiny in Leo's bar: no cracks in the red leather seats of the booths at the back. It's obvious these guys don't need tourists to make money. Shant makes me wait, but I stay casual even though I can feel my ass sweating. This is already wrong. I can't run a job unless I'm the boss, and he's letting me know I'm not the boss.

'Hey.' The voice is high-pitched. It comes from a pair of spectacles peering over the back of the seats three booths away. The face behind them is a boy, kind of. It's one of those staring-down-the-barrel-of-puberty faces that's still making up its mind.

'Hey.'

The face comes up. It looks at me like I'm a cat that wandered in off the street, not sure whether he's supposed to pet me or kick me out. 'What are you doing?'

'I'm, uh . . . waiting for someone.'

'Oh, you're here to see my dad.' Suddenly he sounds bored.

I look again at the eyes. There's a bony hardness around them that could be Shant. The rest must be his mother. 'You're Shant's son?'

'Mmm . . .'

'Learning the old man's business, eh?'

'Yeah.' The word comes out as a sigh. His head turns so the cheek rests on the top of the booth, like he's going to sleep. He's had this conversation before, and he doesn't want to be here. I don't blame him. If he was my kid, I for sure would keep him the hell away from all this shit.

'You should count yourself lucky, kid. You know what my father

18

did?' The face rises from the seat back, curious. 'He ran a furniture showroom on the Rehov Hanevi'im.'

'That doesn't sound so bad.'

'Really? What do you think I did all day? Nothing, that's what. School holidays killed me. To this day, I still get antsy if I smell wood polish.'

'That does sound boring. I just don't know what I'm supposed to learn sitting around here. All I see is people come in, start talking, and my dad gets angry.' His eyes dart around the room; then he leans forward. 'Some of the kids at school say he hurts people.'

Shit. You can tell by the look on his face: he knows – not the ugly detail, but he can feel what's not right. Kids are smart like that. I mean, my dad was a fucker, but the worst he ever did was leave a few bruises on us, and Mom if she got loud. He never buried anyone in an underpass. What can I say? He's looking at me, waiting for an answer, a guy who just walked in off the street, like somehow my opinion matters.

'Those kids don't know what they're talking about. Would I be here if your dad was gonna hurt me?'

'I guess not.' He looks happier, but not much. I guess he probably wanted me to tell him his dad was really the greatest guy on the planet, but he'd know I was lying. Sometimes the truth sucks, but it's what you've got. 'You know, the other guys who come around here don't say more than two words to me.'

'Well, they're idiots. Maybe that's why your dad has to shout at them.' The sound of heavy footsteps on the stairs drags me back to reality. 'Don't worry about learning the business. All that "follow in your father's footsteps" stuff is for schmucks with no imagination. You do you, kid.'

He gives me a grin that looks nothing like his father.

Shant Manoukian appears from an arched doorway with no door at the back of the room, big but lean in a loose tracksuit, all smiles and handshakes. A faint sheen of sweat gives his face a movie-star glow. He looks at the kid for a second, seems about to say something, then shrugs and turns to me.

'I see you met Kyle. Sorry to keep you waiting. I was just finishing up my yogilates.' I never heard that word before Leo said it. It must be some bullshit workout thing. I'm hoping for the purposes of this conversation it won't matter. Whatever, he's not sorry. White teeth flash every time he grins, which is a lot.

'Yeah, Leo said.'

'You should try it, man. Your posture could use a little work.' My spine twitches with the urge to straighten.

'You sound like my mother.'

'Ha! I like you, Levi. You're a funny guy. So, Leo tells me you got a job. What's the deal?'

'Ten K for a week of planning, executing next week, half now, half on completion.'

Shant nods in mock approval. 'You sure you got five K, Levi? That pays for my time but what's the job?'

I give him the same line Mizrachi gave me – listening to the details constitutes agreement to complete the job. His face tells me exactly how shitty that line is. The movie-star head starts to shake slowly, almost sympathetically. He holds up a hand like a traffic cop.

'You're talking about signing up blind. That's not professional. Maybe Uncle Leo said something to you about risks. He looks out for me, but I run my own business. I can take risks; it just costs is all. One hundred K, fifty up front. You got fifty in your pocket, Levi Peres?'

I start making out that I'm good for the money, but when I get to the part about only ten K up front he looks like he's sucking something sour. I stop talking and his expression softens.

'Levi, it's not for me. You're a smart kid; I can see that. Leo would tell me to nod and smile and keep pumping you for info, but I respect you for coming here. I respect you for trying to make this work, but it's no good. Walk away from this. Have you thought about Gaza?'

We shake hands. As I head out the door, Uncle Leo gives me a mock salute with the stub of his cigar. All that respect stuff was bullshit. Shant figured out it's a job they don't want to steal, so he found a quick way to end the conversation. In a way it doesn't matter. They'll forget about the job they didn't do, but they'll remember we had this conversation. After this, Levi Peres can sit down and talk business with anyone in this city, which is great, but it doesn't get me out of my hole with Safar. Only money's going to do that, but I have a manpower problem, and not enough money to fix it.

4.

Clementine

From a distance, the Mission is a white hole in the dark of the Old City. As Clementine gets near she can see the cracks the whitewash doesn't cover. In the gothic-arched doorway the smell hits her: an intense urine tang. The deranged cluster in the shadows, dark piles of shambling rags drawn to this place of succour, but repelled by some ineffable magnetism from the door itself. A pair of yellow eyes, slitted like a cat's, watches her pass from beneath a concealing hood, the expression impossible to read.

Inside, the Mission is true to its name, an outpost for a dying Europe. The walls are the same whitewash as outside but cleaner, with fewer cracks. Six rows of dark wood benches line up either side of an aisle pointing arrow-straight to a low altar covered with white cloth. For the first time since she left France, homesickness touches Clementine. This room could be in Lyon or Grenoble, but for the faint mist of dust that hovers golden in the yellow light.

A pale-skinned woman, the first she's seen since she arrived, appears from a doorway in the wall behind the altar. She wears a simple brown robe tied at the waist with a cord. Her short, red hair is cut like a man's in a style that would mark her as sexually deviant at home, but maybe the rules are different here. The shaven sides show her ears fully, but there is no glint of metal in either of them. For whatever reason, this woman does not embrace the technology the locals favour. She smiles in a manner that grants limited, conditional acceptance of Clementine's right to be here and waits for her to speak.

The silence is wrongfooting. The conversational gambits she'd been running through on her way here all seem too obviously false now. This woman's stern simplicity demands repayment in the same currency. Clementine's concocted stories of a struggle against oppression, of loss and abandonment, evaporate, replaced by a single statement. 'I want to disappear.'

The woman's eyes wander over Clementine's pale skin and inappropriate, form-fitting European clothes. There's a glimmer of something that might be sympathy. 'Are you ready to embrace our Saviour?'

A simple, binary question, loaded with two millennia of history, packed with an infinity of agendas. Which one does this unremarkable woman serve? What will it demand? Choice is a luxury reserved for those already possessed of food and shelter. Clementine does not hesitate. 'With all my heart.'

The woman's smile warms, but her eyes are still calculating. 'I am Hilda. You can help in the kitchen for now. I'm afraid you'll have to stay in the hostel dormitory tonight. You'll need to change out of those clothes. They'll bring trouble we don't need.' She walks with slow, smooth steps, leading the way to a darkened glass door behind the altar. It opens to reveal a small vestry that looks as if it serves as a bedroom. Despite conspicuous cleanliness, it is a tableau of a life improvised. Piles of things, mostly books and papers, cover every available flat surface, including a narrow, hard-looking bed. Hilda reaches into one of the piles, pulls out a brown robe identical to her own, and passes it over. For a moment Clementine watches dumbly as the reality of what she's doing settles on her. Holy orders. Will there be a vow? Some sort of ritual? Will they accept someone like her? All she has is this woman's tacit acceptance. Instead of hopelessness, the thought inspires a wave of calm. This is all she has. Perhaps a freedom from choice is the gift of the Holy City.

There is a pang of loss as she strips off her smart-fabric leggings and vest. Inappropriate they may be, but the temperature-sensitive weave and adjustable wicking properties made them valuable in any climate. The variable colour shift was a useless legacy of her old life – it wouldn't hide her in the city. Clothes like this were hard to find, even in Europe, since the war on the Ural frontier had started up again. The gossamer network of goods between continents necessary for such sophisticated products had taken years to re-emerge after the first war, and now it was gone again.

She hesitates, wary of nakedness in front of a stranger, until Hilda looks away. The world goes dark as the robe slides over Clementine's head. It's heavy, and the coarse fabric scratches her skin where it touches. Her head emerges to see Hilda smiling now, perhaps in amusement at the sight of the slight woman swaddled in fabric, perhaps at something else. The benign opacity of her expression is a mask that could hide anything, or anyone.

The kitchen is spotless but tired. The stainless-steel surfaces are scored with the passage of a decade of cutlery. A small, dark woman stirs two big pots of something surprisingly appetizing. She doesn't wear robes and she seems surprised to see Clementine, but silently accepts her presence, handing her an apron and a dented ladle. From the other side of a green plastic folding shutter comes the sound of moving bodies and murmuring, the stilted conversations of the hopeless, not listening to each other, hitting dead ends, repeating themselves.

The cook leans across the counter and pulls at the centre of the shutter. It clacks noisily up into a hidden recess. The people on the other side are mostly men, already in a line. They know how this works. A few glance up, noticing the unexpected robed figure, but most are focused on the food. They shuffle past blindly as Clementine ladles bowls full of aromatic stew. There's a faint waft of sumac and bursts of something else more exotic, a spice that leaves an almost uncomfortable heat on the tongue. Still, it's good food. The homeless in Europe have been killing rats for more than a decade now. An unwanted memory sends a shudder through her: not just the homeless.

The act of serving becomes automatic and she stops noticing the faces in front of her until one of them hisses thanks. She looks up to see the yellow eyes that watched her in the doorway. They see through the disguise of her robe. The features around them are hidden behind shadows and layers of ragged cloth, the blotched red wrist of the hand that takes the bowl seems almost to strobe out of existence in the flickering yellow ceiling light, but the scars of radiation sickness are unmistakeable.

Clementine suppresses a start of surprise and resumes the mechanistic act of filling the bowls, looking around her to see if anyone else has noticed the stranger. The cook wrestles the dead weight of the second pot, oblivious. The homeless continue their dead-man shuffle.

A few make attempts at conversation when she steps out from behind the counter to gather bowls and spoons, but they're nonsensical, or perhaps in some dialect of the damned she doesn't understand. She smiles dumbly; none of her language training prepared her for this. As she clears away, she looks in vain for the yellow-eyed stranger.

The small, dark cook makes empty conversation as they share the duties of washing up and putting away. She answers Clementine's questions about recipes and ingredients with gentle incredulity at her ignorance, unable to grasp the exoticism of her fare to someone who comes from a place where spices will not grow. The rest of her talk is platitudes and local gossip: political scandals, acts of outrage by a cult she calls 'the Machine people'. The stories mean nothing to Clementine. There is no threat of meaningful dialogue. She has already disappeared.

She follows the cook's directions to the dormitory. A window-less corridor floored with colourless, hard lino takes her there. The geography of this place is unsettling, hard to follow even for someone like her. It doesn't correspond at all to the featureless white box visible from the outside. Walls have been knocked away into nearby buildings and tunnels dug between to link them. It is a warren of the faithful with many entrances. The exteriors are all facades. It makes her wonder who else is hiding here. Or is this just what pragmatism looks like in the ruins of the Holy City?

The hostel dormitory is small and cramped compared to the cavernous dining hall. There are people already here, most dressed in the ragged uniform of the poor. Some chat with cautious famil-iarity. Hilda had explained the hostel's twelve beds were allocated on the basis of a benignly rigged lottery. At 5 p.m. every day appli-cants were invited to draw straws for a place. Recent winners, and known substance abusers, chose from a lot that contained no long straws. Some perhaps suspected their fate was sealed, but it was fairer than chance. Clementine had bypassed the lottery entirely, for reasons as yet unclear.

Fully half her roommates are women: the lottery's work again. They look genderless in the garb of poverty and the skin of their faces and hands is hard from days spent outside in the streets. The eyes of the men follow her hungrily across the room to an empty bed in one corner. Their scrutiny is relentless, their thoughts obvious, but signs proclaiming the Mission's code of conduct hang like silent sentinels on the walls. Nobody wants to find themselves losing the lottery.

Nobody undresses. Instead, there are token gestures towards the rituals of preparing for bed: outermost garments are put to one side; one of the men prays in a style Clementine has never seen before, rocking backwards and forwards while murmuring atonally. Another uses a bowl of water to perform lengthy, ritualistic ablutions confined to the limited areas of flesh accessible without removing further layers. They all seem to move to some unspoken timetable. By the time the fluorescent strip light on the ceiling flickers out, they are already lying still.

Clementine stares at the ceiling in the darkness. She can feel the eyes of the men and hear their thoughts. Still, this is the safest she's been for months, since before leaving France. She thinks of the people she left behind. How many survived? Most would be dead, the bravest. If there were any survivors, they'd likely been sent to join the punishment battalions in the east. Not everybody got the chance to disappear. She was lucky, lying here in a hard bed amongst the hopeless. Still, sleep would not come.

A rustle of cloth and a stifled gasp is the sound of a man masturbating in the dark. Clementine pushes her bedcovers aside and walks to the door, picking her way faultlessly through the pitch black, the path and distance memorized through instinct honed by months of training. In the corridor, she blinks three times rapidly and a film descends over her eyes. Monochrome outlines appear out of what was total blackness and she retraces her steps through the warren until she reaches the smoked glass of Hilda's door and knocks.

A light blossoms behind the glass and the older woman gestures her inside wordlessly. She doesn't seem surprised. Even roused from sleep, she still wears the same gentle, slightly calculating expression. Clementine slips out of her robe and crawls into the recently vacated bed, still warm from Hilda's body. The older woman smiles as she leans down to pull the blanket across to cover her nakedness. The light flicks off, the door clicks closed, and she is gone. Tears of relief and gratitude well in Clementine's eyes. She has to blink three times before they can fall.

5.

Levi

Yusuf is pretending to be busy when I get back, chin on his elbow, bodyweight pushing a dent into the clouded zinc of the bar while he listens to some no-hoper trying to sell knock-off shisha tobacco from India. If the guy bothered to look at Yusuf's face he'd know he wasn't making a sale, but he just keeps talking, stuck on a script that won't work without a clean data feed he can't get this deep in the Old City. Any other week, Yus wouldn't be giving this schmuck the time of day, but he's still smarting at getting cut out of the Silas deal. He makes out like it's all a big fuck-up, but jealousy is what it is. This is the kind of petty shit he does as payback. The tobacco guy only lets up after Yusuf promises to try a sample batch, which is never going to happen. Through me he gets Zanzibar gold leaf at closer to wholesale than is decent or reasonable. That's the other part of our agreement.

The door curtain rattles behind the tobacco guy. Yusuf gives me a look while the rainbow beads swing and slow to a stop; then he moves to the door, fingers picking at the knot of his apron as he walks. Smoke swirls through the chink of light striping his face while he watches the guy disappear down the street. 'So?'

'So what?'

He sits opposite, bulk filling half the table. The way he moves, quick, crisp, he's excited about something. 'So you're still here. It can't have gone that bad.'

'Yeah, it went pretty good actually.'

'You got yourself a cheap thief?' There's an edge in his voice, like I put a little dent in his excitement.

'Not that good.'

'Have you thought about . . .'

'I am not going to Gaza! Will you shut up about Gaza?'

'*Ya rab*, Levi! Forget about Gaza. Did you hear about your girl-friend?'

'Again with this?' It's the girl. I should have known. His ability to drop things is zero.

'Hear me out. A few people saw her come in here. You expect that. Well, it turns out she had a little trouble on her way over: a couple of boys from the Safar crew thought she looked like fun, followed her into the souk.'

'Yeah? That's too bad, but shit like that's going to happen. What's your point?'

'It didn't exactly turn out how they expected.' He's got his fists clenched, he's so excited.

'What do you mean?'

'She ditched them.' He watches my face, waiting for a reaction.

'Ditched them? Ditched them like how? Like she ran away? I mean, good for her, but that doesn't qualify her for shit, Yus.'

'I'll tell you what Omar told me. He was there; his stall's right across the street. She turned into the alley opposite the arcade, you know the one with the carpets hanging out front, and the Safar boys followed her. Two minutes later, she comes out, heads straight in here like nothing happened, and get this – the boys don't show their faces for ten minutes after that.'

'So what? She beat them up?'

'Come on, be serious! Omar's friends with those guys – they talk to him, and they say she disappeared! They turn the corner, it's a dead end, but there's nobody there.'

'You are full of it, my friend. Or they are. It doesn't add up.'

'So she's perfect for you.'

'Ha, ha, you kill me.' A certain percentage of everything Yusuf says is bullshit. If it's second-hand, like from his friend Omar, you can double that percentage, but, by the law of averages, every so often he comes up with something. Safar's boys are just kids, but they're a serious proposition on home turf. If she got away, she did something right. 'OK, you made your point. For the sake of argument, let's say that's interesting. If she disappeared, how would I even find her?'

'Oh, that's easy. She followed your advice. Smart girl.'

'My advice? I didn't give any.'

'Sure you did. One of the regulars saw her at the Mission. Looks like she's working there now.'

I look over my shoulder at where the three old guys are still taking turns sucking at the pipe. 'One of them? I didn't realize they ever moved.'

'You're a piece of work, you know that, Levi? Old Yash has been scoring his dinners at the Mission ever since his wife died.'

'Hold on a minute. Are you telling me one of those guys at the pipe is a different person than was here when I left?'

'And you're supposed to be the sharp one. You think I only have three paying customers? How do you think my business works?'

'I'm not an accountant.'

'No, you leave the adding up to me.' The dome of that big bald head glistens as he shakes it at me. 'You got into this mess because you owe too much money to the wrong people, and now you're at the wrong end of a bad deal. You've got to fix this.'

'Look, OK, I get it. A strange woman came in; she was kinda hot, in a skinny European way, and you're excited. I still don't get why you think she's a solution to my thief problem. You don't know anything about her.'

'I know she made the Safar boys look stupid, and she's faster than Fat Saul.'

'Evolution is faster than Fat Saul.'

'Options, man. Options. All I'm saying is, you don't have many of them.' He's got that big dopey grin on his face, and he's nodding at me like he's waiting for me to agree. It kills me when he's right.

'Look, it's late, it's been a messed up day, and I can't even think right now. If it'll make you happy, tomorrow I'll go to the Mission, see if she's there. If I find her, we can have a conversation. If I don't . . . well, we'll work something else out. Sound good?'

'Hey, I'm just trying to help you here, but yeah, that makes sense.' He sucks his teeth and grimaces, which tells me whatever comes next is going to be a pain in the ass. 'Seeing as you're going out, can you pick something up for me?'

'What?'

'I'm running a little low on whisky. You got some in last week, didn't you?'

'Can you get it yourself? It's just in the stash: in the tunnels in the usual place.'

His face breaks into a sheepish grin. It looks kind of ridiculous on a guy his size. 'C'mon, man, you know I don't like to go down there. Gethsemane always freaks me out. There are people buried in that place, like actual dead bodies.'

'OK, OK, I'll do it. You're pathetic, you know that? It's just a freaking bomb shelter. It's been empty a hundred years.'

'Love you, man.'

'Yeah, whatever. Bye.'

It should be a ten-minute walk to the Mission from my apartment, but Yusuf's detour takes up the hour after breakfast, and the streets are filling up by the time I get going. The route takes you to the north edge of the Old City, where the walls crumpled like paper and the only time people talk about reconstruction it's the punchline in a bad joke. Harsh morning light shows up the worst of it. Broken glass shines like teeth in the windows of skeleton buildings. Sagging wires just above head height carry stolen electricity to a few of the squats, but at night it's mostly dark around here.

The Mission's the least shitty thing in the neighbourhood, which isn't saying much. All the cripples and the kanj-heads are outside, cluttering up the doorway or sliding off like woodlice to wherever it is they hide in daytime. They watch quietly, trying to figure out if I'm a mark, losing interest as soon as they realize I'm not here to empty my wallet. Eventually one of them points me in the right direction.

At first the robe throws me off, but the brown ghost pushing a mop around the crummy dining hall is her. All that cloth hides her legs so it looks like she's floating across the yellow patches of floor between the tables where the bums eat their dinner.

'Hey, Cinderella . . .' She looks up. 'Spare me a few minutes of your valuable time?'

She fixes her eyes on the mop; they follow the shiny streak it leaves on the floor. It smells like a hospital in here. 'Last time we spoke, you said you didn't need a girlfriend. I think we're on the same page.'

The mop goes into the stained metal bucket like a drowning man and unleashes another burst of detergent stink. I grab the handle. She looks at me like she's a second away from reaching for a blade. There's something funny about her eyes, like they're set too deep. She pulls the stick away from me and the head makes a big wet slap as it hits the floor. She's strong.

The thing about being in my business is that you learn pretty quick not to take the brush-off: from girls, from gangsters, doesn't matter. If you need something, you go after it. Also, like Yusuf said, options are something I don't have right now.

'Fat Saul wants his orange back.' The hood of the robe falls back, away from her face, as she looks up at me, eyes wide with suspicion, maybe fear. She wants to ask how I know, but she's not saying, which is good; keeping your mouth shut is an under-appreciated prerequisite for this business. Some people never learn it. The mop stops and settles into a thin pool of grimy water as she leans on it, listening. 'Are you even earning any money here?' We both know the answer to that question but still, the point needed to be made. 'One week, two thousand shekels, and don't worry, it's nothing nasty.'

The money gets her attention, like I knew it would. I can see she's still thinking about it when the mop starts moving again. How clean does a floor need to be? It's only bums that eat here. 'Don't they ever give you time off in this place? Listen, I can see you're busy with some important work right now, but when you're done, come see me down at Yusuf's tonight. We can have a proper conversation. I'll be there 'til seven o'clock.'

The place is empty apart from the regulars when I get in. Yusuf's watching war porn on the news feeds. One look is enough to tell you tourist season won't be happening any time soon – Machine crackdowns on insurgents in France and Norway, Sino-Sovs still getting pushed back on the Kazakh front. He finally drags his eyes off the screen when the picture cuts from footage to a talking head.

'Hey, Levi! Did you—'

'Don't say it! I know what you're gonna say and I don't need to hear it. It's under control. That's all you need to know!'

'I was just going to ask if you got the whisky.'

'Yes! Yes, I got your whisky, OK? And yes, I went to the Mission. I did exactly as you said. There, OK, I said it. Happy now?' I know he's just pushing my buttons and I shouldn't give him the satisfaction but sometimes I can't help it. I mean, it's one thing to give the guy a little excitement in his life when he's stuck behind the bar all day, but you'd have to be a saint to put up with his I-told-you-so shit.

'So . . .'

'She's coming.'

'When?'

'Tonight.'

'I guess we'll see.'

'Yeah, I guess we will.'

By the time she walks in, its twenty to eight and Yusuf's already collected on the little bet we made about whether she'd show. The robe's gone, and she looks different, dark blond hair combed back like a man's, I guess so she gets less attention, but she's wearing those weird tight clothes again. Maybe they're not so strange if you're from Europe. I don't know – we used to get tourists, now we get refugees, but she doesn't look like either.

'Good to see you, babe, but you know, punctuality is important in this line of work.'

'Yeah, sorry about that. I brought you an orange.'

There's an orange on the table and I don't know where it came from. I didn't even see her fingers move. In those clothes there's nowhere she could hide one of Fat Saul's big Jaffas. This could still be a good day for Levi Peres.

6.

Silas

A shining stalactite of drool extends from the lip of the broken being in front of him. In a minute it'll break and land on the office rug, which supposedly belonged to a Persian King: Cambyses or something. At moments like this, his father's words come back to haunt him. The old man used to say: 'The problem with money is that you have to earn it.' After a lifetime spent trying to prove him wrong, this moment serves as a dismal affirmation. Meeting the customer is perhaps the harshest of the many unforgiving practicalities of business, and today it manifests in the form of three figures of indeterminate gender filling Silas's office. Metal obliterates almost all trace of the people they used to be, sculpted into shining limbs and crania, leaving only the merest patches of exposed flesh necessary for cutaneous respiration. The nearest one, the dribbler, has taken a step further to abandon his humanity; sludgy nutrient sacs on his back are proof he has overcome the tyranny of desire for food, but the feeding tube running into his mouth prevents his lips meeting completely. Hence the carpet issue.

Of all the many stripes of loon who form the patchwork fabric of the city, none irritate Silas as effectively as the Cult of the Machine, but personal preferences cannot be permitted to intrude on business, not when these sums of money are at stake. If his visitors notice his carefully veiled animosity, they give no sign. An inability to perceive the emotions of others is a weakness that almost always afflicts those who consider themselves superior, and the Mechanicals are no exception. They glory in their semi-synthetic endocrine and lymphatic systems, crudely re-engineered to interface with their creaking prosthetics. Anyone with an ounce of self-worth would permit only as much intrusion into their body as is necessary for the essentials of communication and medical care, but the Mechanicals would have you believe that slaving your nervous system to a Korean-built micro-processor in a box at the base of your skull somehow makes you more than human, rather than less. Their very presence here, in his office, gives the lie to their bluster. If they'd attained any Machine-like detachment, they'd sit back and wait for delivery, but no, they're worried. A skilled observer can discern the signs; it's just a different kind of body language. Real people fidget or mess their hair. These damaged appliances emit heat. The dribbler speaks first.

'We want you to bring forward delivery of the device.'

The feeding tube gives the poor thing a lisp. Manners dictate Silas endeavour to look it in the eye. The oval face is pale and veined from tissue rejection and the steady diet of immunosuppressants taken to counter the body's response to contamination by metal limbs and digits. The reality of cheap, backstreet augmentation is something the Cult doesn't show to potential recruits, but progression depends on physical demonstrations of commitment, and the faith doesn't pay for new arms for the rank and file. If they survive to reach middle management, they all look like this one, give or take a tube. It won't have long left in its current form; it'll either 'ascend' and be admitted to the factory-labs of Europe by its masters, where they'll remove the last vestiges of human flesh and graft its electronically preserved consciousness into a bio-engineered form within an exoskeleton of shining metal, or it will die of something resembling AIDS. The Machines who inspire this worship are an

37

abomination, a wrong turn humanity might have avoided in a better world, but their power is more real than any god's, and their ersatz faith certainly incentivizes the workers.

Silas shrugs. 'You know the schedule we're on. The job entails expenses. If you want me to stick to the dates, I need you to cover my operating costs.'

'It is yours. You should take it and give it to us.'

'We've discussed this. The Antikythera Mechanism is not mine, it belongs to the city.'

'But you could take it. Give it to us now. We will pay you more.'

This is where difficulties arise. The Machine Cult are decidedly less than human when it comes to acknowledging such minutiae of existence as holding down a job. You could view that as evidence of the changes their body-modification has wrought upon their minds, although Silas rather suspects they haven't changed at all – the people who inflict this upon themselves are the ones who couldn't cope with all the messy uncertainties real life entails. The extinction of flesh reduces the uncomfortable variables of self, but the external world is harder to control. Reality is stubborn and unforgiving, and today Silas is its avatar.

'Please, there is a schedule. Deviating from it will bring trouble none of us want.'

The taller, healthier one in the middle of the trio pipes up. 'Another two million. Bring it to us tomorrow.' The end of the last word disappears in a wet gurgle. They are not flexible thinkers – they struggle to let go of an idea once they've latched onto it. The mistake would be to think they are stupid. The one at the back, not talking, is doing a reasonably surreptitious survey of the security arrangements. The slow, lateral turns of his head suggest he has some sort of scanning augmentation built in around his eyes, perhaps even total replacements. If they've received surveillance technology from their patrons in the West, any locally available counter-measure will be useless.

'I have removed the Antikythera device from public display as a precursor to our enterprise, but it is not on these premises. If you wish to withdraw from the arrangement previously agreed . . .' Silas stresses the word any sane human being would recognize as significant. ' . . .you should feel free to make your own arrangements. After all, no money has changed hands. I feel I should add, though, just so you fully understand the parameters within which you must make your decision, that in addition to their standard weaponry, I have equipped the museum's guards with dart guns capable of delivering a discreet dose of phenobarbital.'

They stare blankly.

'Really? No? Well, allow me to enlighten you. It's a remarkably cheap and effective way to negate immunosuppressants.'

The heat from their bodies becomes palpable as nervous energy is reprocessed into something their systems can handle. They remain perfectly still. Without the drugs, their bodies will reject the metal they've forced in, attacking it like cancers. It is a grim, painful death, but, more than that, it is an undoing of everything they've become – a forced recognition of its artificiality and wrongness. Those darts are existential terror for a shekel a shot.

One of them takes a step forward, his shadow darkening the desk. It is another weakness of the Machine Cult that they overestimate their ability to intimidate. In their infuriating way, the Cultists are a fascinating case study in the gap between the imagined perceptions of others and reality. They imagine they wield the power of their inhuman masters in the West – the unspoken threat of it hangs in the air – but it is bluff. The writ of the great powers does not extend to the Holy City. If it did, Jerusalem would be just another factory, but instead their proxies are ruining the carpet.

'So, gentlemen, to my expenses: I require five hundred thousand to cover my initial outlays on personnel and equipment, and another five to fund the next stage of the operation. That will suffice until delivery, at which point I'll have to insist on payment in full prior to handover.'

Their stare is unwavering, but eventually the one at the back speaks. 'You must be there.'

'No. My terms of delivery are non-negotiable. The associates I have engaged are quite capable of getting the item to the coast, or any other chosen extraction point. My government commitments do not permit me to leave the city.'

The frustration of it is that he has had this conversation with them before, in various forms. They must have hoped their physical presence would alter its outcome this time, but the truth is that they came here with no leverage. If you were inclined towards sympathy, you might even pity their predicament. They are laying out a huge quantity of money given to them by creatures of utter ruthlessness and unimaginable power. For them, failure in this enterprise carries not just a certainty of death, but a denial of the afterlife they have dedicated their existences to achieving. Like any purchaser, they want to feel they are in control. In a commercial transaction a good salesman will foster the illusion, but this is the point at which criminal enterprise differs – even the appearance of ceding control can be fatal. Silas makes a show of looking at his watch, a usefully pointed anachronism for the present audience.

'You'll have to forgive me, I'm afraid I'm going to have to bring this meeting to a close. If you can be sure to have the money wired to my account by close of business today, I will be sure to keep our little operation on schedule.'

7.

Clementine

Levi's thin fingers close around the bright fruit as if to test its reality. He pinches the green leaf from its stem and sniffs it before leaning back, apparently satisfied. At the edge of her vision, the other one watches from behind the bar, his face halved in blue chiaroscuro by light from a screen showing some foreign sport. A bank of three refrigerators against the wall hums as freon courses through the tubes of their heat exchangers. One is a semitone deeper than its fellows and rattles faintly at thirty-second intervals. A dripping tap plays counterpoint to the chorus, but otherwise the room is silent.

At a nod from Levi the barman bustles out from behind the counter like a heavily muscled housewife. Clementine hovers, uncertain where to sit, resisting the urge to blink and peer into the room's darker recesses. A squeal of tortured wood from behind makes her jump as Yusuf slides a splintered wooden bar down between two staples on the door, sealing them all in.

'Closing early tonight. This is a private conversation.' His smile summons the memory of yesterday. His kindness had been a chink of light in her despair, but that meant nothing now. These people were criminals; that much was clear.

'Over here.'

A sudden circle of light illuminates a small round table in the corner of the room. Levi hunches over something, just as he did before. That time it was trinkets, now it's two data slates hard-linked by a physical wire: old-school, but secure. Whatever is in them is supposed to be secret. The yellow glare from the ceiling lamp prevents her seeing what's on the slates. Levi extinguishes the images with a tap of the finger and looks up as she approaches.

'So, how are you doing? You like it there, at the Mission?'

'I'm here, aren't I?' Guilt darkens Clementine's words. Nobody at the Mission made her sign contracts or swear oaths, but this still feels like a betrayal.

'Yeah, I guess you are.'

'So are you going to tell me about this job?'

'In a minute. The thing you need to understand is that once I tell you the details, there's no backing out.' He looks over her shoulder to where Yusuf still stands next to the barred door, and then looks to her, waiting.

'You want me to say "yes" without knowing what I'm agreeing to?'

'Basically, yeah. Don't worry, it's only a little bit illegal.' Levi chuckles at his own joke, but Clementine turns away, stares at the floor. The attempt at humour throws the reality of her choices into stark relief. It's this or the mop and the kitchen forever, serving the ghosts as they pass through.

'Levi, we don't know each other. We can't really talk about trust, or agreements, or anything like that. There's no reason for me to trust you, or vice versa, so let me tell you where I'm at, and then you can decide for yourself how much of a risk it is to tell me about this job. How's that?'

His mouth narrows into a line and his gaze flicks to Yusuf and then back to her.

'OK, tell me "where you're at".' His words mimic Clementine's still shaky Arabic accent.

She forces a smile. 'I'm broke, I spent last night in a homeless shelter, and the locals seem to regard the only clothes I own as some kind of sexual invitation. I need the money.' Her smile sags beneath the weight of reality in those words, but she holds it in place and fixes Levi's gaze, waiting for him to speak.

'I think we can do business.' His grin is a salesman's, closing an easy deal. He taps the corner of one of the screens, and both of them shine into life; then he flips them around to face Clementine. They are photographs of the interior of a building taken from its own security cameras. 'I need you to get into this building – it's a museum storage facility – and retrieve an artefact. Think you can do that?'

'Yes.'

He laughs again. 'Confident, that's good.'

Her fingers slide across the table to touch the tablet, but Levi jerks it back, caging it with his own hand just beyond her reach.

'Keep your hands to yourself. You see what I need you to see, no more.'

'If you want me to plan a break-in, I need to see everything.'

He shakes his head and smiles, but there is no warmth in his expression. 'I think you're labouring under a misunderstanding. I don't need you to plan anything. I need someone quick and smart to do the legwork, that's all.'

'How do we get past the security? There'll be alarms, cameras . . .'

'You won't need to worry about any of that stuff. It's taken care of.'

'I worry if it's my picture they're taking.'

Levi's mouth pinches like he's tasting something sour; then he shakes his head again. 'I already told you too much. Get out.' He spits the last word and leaves a silence, waiting for her to move.

His anger vents in sharp, shallow breaths, a warning hiss, but Clementine doesn't shift. The thought of tomorrow morning's cleaning routine echoing infinitely into the future keeps her rooted to her seat.

'Go on, move! If you breathe a fucking word to anyone, we will find you. Nothing moves in this city Yusuf doesn't know about it.'

Her head jerks around at the mention of the other man's name. He's still standing watchfully by the door, barring her exit, but there is no malice in his pose. The tablet lies tantalizingly out of reach, but she can almost taste the trickle of current flowing through the solid-state circuitry from the tiny block of lithium at its core. Just a little nudge . . .

Blue light from the tablets suddenly illuminates Levi's face. He blinks in disbelief. 'What the fuck did you do?'

'Like I said, I need see everything.'

Heavy footsteps from behind warn of the big man's approach, but Levi holds up a hand, and they stop. She feels the looming presence no more than a metre behind her.

'May I?' She gestures to the tablets shining through Levi's caged fingers and he nods cautiously, pulling his hand away.

The moment her index finger brushes the tablet's casing, data rushes up to greet her, coursing through the fingertip interface into her grey matter, flowing in a stream of firing neurons into the tiny auxiliary processor at the base of her frontal cortex. An itch in her brain is a long dormant sub-routine kicking into life, processing, sorting through thousands of files. The storage is archaic: pointless partitions and fragmentation make it needlessly cumbersome, but a few microseconds suffice to realize it is mostly redundant information. Almost all the files are copies of each other with small, pointless modifications. This data is an illusion, a pantomime of rigour.

'This isn't everything.' Clementine's voice comes out in a lifeless monotone.

'What do you mean? I have contacts. This is the skinny.'

'Look.'

The micro-projector on one of the tablets sparkles into life, and the photographs from its data files flicker into the air above the table on its beam of light. One after the other, they seem to hover, connecting with each other through some algorithmic alchemy to form a glowing three-dimensional wireframe of the target building that rotates slowly between Clementine and Levi.

'Fuck.' She turns in her chair at the sound of Yusuf's voice. The big man is staring at the ghost building she's conjured, mouth wide open.

'How? How do you do that?' Levi's stare is intense, but his voice betrays a note of excitement.

'It's easier than the orange.'

'That's not an answer.'

'You're right, it isn't. Is that going to be a problem?'

A calculating look comes into his eyes, and he shakes his head. 'What's going on here?' He points to one of five blurred areas in the rotating schematic. It stops, and the relevant area enlarges, obeying an unspoken command.

'This is how I know you're not being given everything – there's no source data available for me to process into the larger model. Is there a reason your contact wouldn't give you the whole picture?'

'Maybe. Maybe these areas just aren't important.' He waves a hand, and the model continues its rotation. 'This doesn't change anything.'

'I think it does. I think my fee is four thousand.' Clementine pulls her finger away from the tablet and the schematic winks out of existence, casting them both into gloom. Levi emits something like a growl, a sound of reluctance from deep in his throat; then he leans forward, face cracking in a sudden smile.

'Yeah, yeah, four thousand is cool. You bring a lot to the party. I can respect that. I think we should regard this as the beginning of a business relationship.'

'No, I do this and then I'm out.'

'Let's just see how this goes and then maybe consider it further down the line.'

Clementine breathes deep and shuts her eyes against memories: a year of running now. This is not her first opportunity to make money through crime. There were offers in Marseille as soon as people got a hint of what she was. Now, at the end of the money, choices are fewer. 'This is not a career opportunity for me.'

'I understand. I'm just saying things can change, that's all.'

'I hope we understand each other.'

'Yeah, whatever, now do your thing.'

Clementine gestures the light model into being and it resumes its rotation between them, white lines of the wireframe scrolling across their faces like moving scars. Levi points as he talks.

'It's a warehouse – the main storage facility for the state Museum of Antiquities. It's split between three floors, each corresponding to a different level of security – A, B, and C, but the order is all messed up. C is the low-level stuff you might just dig up if you get lucky – coins, pottery. It's on the ground floor – not heavy security but there's only one door in, and there's a guard on it 24/7. I'm guessing some pressure sensors and beams – nothing crazy.'

He watches for any trace of a reaction. Clementine stays silent, mentally cross-referencing what he's telling her with data already absorbed from the tablets, searching for inconsistencies. There are none. As far as she can tell, the picture they have is not false, merely incomplete, but that could be equally deadly.

'The floor above C is A. I told you it was messed up. A is the really valuable stuff – this kind of thing, it's either on the cover of the museum brochure, or they deny its existence, or maybe both, I don't know. B is our destination, the top floor.'

'Why aren't we going for the valuable stuff?'

'Because this is a real job. We're getting what the client wants. That's it.'

'Who's the client?'

Disbelief flattens Levi's voice. 'You don't know. You're never going to know, so don't ask.'

'Fine, you're right. I don't need to know the backstory, but I can't work with these gaps in information. A single unexpected camera or sensor could turn any plan I make into a very bad idea. These are problems I can solve, but I need to take a look and make some guesses at what we're dealing with.'

'Now?' He looks uncertain, the brittle pride of a few moments ago cracked in the heat of practicalities. A good sign.

'No, daylight's better. We've got time, haven't we?'

'Yeah, time is one thing we got. Do what you need to do.'

'OK. Give me a couple of days to work things out, then I'll meet you back here after lunch. I've got to serve breakfast at the Mission and clear up.'

'For those bums?'

'For those bums.' She owes that much, and more, for the kindness she's been shown. This is already enough of a betrayal, and they have problems of their own. Before she left to come here tonight, Hilda had been worried about something: one of the elders, a man she called a prophet, had been arrested.

Levi's nose wrinkles as if he can smell the urine tang of the Mission gatehouse. 'I could, like, advance you a little money – you get yourself a proper room somewhere.' He hunches back into that jacket and it swallows him. All his edges are blunted but he still looks nervous about something, smoking with no hands while he fingers the tablet. The tip of the straggly cigarette glows to the sound of a sharp inhalation. Is he trying to make nice after the confrontation, or is this some convoluted attempt at a pass? No, he's smarter than that. Then the realization hits her; she's become an asset worth looking after, and even this utilitarian kindness fits him about as well as that jacket. It's not comfortable.

'See you soon, Levi.'

8.

Silas

A red light flashes, urgent but ignored at the corner of the desk. For almost twenty-two delicious minutes he has sat, transported by the magic of the screen, but as the play nears its end, its analgesic comfort starts to fade, and the pressures of an endless day loom as a faint ache at the edge of perceptible sensation, a warning of what is still to come. That pitiless light will be someone else wanting something, imagining their desires correlate with his priorities. For a few more stolen moments, he pushes the unwelcome thoughts away, focusing his full attention on the scene unfolding before him.

It is the culmination of an arc unfolding over six episodes. The alcalde, an unremittingly villainous official in charge of a generic rural settlement that could be anywhere from Panama to Peru, is about to reveal to the lovely Consuelo that she sacrificed her virtue for nothing. Her beau, Pablo – the man she hoped to save – is already dead. The denouement can take different forms but it is always an exquisite variation on the theme of moral compromise. For those too depraved to appreciate the melodrama, the Lat-Am import soaps offer two choices: alternative streams present the same storylines rendered as pornography of varying hideousness. The work must be wearing for the actors, but it creates a perfect product, a culturally pliable opiate for the worn workers of the Sino-Soviet bloc or their bourgeois counterparts in the West, perhaps even for the demi-human elite, although it's hard to imagine what currents of emotion circulate in the hormone-regulated soup beneath their metal shells. The episode ends with a lingering close-up of Consuelo, her delicate jaw quivering with grief and shame. Silas leans back into the punched leather comfort of his chair to savour the image for a moment before allowing work to intrude.

'Sybil.'

Unusually, his assistant fails to respond to the summons.

He lifts his feet from the desk, squares them on the floor in preparation to stand, pushing back the niggling urge to snap at her. There will be some good reason for her silence, and displays of hostility should be saved for the moments when they can serve some purpose. He pokes his head through the doorway separating their domains.

The spectacle of Sybil, with her artless mousy hair and dull, faintly bovine eyes, often provokes disappointment in visitors who come here. But in truth, she's an asset infinitely more valuable than any office decoration. Sybil treads the razor line between blind obedience and initiative like no other. This quality requires a total absence of self – no guiding principles, no emotional attachments – an ability to make critical judgements, coupled with the capacity for selective blindness necessary for ruthless action. The trust he places in her is near total.

'Sybil dear, when's the diplomatic pouch from São Paulo due?'

She nods acknowledgement of the question but does not instantly respond, enmeshed in an incomprehensible array of tasks, all no doubt urgent and essential for the furtherance of his agenda. For more than a minute, information flows through her, sucked in through fingers jabbing and stroking at the floating arcs of data, outputted through clipped voice and text. Her effortless, natural manipulation of unseen lives exhibits a level of technical and managerial competence he could

49

never attain, yet, he reflects, it is Sybil who performs his bidding, not her his. Proof, if it were needed, of the myth of meritocracy. Or to look at it another way, he possesses merit of a different kind he suspects Sybil will never own; he simply does not care that she is better.

'Sorry about that, I thought I had a few minutes. I can never get my head around how short those episodes are with the commercials cut out. What's Consuelo up to?' The data arcs floating in front of her dim and become transparent.

'She just found out Pablo's dead. She's taking it pretty hard. I don't suppose the next month's instalment is in yet?'

'I'm afraid not. Two or three days would be my best guess.'

'Oh well, work it is then. What was that light about? The Cult again?'

'Actually, no. It was Vasily Tchernikov.'

'Vasily? What does he want?' Like anyone worth knowing, Vasily Tchernikov wears more than one face. Publicly, he serves as the cultural attaché within the embassy of the Sino-Soviet Republic of Humanity, but the niceties conceal a more demanding role as station chief for their intelligence operation within in the city. Until recently, someone like him would have regarded Jerusalem as a dead-end posting, but of late the Republic has been making an effort to cultivate client states outside of the Machine sphere of influence; this makes him an asset worth maintaining.

'Something about repatriating some statues recovered from Palmyra. He says the Russian envoy in Damascus is insisting they be returned. Their presence in our Museum of Antiquities is "naked cultural larceny".'

'Vasily said that?'

'No, that was Damascus.'

Silas stays silent, taking a moment to savour the subtext of what is, on the face of it, a banal request for a few lumps of badly eroded sandstone. The Damascene government styles itself as the flag-bearer for a new style of democracy in the Middle East, but in truth they are masters of an irradiated shit heap, dancing to the tunes of their masters in Sverdlovsk. Of all the Republic of Humanity's client states, Damascus is the runt of the litter. The statues will no doubt be part of some gambit to claim cultural consanguity with the dead nations who used to occupy the real estate – a preamble to making wider territorial claims.

'Fuck them . . . No, wait a minute – these statues – are they any good?'

'They're unique: representations of Moloch recovered from the ruins of the temple of Baal in Palmyra. To the Shias and the Haredim they're blasphemies – both regard them as representations of Satan – but culturally they're significant, so we have them on display.'

'So getting rid of them could actually make a lot of people happy?'

'And annoy anyone in the city who cares about real history.' A mischievous smile curls the edges of Sybil's lips. This is what visitors to Silas's office do not see – the perfect sympathy, the way she moulds herself to his needs. It is a gift almost beyond price.

'You're making this decision too easy. Call the relevant curator. Tell him to pull the Moloch stuff from display and get it ready for transit.'

Sybil's gaze drops and she shifts awkwardly in her seat. 'Ah, I'm afraid that won't be straightforward. Boutros wasn't in today. Nobody seems to know where he is.'

'Boutros?'

'The "sanctimonious plank" who raised an official protest when you moved the Antikythera Mechanism into storage. He hasn't turned up to work since.'

'I imagine it's some sort of protest. Never mind, with any luck, he'll keep himself out of the picture for a while. Honestly, the fuss that man makes, you'd think he owned the bloody thing. And he used to seem such a reasonable sort too. Well, you'll have to get someone else to deal with the statues. It doesn't take a PhD to cover a statue in bubble wrap and tape . . . and call Vasily. Tell the Russian bastard he owes me a favour.'

'Of course. Would you like to run through your schedule now?'

'No, I need you to make some excuses for me. I'm going to court.'

Her head tilts. 'Court?'

'Our esteemed Chief Justice is presiding over a case that could cause him a little trouble. I might just catch the end of the evening session if I'm quick. I sense an opportunity here and I don't want to miss it. Is there anything that can't wait?'

She makes a face and swallows the answer she wanted to give. 'Just some griping. Nothing I can't handle.'

The prophet's eyes shine with the moist intensity of the unhinged, as if some hidden wellspring of emotion was constantly threatening to overflow. Beneath weeks of hair and dirt he is still a handsome man, an anomaly in a courtroom packed with decaying function-aries of the legal system. When he speaks, his teeth glint bright white between lips cracked and darkened by the sun.

'The Lord will be my judge.'

The actual judge seems unaffected by the implied insult. From Silas's seat in the galleries, Amos Glassberg might be a statue of Solomon, a lean figure swathed in purple fabric that can serve no practical purpose but to evoke the required history. The whole courtroom is an absurd parody of something imagined from the city's ancient past. Faux marble covers the walls and the steps leading up to the raised judge's chair. In places it is cracked and warped. Where moisture leaks around the outlets for the air-conditioning units, it darkens with mould. The cool they bring is worth a little rot. The heat of human bodies pressed together in the galleries is relentless.

Of course, the Solomon schtick is all part of Amos Glassberg's carefully cultivated image. The city's Justice Minister might be boredom incarnate, but he possesses a canny instinct for what the people want from the law, and in public he always maintains the stoic visage of a father governing quarrelsome children. Jerusalem doesn't do kings anymore, or even heads of state – the idea of all that power in the hands of one person is unacceptable to everyone who knows it won't be their man. Glassberg is as near to a ruler as the city's broken democracy permits. Other ministers have their fiefdoms, but all are answerable to the law. He rests an elbow on the elaborately carved arm of his judge's seat and addresses the man in the dock. 'I see. And which Lord would that be?'

A gentle smile calms the deranged face, hinting at some hidden joke, but Glassberg ignores it. He has seen too many messiahs fall into the trap of thinking this is a real conversation. This one is only the latest in the recent wave of immigrant Christian criminals to fill the courts. At moments like this, it is all too clear the centuries have not diminished the city's fearsome appetite for martyrs. Their particular faith seems to be of no consequence. Prophets, poets, and crusaders have all placed Jerusalem at the centre of Creation, and the people of the city love and fear them for it. The trouble is, however bright the ideal shines, the intellectual property is still tied to this grubby real estate surrounded by desert. When the conceptual city collides with the reality, the spectacle of collision draws the public to the courtroom like flies to a slaughterhouse. Glassberg knows this. Despite the staid exterior, his feel for the ebb and flow of the city's passions rivals Silas's own, which is why he must go.

The judge's gaze turns from the prophet to the prosecutor, a heavyset, middle-aged man uncomfortable in a tunic that reveals legs which, on balance, would be better hidden. 'What is the charge levelled at the accused?'

'Conspiracy to commit acts of terror, sedition, and criminal damage, your honour.' He straightens his skirt and tugs unconsciously at his wig. The outfit is another stab at Bronze Age retro, supposed to be an authentic representation of priestly garb from the era of the First Temple, but cheaper than the ministerial robe, and about as authentic as this courtroom. In another city, you might mistake the prosecution team for inept middle-aged transvestites, but history in Jerusalem is currency, and even a forgery is worth something.

'What form did this "terror" take?'

'On the second of August, he led an occupation of the Talbiya branch of K-Nect-U implant clinics. His followers vandalized the property and destroyed implants valued at almost two million shekels.'

Glassberg leans back in his seat. A sigh of impatience escapes him. 'Counsellor, what you are describing is a public order offence, culminating in criminal damage. I hope there is a reason you have elevated this to the city's highest court. Furthermore, I hope that reason is unconnected to the cameras we have present.'

A murmur passes through the room. Glassberg has addressed the elephant directly. He does that. Anyone who's spent time in his courtroom should know it, and yet somehow it always surprises people. It is one of the gifts that make him dangerous.

The prosecutor squirms. His plastic smile does a poor job of deflecting the implicit accusation: that the trial is political pantomime for the cameras, headline fodder for news feeds fuelling the fears of the anti-immigrant brigade. 'Please bear with me, your honour. The list of charges is extensive.'

Amos is merciless. 'But succinct; at least it will be if you wish it to be heard in this court.'

The crowd in the galleries around Silas trembles again, sensing conflict.

'Two days after the occupation, the clinic was burned to the ground. The perpetrators are in custody, and claim they were acting on the orders of this man.' A stubby finger points at the prophet.

'And obviously you've obtained evidence to corroborate their claim?'

'I have their sworn testimony.'

'I'll take that as a no, shall I?' The prosecutor opens his mouth, but Glassberg cuts him off. 'Well, we'll see in due course, won't we? Is that it for charges? You mentioned sedition?'

'When officers attempted forcibly to remove the perpetrators from the clinic, he claimed their authority was invalid, and multiple witnesses heard him instruct his followers to heed the call of a higher authority which he alone can interpret. It is both a blasphemy and a violation of civil law.'

'More or less the usual then?'

'Your honour . . .' The man adjusts his curled wig in a misguided attempt to assume an air of dignity. 'Cases like this strike a twin blow at the very fabric of our society. The clinics are vital for the installation and maintenance of citizen comm-plants. Without them, commerce suffers, and law enforcement loses a vital tool. Chaos and ruin threaten. This, I believe, is more than sufficient justification for the charge of terrorism.'

Silas bites back a bark of laughter at the legal hyperbole. There is more than a touch of the absurd in the spectacle. Glassberg's dignified disdain sets it off perfectly. He sees what's happening, but can't help being the straight man in the deadly theatre unfolding around him. He knows what will happen outside the court, as the pantomime of manufactured outrage reproduces itself in earnest on the streets. A man like him cannot see past the fire and blood to the opportunities they bring for anyone possessed of will and imagination. His lean jaw tightens, and his gaze tracks pointedly from the prosecutor to the cameras at the back of the court.

'Are you finished? I assume that little tirade was the reason we're all gathered here. I imagine there was enough there for it to have the desired effect?'

Silas grimaces. This is what makes Glassberg an obstacle, for all his plodding predictability. In a sentence he can steal the wind from anyone who tries to play the part of demagogue in his courtroom, and he does it without putting so much as a dent in his reputation for impartiality. The rebuke sends a thrill shivering through the crowd. The prosecutor looks around the room, pretending to gauge the mood while he searches for a rejoinder. He starts to say something, stutters and falls silent. The threat of a contempt charge hangs unspoken in the air.

'Right, shall we move this along? I'm sure we'd all rather be doing something else.' Glassberg assumes a breezy businesslike air. 'I'm throwing out the conspiracy charges and the sedition. There are a hundred lunatics saying the same thing on every street corner in the city, and I fail to see any benefit in turning the city's prisons into asylums or, indeed, into refugee camps. The charge of criminal damage is, I note, uncontested, so we can dispense with a lot of the formalities.' He sits up straight and addresses the prisoner in the dock. 'The accused will pay a fine of one hundred shekels and understand that any further instances of this behaviour will be more severely punished.'

The man in the dock smiles placidly as the bailiffs lead him away to his liberty, quietly certain his fate is the result of divine providence rather than any trivial human agency. His followers at the so-called 'Mission' will pay the fine without blinking. This is not their prophet's first appearance in Amos's courtroom, nor will it be his last. Nobody wants them in Jerusalem, even the Christians they claim fellowship with scorn them, but still they persist, funded by some foreign fanatic who hopes to earn his own place in heaven by importing religion to the Holy City.

Fury darkens the prosecutor's face. No doubt he imagines he will exact revenge for this humiliation in the city's looming elections. The prosecutor's chair is the traditional stepping stone to the Justice Ministry and the judge's seat currently occupied by Amos Glassberg, but he is the wrong man in the wrong place. His support from the traditionalists of the Syriac and Orthodox traditions will not be enough. The landscape is changing; new faiths disturb the old balances – in that sense the transparent evangelism of the Mission is no different to the Cult of the Machine: both sweep up human refuse and recycle it, building armies of the grateful. They don't dare wield their influence openly yet, but it is only a matter of time. Power, once gained, does not go unused. Already, in subtle ways, they force change upon a city that resists it by nature. And so they must endure the painful lessons learned by all the faiths that came before them, lured by the conceptual Jerusalem, and damned by the real.

The foreign churches will burn tonight. Frightened people will start the fires, their fear will spread like the flames, and then they will look for someone to make them feel safe from themselves. The city's fractured politics have long made it impossible for any one faith to govern, but for the right man, for someone with a vision for Jerusalem as more than a backwater city-state at the edge of the developed world, the cracks in the old order offer a chance to sow the seeds of a new era.

9.

Clementine

Something twists the night air around Clementine, dragging it through the narrow channels of the Old City's streets, raising tiny dust devils of grime that disappear in the dark. A storm blowing in from the desert? No, something else. She follows the flow, drawn by the sense of something unfolding, until the bark of human voices reaches her. The shouts sound faint and distant, but it's an illusion spawned by the wind blowing away from her; nothing is ever further than a stone's throw in the clogged vessels of Jerusalem's ancient heart.

She hears the crackle like snapping twigs before she sees the glow, a nimbus of orange floating above the rooftops like a second dawn: fire, sucking the air from the alleys, gorging on the tainted oxygen. The calculation of its position comes to her unbidden, and panic sours the back of her throat; the flames are coming from the Mission. She runs easily, slipping through pools of darkness between scattered bubbles of yellow sodium light, the movement a liberation she could never enjoy in daylight hours.

A small crowd lines the edges of the square around the Mission, watching the chapel roof burn as if it were a sacrificial pyre. A few figures, some robed, some ragged, scurry around the base of the white walls, leaning ladders against the gables the fire hasn't touched yet, running thin hoses to grime-encrusted hydrants, relics of another age. At the centre of it, she recognizes Hilda's bulk silhouetted against the flames: still, solid, a bulwark of calm amidst the panic surrounding her.

'What can I do?'

The older woman jerks around at the sound of her voice. Her gaze sweeps up and down Clementine's foreign clothes, the question of where she has been unspoken.

'It looks like it's just the roof so far. If we can stop it spreading, we can still save the Mission.'

'What happened?'

'Later, Clementine. We'll talk.' Her voice is stern, but unthreatening. The anger in it is directed elsewhere. 'Get to one of the ladders.'

She follows Hilda's pointing finger to a patch of white wall already darkened with soot. Two ladders lean against it at either side of the patch of blazing roof. One wobbles dangerously as a man bearing a thin green hose climbs to the top. She clutches it with both hands, but still it totters with every step the reluctant firefighter takes, threatening to slip away from its two tiny points of contact with the cobbled ground. As she leans her body against it, his movement vibrates through the quivering wood and into her, her entire bulk still insufficient to prevent the ladder's metal feet scraping against the stone.

At the top, the man waves a signal and someone at the hydrant gives a lever a quarter-turn. The hose gurgles next to Clementine's ear and water trickles from the tip, bringing shouts and urgent gestures from the holder. The small robed woman operating the pump hesitates before giving the lever another quarter-turn. There's a rushing noise and suddenly the water line starts twitching like an angry serpent. For a terrible moment Clementine imagines the hose's plastic splitting like a bean pod, unable to withstand the pressure within, but in seconds the trickle becomes a fierce, sparkling jet.

The ladder trembles against her as the hose-wielder shifts position to direct its flow into the heart of the blaze. She can see he's trying to climb higher onto the ladder's last rungs, but he keeps stepping back, sending new vibrations down through the wood. It must be the heat from the flames forcing him away. Her fingers grip the zip of her bodysuit's high collar. She could pull it up to cover most of her face – it's not fire-proof, but the nano-weave is tough and the insulation would stop her feeling the heat for a few minutes. She could do it. A few yards away, Hilda directs another shopkeeper's ladder towards the blaze, but it's too short for the Mission's high walls. The debt she owes to these people burns in Clementine's chest, but heroics bring attention. She might not get another chance to disappear.

The wail of a siren drowns the thought. A red-painted, six-wheeled vehicle creeps from one of the alleys with a slowness that belies the urgency of its cries. The Old City's narrow lanes do not permit speed. It stops directly behind Clementine, and something like a shiny gun on the roof of its cab swivels to point up at the fire. There is a roar of pumps and bright white foam arcs, dreamlike, into the heart of the blaze. It spatters onto the men on the ladders, but seems to land like soft snow, doing no harm. The fire simply dies. Its absence leaves silence, and Clementine stares in wonder at the roof, the nubs of blackened beams poking through the foam like boulders in the snow of a sudden, surreal winterscape, where moments ago flames crackled.

The spectacle over, the crowd around the edges of the square fades away. The fire truck simply reverses back into the alley it appeared from with a whine of electric motors, presumably guided away by its driving AI. The ladders are carried away. The reluctant firefighters become themselves again, the memory of the blaze persisting only as an acrid stink in the air. Clementine follows the trickle of robed figures retreating into the Mission.

When she gets to Hilda's room, the older woman is sitting on the chair in front of the desk, not the bed, where they usually talk. 'Where were you, Clementine?'

For a moment she struggles to speak, wrongfooted by the question. Her comings and goings seem trivial after the Mission's brush with catastrophe, but Hilda's voice makes it clear she is quite serious.

'I . . . I went to see some men about a job.'

'At this time of night?'

'They run a bar.' The betrayal is acid at the back of Clementine's throat.

Hilda stares for six heartbeats before nodding silently to herself, as if in response to some internal dialogue. 'I suppose that's your right. This isn't a prison. Why didn't you tell me?'

'I'm sorry, I didn't realize it mattered.'

'Maybe it doesn't. Maybe I'm a fool . . .' Hilda's words trail off.

'I don't understand, Hilda. What happened here? What's going on?'

'Perhaps you can tell me?' For a moment, the older woman appears lost in thought. 'No, no, forget that.'

Clementine's eyes close, her hands rise unconsciously to cover her nose and mouth as the implications hit home. Of course, what was Hilda supposed to think? This woman arrives, a self-confessed fugitive, and a day later, someone sets fire to the roof of the Mission. How could she not think there was a connection? And the timing – by pure coincidence it all happens just after she snuck out.

'I don't . . . I don't know anything about this. I don't think anyone knows I'm here. This . . . the fire – it's not what they would do.'

'Perhaps you should explain.'

'I'm sorry, I can't.' Clementine lowers her hands away from her face and lifts her gaze to meet the other woman's scrutiny, those green eyes boring into her from beneath the shock of copper hair. The temptation to confess threatens to swallow her. But it would be selfish; the knowledge brings danger. 'Perhaps it would be best if I go away for a while.'

Hilda flinches and gives a barely perceptible shake of the head. 'You don't have to.' The corners of her mouth relax. The anger that possessed her moments ago seems to flow away, dispelled by some internal discipline or ritual of acceptance. Clementine watches, fascinated by the subtle transformation. There is still so much unsaid. What is it that moves this woman to care for her above the strays who wander through these doors? She'd thought at first it would be sex, but the bed has remained hers alone.

'Who would set fire to the Mission?'

Hilda smiles sadly. 'I'm afraid there's a long list of suspects.'

'Why?'

'That's easier. We don't belong here, that's one thing a lot of people in this city agree on.'

'I don't understand. The work you do . . .'

Hilda takes a breath. 'It's hard to understand the city until you've lived here. The work we do, helping the helpless, is a visible reminder of all the ways the city doesn't work. People would rather turn a blind eye than see their own cruelty laid bare, and our beliefs frighten them.'

'I thought you were Christians.'

'Let me show you something.' Hilda stands from the chair and steps over to the bookcases against the far wall, her fingers ghosting across the spines of old volumes bound in cracked leather. The titles are unfamiliar: *The Revelations of Glaaki*, *The Pnakotic Manuscripts*, *De Vermis Mysteriis*. 'These books are our most treasured possessions, but they are not Christian scripture. Indeed, many Christians would consider them heretical. We gather knowledge because we accept there are truths in all faiths – they are all paths to connect with something greater than ourselves. We believe we all worship the same creator, whatever you wish to call her. So, yes, we are Christians, but we're the wrong kind. We are not pure.'

'That doesn't sound like a threat.'

A long sigh escapes her. 'If you've survived a thousand years by telling everyone they're damned unless they accept your trade-marked God, our mere existence is a threat to who you are.'

'So the fire . . .?'

'It's only the beginning, Clementine. I'm afraid there is worse to come.'

10.

Silas

The city burned bright last night. Four animated sparks of yellow twinkle in digital imitation at the corners of a cold blue street plan, shimmering in the air an arm's length from Amos Glassberg's desk. He blinks periodically in response to the recurring glitch that makes a section of the map flash bright white, a sudden annihilation. The sparks mark the sites of four fires, all at or near Christian sites of gathering or worship. You could link them by drawing the shape of a cross if you were so inclined.

'Thank you for coming, Silas. I know it's early, but last night was the worst violence we've seen this year, and there's more coming.'

He stands by the wall display, his spare shadow darkening one corner of the map. An aquiline nose and short, steel-grey hair combine to give him the appearance of a cleaning implement, which, in a sense, he is. We don't get on, but it is a mark of the man that he will turn to me for insight despite our personal incompatibility. His devotion to the city does not permit him the luxury of picking favourites. Still, his appeal for help marks the night's events as exceptional. The most recent blaze still smoulders. He looks away before turning back to speak.

'I'm sure you're aware of the theories flying around. The less responsible news feeds are already calling this the opening salvo in a new war of faith.'

'Amos.' His head turns at the uncommon use of his first name, even though as ministers of state we are theoretically peers. 'I'm glad you called me in, we don't get many opportunities to talk.'

He nods at the platitude. In theory we are supposed to attend regular shared briefings. City convention dictates the holder of the title 'Minister of Antiquities' is responsible for running the city's approximation of an intelligence service, which is supposed to assist law enforcement as and when required. When I took the job on, intelligence gathering was an inconsequential addendum for a city largely spared foreign influence, but times change, and I have tailored the role to fit them. The network of informants and contractors I have built up is of questionable utility to the public, but intelligence work is by its nature covert, so no one delves too deeply into what they actually do. The only downside to the arrangement is I must occasionally provide a morsel of genuine information as a fig leaf, and even if he does not suspect my involvement in the current unrest, Amos Glassberg will not be satisfied with banalities.

'I understand you're worried about the fires. Who wouldn't be? But I'm concerned they're a sideshow, meant to distract us from more pressing issues.'

'Pressing to whom, Silas? I asked for this meeting in the perhaps misguided hope you could tell me something about the fires. Would I have better consulted our fearless chief of police?'

He watches, studying me for any sign of vulnerability. The goad could be a simple attempt to play to my arrogance, or he could be digging deeper. It is not impossible I have been lured here under false pretences. Amos has historically been too preoccupied with the city's ongoing crises to look closely at ministries beyond his own, but complacency is a luxury I cannot afford.

'That would not be appropriate . . . I fear he may be involved in illegal activity; that's why I wanted to talk to you personally.'

'Fear? You?'

'Not for myself. For the city, of course.'

'For the city. Obviously.'

He knows I'm hiding something. He doesn't know what. I must tread carefully. An uncharacteristic display of civic duty would arouse suspicion, but if I play my part as avatar of necessary evil, pragmatism and duty will force him to rise to the bait. Of course, any information from me will be suspect, but corroboration is not hard to arrange, and the spectre of high-level corruption in the police force cannot be ignored. Taking action will hurt him; Ayed, the venerable police chief, is the closest thing he has to an ally, but a martyr like Amos does not shy from pain. The script practically writes itself. Even at the highest levels, police pay is meagre. Ayed has four daughters; one of them was involved in that messy scandal with the rubber costumes, and an opportunist who caught the incident on camera is bleeding him dry to keep it off the news feeds. All I have to do is let Amos draw the dots.

'And what urgent action must I take against the man who is your primary obstacle to becoming even wealthier, Silas? I don't understand you at all, you know? As far as I can tell you don't even do anything with the money.'

'These are matters of state, Amos. You would do well to take them seriously.'

'I asked you here to talk about the fires. If you don't know anything, you might as well leave. We're both busy men.'

'And I wouldn't dream of wasting your time, minister. I've requested a briefing from one of my analysts who's been looking into the matter, but he's running a little late. I was merely trying to make best use of the opportunity to talk. Communications between our departments are not what they might be.'

He nods acknowledgement, mollified or unwilling to press the point; I cannot tell which. This testiness is unusual. In another man, I'd say I'd touched a nerve, but it would be unlike Amos to show it. Could there be something else, deeper, troubling him? Is it possible the years spent papering the city-state's cracks are finally taking a toll? He has always seemed eternal, immovable – a foundation stone for the city's government while other ministers come and go – but the city is changing. The new faiths upset the old balances. The preliminary police report into the fires suggests a radical faction within the Greek Orthodox community may have been responsible for at least one, and the Machine Cult tops the list of suspects for the remainder. It's all so wrapped in caveats as to be functionally useless. A discreet cough from the doorway interrupts the train of thought. A man in a grey suit hovers.

'You're late, Belloc.' My rebuke elicits a subtle wince.

'My sincere apologies, ministers. I was in the field, gathering data. I felt, in the circumstances, accuracy was a more pressing concern than punctuality.'

Amos gives a nod of acceptance. Belloc is a boring little man, but he's a useful asset for occasions like this, where the important thing is that work is seen to be done. He wears the air of carefully cultivated anonymity common to analysts who prefer the thrill of secret knowledge to any vulgar outward display. If you didn't know he was a spook, you'd perhaps think he was back-office staff in one of the financial institutions. He walks busily across the room to where the digital display still flickers.

'May I?'

'Please, go ahead.' Amos straightens his spine and steeples his fingers, assuming a pose of quiet authority.

'Where should I begin? Do you want detail?'

'No, I'll ask for detail if I need it. My question is "Why?". Why is this happening now? We've always had our troubles – this is Jerusalem – but something is different now. I need to understand what it is.'

'Data is still coming in, but what we have does lead in a certain direction.' The map on the digital display flickers out of existence, to be replaced an eye-blink later by a page filled with graphs and charts. 'As you're aware, the insurrection in Southern and Western Europe has driven large numbers of Europeans to claim refugee status.' The deadpan delivery pauses for Belloc to gauge his listeners' ability to absorb the flow of information. Amos gestures for him to continue. 'In raw terms, the numbers we're facing in Jerusalem are not large, even for a small city-state, but the cultural impact they have is disproportionate.'

'I can see that. What is it about the newcomers that pisses people off? We've had Christians in Jerusalem for as long as there have been Christians. What difference does a few more make?'

'It's a matter of cultural homogeneity. The Greek, Armenian, and Syriac Orthodox Christians can trace their roots here back to a time before the old state of Israel, or even Islam itself – they're part of the furniture. They behave like people from the Middle East because, in large part, they are. The Missionaries, while they call themselves Christian, and observe much of what we would call classic Christian ritual, are importing a foreign brand of syncretism that potentially poses a threat to all the established religions. The one thing they can agree on is that they don't like the newcomer.'

'So you're saying it's a matter of theology? I thought rioting about that stuff went out with the Byzantines.'

An uneasy smile curls the corners of Belloc's lips. 'If you can forgive some speculation . . .'

'Go on.'

'It's not the message, it's the messenger.'

'What do you mean?'

Belloc pauses, nesting his chin between thumb and forefinger. 'The Mission is almost entirely run by women, both in its charitable endeavours and its commercial offshoots in agriculture outside the city. In Europe that wouldn't raise an eyebrow; the wars have slashed the number of men in the workforce. Here, it is visibly foreign, an enclave of a world we rejected on a societal level, and it is growing.'

Amos sags. 'Good grief, how fragile are we that we're threatened by a bunch of women running their own soup kitchen?' Belloc opens his mouth. 'No, no, I know there's more to the Missionaries, but still, it's enough to provoke despair. Thank you, you can go.'

The analyst gives a bow and turns to face the still-open door; then he hesitates. 'You don't want our provisional assessment of responsibility?'

'Is it anything more than a list of the usual suspects seasoned with speculation?'

The frankness of the question raises a smile from Belloc: a warm, genuine expression I've not seen in his briefings with me. He appears to think for a moment. 'No.'

Amos raises a plastic-bound folder containing the police report from his desk. 'I've already got one of those.' He waves it in a casual dismissal. 'Oh, one more thing. What's your name?'

'Belloc, sir.'

'Thank you, Belloc. You've been most helpful.' He turns to me. 'You know, Silas, I never cease to be impressed by the quality of your people. Perhaps the rest of the city government might benefit from adopting your ministry's recruiting practices.'

The pointed ambiguity is unmistakeable. The people who come to work for me do so for money, or for power, not for any high-minded ideals of public service, and yet, for now at least, Amos seems satisfied to reap the benefits. The sound of footsteps on polished cedar wood confirms Belloc's departure. I count to thirty-six, letting the silence stretch between us before turning in my seat to face Amos. He looks tired.

'What do you want to do?'

He shakes his head, and the bushy grey brows furrow. 'About the fires? Or about the rest of the bloody mess out there?'

'Either.'

'I'm not sure what I can do, Silas. Jerusalem has survived three and a half thousand years of history: plague, famine, and war. The city has outlasted all the empires that laid claim to it, but it has never had to contend with women who do not know their place.'

11.

Clementine

The museum storage facility is a cave of wonders cloaked in anonymity. It has the same battery of cameras covering the approaches as any of the other warehouses or light industrial units nearby, and probably a fat guard inside, not watching the feed. They are not the problem; the problems will come in forms I cannot see.

Metal pierces the nodules of scar tissue along my spine. The sharp tips of my dorsal antennae emerge bloodlessly through skin and clothing, but not without pain. Apparently I wanted it that way, a recurring, jagged memento to humanity forsaken. I still have gaps from the time before the operation. It seems stupid now, but acts of creation are haphazard things: no chance to learn from mistakes.

The aerials resonate, electrons flow between dipoles within the metals, and the body's hurt fades, drowned in a flood of new sensation, the stink and hum of multi-wavelength transmissions as interpreted by my nervous system. The human brain is not equipped to perceive or interpret microwave and radio frequencies directly, but it takes only a minor augmentation to process them into functioning analogues of sensory input, primarily tastes and smells.

71

Still, I don't have much time. The activity exhausts and terrifies the animal brain: like a glimpse of the sacred, it will leave you deaf, dumb, and blind if you stare too long.

The warehouse is an eye of calm in the sensory storm of the city's transmissions; the wireless networks, the phone calls, the radio chatter, they all slide around its edges. It must be shielded; a vast cage of copper or silver concealed within those grey walls renders it opaque to my senses. There will be a data link somewhere, hard-wired, buried and sheathed, no doubt, but if I'm right about this place, I won't need to start digging up the pavement.

A rudiment of my consciousness concentrates on maintaining a nonchalant walk past the unmarked entrance, as if I were heading towards the plumbing supply centre at the end of the lot. That part of me is essentially a minor sub-routine now, performing an unimportant, achingly repetitive task while my higher self works at the speed of thought. In this state, normal vision becomes the opposite of a dream, images totally real but empty of meaning. The hacker's art is to inhabit two worlds and to see the moments they intersect.

Blue light bathes a jowled face behind the reception desk. It does not turn at my passing, absorbed in a vidfeed that numbs the tedium of a job the guard must hate. My nose wrinkles at the reek of the trickle of data flowing to the device in his hands; no security system devised by man can withstand the relentless destructive pressure of boredom. There is my intersection.

My body continues its slow, meaningless progress while my higher consciousness follows the flow of sports updates and tepid retro porn into the device and then emerges into the cool, clean waters of the warehouse's sealed internal network. Three distinct odours assail me: inhuman presences dwelling within this cloistered pool. Two I recognize; one is unfamiliar. A sharp, citrus tang is a top-of-the-line Shimezu AI running the visual-surveillance systems. That's a nasty surprise – something like that belongs in a war zone or a bank, but it shouldn't matter, I'm not here to fight. As long as

I remain passive, I should be undetectable to the watchdogs, bathed in the odour of used data. A menthol reek is the wave patterns of something Chinese-built: a respectable generic clone of a security system created for some other purpose. The strange smell is like toffee, but musty. Maybe something locally built? It feels old.

I try sending it some neutral data packets routed through the city's municipal net and the guard's handheld device. There's no response, no sign this thing's even aware of the data. The other AIs are bristling with transmissions across the wavelengths, checking feeds from security cameras and microphones, but this one's like a sleeping dog. I tiptoe up to it, telling myself not to fall into the trap of my own metaphor. The sense-analogues are one thing – a reliable algorithmic transposition of one form of data to another; but metaphors are guesses, products of self, not process.

The interface is straightforward. This thing isn't asleep, it's just really stupid, barely even a proper AI. It self-identifies as the warehouse interior, taking inputs from tactile and pressure sensors in the floors and shelves, comparing them against pre-set norms and that's it. Its output is pretty much binary – is something touching me or not? Apart from answering that question 1,200 times per second, all it does is recalibrate every time something new comes into the warehouse: learn the new object, reset parameters, yes-no yes-no yes-no until doomsday.

I disconnect before the warehouse interior wakes up. The antennae retreat into their half-inch-wide housings within my vertebrae without sensation. An errant foot hits the floor too hard, my body clumsy and tired from too long on autopilot. At a safe distance, I turn around to look at the warehouse's physical reality, human senses and human thoughts wrestling with the uncomfortable data won through my intrusion, trying to marry it with what I see. The building sits on a kind of raised concrete foundation to put its floor level with an average truck bed. There are steps at one side of the platform leading to a blue metal door with a square window and an intercom system. The big stuff comes in and out through a rolling metal shutter-door facing the truck bay: superficially an easy way in but there'll be multiple layers of redundancy on those sensors. It would be good to see a delivery happening, but I've hung around too long already.

By the time my perception's realigned with my physical self, I'm at the plumbing store, guided by some primal instinct to queue. A man in a long brown overall is looking at me like I already stole some priceless treasure from their shelves of grey PVC tubing. I buy some copper wire to look respectable; then I walk half a mile to get out of the local sense-nets before calling Levi. Interface with the voice network feels painfully slow after the freedom of my intrusion, but in reality it is only seconds before we connect.

He cuts me off without a word – busy, or spooked by a contact he doesn't recognize. I don't have time for this. I push aside my fatigue to force open a connection via the city-net. The security protocols of his implant are as archaic as most of the software in Jerusalem. The line between us stays silent, not even the sound of breath, but he'll know it's live.

'Wait . . . What?' The first words I hear are confusion as he tries to disconnect. 'How the fuck? I can't . . .' He starts talking to someone else. 'I'm sorry, I've just got to take this real quick.' A pause. 'OK, dickwad, I'm not going to ask how you pulled whatever this shit is, just tell me who you are and what you want.'

'Relax, Levi. It's me.'

'Oh, it's "me". That's obviously OK then.'

'Levi . . .'

'Just so we're clear, it's not fucking OK for you to be in my head. And how the fuck did you do that? No, never mind, I'm busy right now.'

'What? I'm not supposed to call you? We've got a job to do.'

'Believe it or not, I have other things to do, also relating to the job. What's this about?'

'I'm going to need some kit, something bespoke.'

'Something else? Listen, I'm not going to be able to cover all these expenses. These jammers and transponders and whatnot are already bleeding me dry.'

'I'm not talking about optional extras here, Levi. This is how we do the job. Don't worry yet. This thing might not cost if we're smart about it.'

'OK, hit me. What is it?'

'We need to make a delivery to the warehouse.'

'A delivery? What are we going to deliver to that place?'

'It doesn't matter. The important thing is, whatever we deliver has to weigh, let's say, five kilos, and we've got to be able to make it disappear.'

'Disappear? What the fuck are you talking about?'

'You'll work it out, Levi. You're a smart guy.'

12.

Levi

What kind of a name is Clementine anyway? She sounds French, but when did they start naming people after fruit? How does she know she needs this shit? If I had the luxury of time, or options, I'd be asking some questions about my new-found partner in crime, but I don't.

The Old City looks empty for the eighty minutes between the day's first two rush hours. Dawn comes late in these streets; some days, it doesn't come at all. In October the sun gets just about high enough to shine over the jumble of rooftops around noon and the light never makes it to street level. No point me rushing. The guy I'm seeing is still going to be waking up. Moshe's an old-fashioned stoner. He's a good guy, maybe the smartest I know, but if he's not talking he's sleeping. His apartment is way over the other side of town. We both moved away from family: difference is, he made money. Now he's in one of these fancy new developments on the cleared bomb sites. They say the contamination is all cleaned up now, but I also heard people say there are rats in the basements with two heads.

There are seven gates out of the Old City now. They were already too small and too few before the walls got blown to shit, but three thousand years of history makes sure improvements don't happen. The most recent addition predates the automobile by maybe four hundred years, and the one thing everyone in the city can agree on is whoever put it there is going to hell, so we've still got tiny gates in busted-up walls that no one's ever going to pay to fix. Only one of them heads the right direction for Moshe's – the Dung Gate. Apparently it's historical.

It's bright as soon as you get out. The road follows a twisting stream hidden by the trees that cling thirstily to its edges. Look in any other direction and all you see is this yellow space around you: yellow dirt, yellow rocks – it's a bad road through a two-mile band of dead earth before you get to the suburbs. The only life you see is lizards and crows. Fuck knows what they eat. Each other, maybe?

The cluster of fancy new developments casts a shadow that kind of hovers over the badlands – like it doesn't want to touch the bad dirt. The buildings are all metal and glass with this strip of green all around that just screams money. As you get closer you can see the strip is more like a field – a whole line of gardens. I hear they reconstructed the aqueducts all the way to the Sea of Galilee just so Moshe and his neighbours could keep their orchids nice, maybe hit up a round of golf.

The funny thing about these towers is, you can walk right in the front door from outside. No one stops you, and there's all these couches and chairs in the lobby where you can just sit like you own the place, so that's what I do. It takes about a minute for some goon in a comedy peaked cap to appear and tell me to get out. I enjoy the look on his face when I mention Moshe. Moshe will pretend to be pissed that I brought him into it, but he loves this shit – what's the point of being a somebody if your name's not getting thrown around? The goon goes away, and I sit down to wait.

When he comes out of the elevator, Moshe's wearing his serious face. 'The fuck you doing here, man?'

'Nice to see you too, Moshe. You know I walked a long way to get here? This isn't exactly the heart of the bustling metropolis.'

'I know where I live, Levi.'

'So that's it? I come all the way here just to get the cold shoulder? Maybe I should have come around your office instead?' Moshe's a good guy really. He just needs reminding of two things: we go way back, I'm a pretty useful guy to know, and I don't give up easy. OK, maybe three things.

'Shit, Levi. You could at least fucking call.' He shields his hands with his body as he punches in the code to his door, which I take as a personal insult on two levels – one: that he ever thinks I would rip him off; two: that he thinks I'm dumb enough to think a shitty code lock is his only security.

The door opens up and my spine goes rigid and my fingers cling to the frame. There's no floor to Moshe's apartment, no walls, just empty space and a fourteen-storey fall into what looks like a duck pond. 'Moshe, the floor, you asshole!'

'Oh, sorry. I forgot.' He claps his hands twice and the floor appears as a layer of dull graphite grey. The furniture stops floating in mid-air and my fingers come away from the door frame, taking with them little chips of lacquer where my nails dug in. *Forgot, my ass.* The walls are still invisible, not even a trace of the glass or the steel beams. I can't believe people pay to live like this. He perches, leaning forward on the edge of a soft couch that wants to swallow him, and gestures for me to do the same. 'So, what are we talking about, Levi?'

'Baseball.'

'Baseball?'

'Fuck baseball, man! I'm here to talk about getting some gear. What did you think?'

'Oh, I don't know. I thought that maybe, since you're always reminding me "we go wayyy back", this might be a social call.'

Touché. 'Don't be like that. This is serious. I need some gear, man.'

'OK, I'll bite. What do you need?'

'Two things: a microwave TX relay and a variable spectrum jammer.'

He looks at me like he just noticed something nasty growing out the side of my head. 'And what kind of party are you planning with those toys?' It's a rhetorical question. He doesn't need to know. That's the deal. 'That's a funny order for a couple of reasons. You know the microwave relay is legal, right? You start walking now, you'll be in Radio Shack in forty-five minutes. They'll sell you one.'

Obviously, I did not know that. It did not occur to me that my thief would be asking for stuff from the hardware store. 'What if I don't want my face on the Radio Shack CCTV as a guy who just happens to have bought one of these gizmos right now? You think of that?'

Moshe's face says my save kinda worked. 'That other thing – the jammer – that's a totally different deal. That's explicitly military-grade tech. Just owning one of them is enough to see you doing time.'

'Which is why I came to see you, my friend.'

'OK, let's say I can help you out. What's my end of this deal?'

'That's up to you. We can make this a cash deal, or I can get you the things you want?' I know what his answer's going to be, but the cash offer makes it look like I got alternatives if Moshe doesn't want to play.

'Cash? You got fifty thousand shekels in that big leather jacket, Levi?'

I give a shrug that looks like maybe, but Moshe knows it's no. It doesn't matter. Moshe doesn't want my money. The thing you've got to understand about Moshe is that he's a good guy who likes to play at being bad. The important word here is 'play'. I will take him out for some crazy nights of bad drugs and hot girls, and I will make sure he doesn't get ripped off, and nothing happens that could get back to his beautiful wife, or to his generous employers. Moshe doesn't really have a job. I mean, technically, he's some kind of a professor at the university, but he doesn't have to teach students or any shit like that. What he's got are a few ideas that people with money think are so fucking awesome that they'll throw cash at him, just in case he ever turns them into realities. It's a great scam. Who knows? One day, he might even build one of whatever the fuck they are.

'I got big plans for you, my friend. Insanity. We are talking total insanity.' I've barely even started the spiel, and Moshe's already smiling, and I'm thinking of what fucking insane debauchery I'm going to have to invent to get him excited and why I didn't work this out on the way over, when my line buzzes. I tap my comm-plant to cut the connection but it starts up again. Moshe's starting to look pissed off, like I've shown him the food but I'm not letting him eat.

'I'm sorry, man, I have to take this. I'll be, like, twenty seconds.' It's Clementine – some shit about needing more gear. This job is going to kill me. By the time I finish the call, Moshe's not quite holding the door open for me to leave. 'I'm real sorry about that, man. Let me tell you what's up. It is going to be wild. Have you ever been to the Aurora? You should see this place, it's incredible . . . Oh, before we get into it, that was my partner on the line. I got to add one more thing to the list.'

For a moment his face does that screwed-up thing that means he's actually pissed off, but it goes, and I know I've hooked him. 'What is it, Levi? What do you need?'

'I was hoping you might tell me, old friend. I need to make something that weighs, let's say, five kilos, disappear . . . and re-appear again, like it was never gone.'

'Disappear? What are you talking about? I'm not a magician, man.'

I take a slim silver case out of my chest pocket and flip open the lid. His eyes go wide like he just popped one of the pills inside. He's enough of a connoisseur to recognize a pick 'n' mix of the finest chemicals money can buy. His finger hovers over a pink bomb of opioid jelly like a tiny dessert.

'You know what? I can cancel a few meetings.' He pinches the capsule from the box and tips his head back to swallow it dry, letting out a deep sigh as it goes down. 'Abra-fucking-cadabra, man.'

13.

Clementine

The Mission is near empty, the city's desperate borne away on soft breezes of tropical air from the Nile Delta and South Sinai. Or perhaps it is something else that keeps them away: a faint sense of danger, like the smell of burnt wood, lingers since the fire. Whichever the reason, only a handful of dark swaddled bodies surround the stone arch of the entrance tonight. Hilda says this is what happens whenever a warm spell slows the onset of winter. They still come for the food, but they evaporate into the gentle night as soon as their bowls are empty.

As I settle into the routine of clearing dishes from the empty places in the dining room, part of me wants to run from the decision I have made, but instead I drift between tables like a ghost bound by the ties of emotion to haunt this place. My path is set; money is the only thing that will keep me safe if I have to start running again. Even if I stay, backing out of my crime would make me enemies in this city; that is another thing I cannot afford. Eventually, the fear fades, dulled by the meditation of repeated movement as I pile dirty dishes next to the slowly filling sink.

Leftovers fill my nostrils with the odours of sumac and tarragon. Even though it's only been a few days, it doesn't seem like foreign food any more; the only trace of the exotic is the barely detectable tang of the city's dust: that never goes away. If I was local, I wouldn't even know it was there. The smells sour and dim as I immerse the cooking pots in soapy water. The food here is good – better than the ordinary working people get at home. The faithful grow most of it themselves on farms outside the city – beans for the Lord.

My fingers pause on an indentation in the hard green plastic of the kitchen shutter before closing it; the memory from that first night of the yellow-eyed figure, his blistered hand reaching for a bowl, comes unbidden. It feels like a fiction now, stress perhaps, but it was so clear. Does the human mind conjure such unelaborated hallucinations? Why do I keep it to myself? Some peculiar property of the memory makes it feel forbidden.

In her room, Hilda's still up, hunched over her desk in a triangle of yellow light. She starts at the sound of the door opening, which is odd, because she's expecting me. After months of travel, the routine we have wordlessly slipped into is a quiet joy. I sit on the bed and she looks away. The evenings have become our time to talk, for her to teach me about the Mission and the city, but for some reason silence hangs heavy between us tonight, something beyond our tacit understanding not to discuss the past. Guilt for my nascent crime is a bitter taste at the back of my throat. Surely she cannot know?

I wait on the bed while she lays down the pen in her hand and stacks papers. A minefield of piled documents covers the floor between us. She perches on the edge of the mattress, an arm's length away.

'Clementine, I've got some bad news . . . well, perhaps it's not that bad. It might turn out well. It depends how you feel about it.'

'How I feel?'

'I'm sure you understand things are getting difficult in the city. Well, we've had a meeting about it and we've decided we have to move.'

'Move?' I'm repeating her words stupidly. This is not the conversation I expected. I'm out of practice when it comes to meaningful conversation, or I never learned.

'Oh, I was afraid you might feel like that.'

Like what? I haven't said anything. 'What's going on, Hilda? Is this about the fire?'

From somewhere she summons a bright smile. 'In a way, yes. We're going to scale down activities at the Mission; we're keeping the kitchen and the clinic open, but the dormitory's shutting down and we're moving all staff off site.'

If I wasn't sitting down I'd feel dizzy. I've only just stopped running. I started to put down roots without even noticing and now they are being torn away. How could I be so stupid? 'When did you find out? When is this all happening?'

'A couple of hours ago, while you were doing dinner. It's happening tomorrow.'

'Tomorrow . . .' My voice is so much harder than I want it to be.

'It's not really a choice. I have to think about everyone's well-being.' I sit up straighter, but I can't look at her. It's that fearless, open gaze. It's too much. It takes everything. 'Clementine, I think you should come with me. I think I can make that work.'

Hearing those words sends a shiver through me. I am wanted, cared for in some human way I could never have imagined. The moment of heightened sensation makes me briefly aware of the metal in my spine; I feel it as shards of a cold, jagged barrier to ever belonging. When I chose this body, intimacy was an abstract concept to me. The ideas I had were gleaned from stories which painted it as a by-product of sex. This is something else, a filling of a void in me I did not know existed, but the comfort comes tainted with the fear of loss. The joy hangs on the care of one single, fallible human.

I lean forward, uncertain, and put my arms around Hilda. She returns the sitting hug awkwardly. Then I remember she said 'tomorrow'. I have a robbery to carry out.

She looks at me, green eyes wide with expectation. There is something about her gaze that transcends those big hips and the blotches of redness in her complexion. I can only call it beauty. It is entirely unrelated to the arbitrary dimensions and second-hand aesthetic judgements of this body I chose for myself. How could I have not understood? This is what my kind have lost, turning our backs upon the physical. It is something precious beyond measure, and we don't even know it's gone.

'Hilda, I can't come straight away. Can you give me a few days?'

'Oh.' In the sound of a single word, I hear the gravity of my mistake. Care for another is a tendril of emotion extended from the human self. I have sliced it at the root. Now she grimaces at the wound. I'm not equipped for this. I'm grasping for metaphors to make things clear, but they're treacherous guesses at the truths I want to express. I need an algorithmically verifiable analogue for these emotions, but there is none. Suddenly, I want to explain, tell her everything, but that's impossible. The truth would put her in danger: more than she already is.

'I'll come, Hilda. I'll come as soon as I can. There's just something I have to do in the city. It will take me three days – four at the most.' Even though I believe them, the words still feel like a lie. Why is that? Because I know they're not believed? Do I somehow sense that external reality, and internalize it as emotion? Are these thoughts the product of ineffable human senses infinitely more sophisticated than any of the devices within me? Or are they a fantasy, constantly feeding upon itself? I cannot know.

'What is it you have to do?'

Become a thief. Steal from the city that has taken me in. Make money because I might have to start running again any day now. All these things I don't say. 'I have a job.'

'You have a job here. There'll be work at the farm.'

'I can't eat leftovers forever. I've got nothing but the clothes on my back. I need to be able to live in this city. Don't worry, it won't take long and it pays good money.' The words are empty, but they are all I have. Hilda's clouded eyes show she's stopped listening.

'I can't help you if you stay in the city.'

'I understand.' This lie feels true, even though I never understood what I did to deserve her care. I force a smile onto my face and push myself off the bed. While I change out of the robe, Hilda busies herself stacking papers, gathering the Mission's impedimenta to prepare for the move. I have nothing to pack. Travelling light has been a tactical necessity for as long as I've been in this body, so I can always leave quickly, but now I find myself wishing for something – an object, a token to tie me to this place and this person. I pause at the door to see Hilda looking at me.

'Stay safe, Clementine.'

The fine down on my exposed skin prickles in the chill night air outside the Mission, each hair a vestigial remnant of humanity's ape ancestors pointlessly reproduced on a body that will never achieve authenticity. The white facade of the building glows softly in the dark, oblivious to my presence, its refuge lost to me, perhaps for good. The list of alternatives is short; I am still a stranger in this city.

The tidal pull of the familiar draws me to the only route I know, to Yusuf's place. My feet follow the well-trodden path at their own pace, without urgency or intention – the habits of caution from almost a year as a fugitive are too quickly lost, drowned in the comfort of routine.

Two stars appear in the gloom before me, head height, unmoving, then gone. They reappear, closer now; the scintillations are tiny spheres of light fixed on the wall of an ancient cistern curving away from my outstretched arm. My hand seeks its solidity, but the mortar between the stones crumbles where I touch, and the lights vanish again. A single step takes me to where they were. Even at night, the wall radiates the cool of the thousands of gallons stagnating within. Two inhuman eyes open, centimetres from my own, ellipses of black outlined in a scattering of gold, hovering in the dark. The eyes are vast, but the body beneath them is no bigger than my hand, vivid red barely visible against the brick, an amphibian intruder lured from its home to this counterfeit oasis. The creature's invisibility is a function of a perfect stillness that seems almost inorganic. The blackness at the centre of the orbs encircles all of me in distorted silhouette. A vast pink tongue flashes out at bullet speed to strike something hovering unseen in the darkness, and a whine at the edge of hearing, previously unnoticed, stops suddenly. The hunt is over and the eyes close, rendering the watcher invisible. The Jerusalem night sighs, heedless of the murder. I am a part of this ecosystem now.

From somewhere ahead, beyond the crumbling cistern, a soft murmur echoes and dies, trapped in the Old City's maze of streets. A faint nimbus of orange light briefly illuminates the end of the alley and three human shadows pass before it fades away, offering no clue to its origin.

The alley ends in an open space, but still no starlight reaches the cobbles. Looking up, I realize I stand in the domed shadows of the sacred patchwork they call the Holy Sepulchre. The orange glow spills around the edge of one of the building's corners. I can hear the noise of bodies moving and hushed speech, a chorus of whispers. Instinct pushes the sharp tips of my antennae through skin into air. An act of will retracts them. The act of observing through the spectra carries a risk of being observed by anyone with technology more sophisticated than the locals possess; I must rely on human senses here. This body was optimized in its construction – visually, aurally – to beyond human norms, but still it feels a dull tool with which to confront the unknown. It trembles with the treachery of adrenaline. In my previous existence I would have sneered at this.

I should walk away. Investigation presents a needless risk, but I have fled for so long to reach this city. I cannot flee the unknown forever. My back stirs centuries of dust from the walls as I edge around the corner and then light dazzles me, forcing my eyes shut.

It must be a thousand candles held aloft on outstretched arms. The light they cast dims in just a few metres but together they are a blinding forest of stars, so bright it obscures the bearers beneath. There is something strange about this crowd, their stillness, their hush, the way the light gleams from shoulders or heads, as if they were clad in mirrors. As my eyes adjust, I become aware I am not the only watcher. Three impressively bearded priests stare down from the church's steps, radiating disapproval but saying nothing. Closer to me, dark figures watch from the doorways.

'They're taking a risk coming here.' One of the shapes leans into the light as it turns to face me, a short man with a faint scar marking his top lip. His voice is low but quavers with adrenaline. He leans forward, weight on his toes, fists clenching and unclenching.

'Who?' A single syllable betrays me as an outsider.

He looks at me now, face half lit in the orange candle glow. He shrugs. 'The Cult of the Machine. The metal arms, the shiny heads – who else they going to be?' He nods at the crowd. They seem unconcerned by the watchers, all facing an object at the centre of their gathering, an almost man-sized sculpture borne on the metal shoulders of four of the faithful. Slabs of pitted iron form the stylized shape of two mechanical gears, overlapping one another like a Venn diagram. An unblinking eye fills the intersection.

'The Machine?' The urge to run is overwhelming. My limbs tremble with the strain of suppressed movement. This must be close to a thousand people marked with a symbol I have spent a year fleeing from.

'They think your body is what drags you to hell, so they're trying to leave theirs behind.'

A sickening realization hits me. This is worship. These people have gathered here to show their faith in gods I know to be false.

The Machines were men once, born as creatures of flesh, but these people are destroying their bodies in crude imitation of something they cannot understand. Somehow, even in a land hostile to their kind, the Machines have found a way to exert their will.

As I turn away, one thought eclipses everything.

They're here.

Not the Machines, at least – not yet – but their disciples: primitive, ignorant, but still dangerous.

I am not safe.

I kill the urge to run as soon as I'm out of sight of the church. Instead, I subject myself to the calculated agony of a slow, serpentine route, stopping intermittently to check for tails. It takes more than an hour to get to Yusuf's. He's closing up, but the door's still open. 'Hey.'

'Hey.'

'Is Levi around?'

Yusuf usually watches me the way men do, but when I walk into the light he tilts his neck strangely, like he's trying to see around me, as if my encounter with the Cultists has left me marked in some way. He blinks and shakes his head. 'Nah. He left more than an hour ago. He doesn't live here, you know . . . officially. This is more like his office.'

'I need to talk to him.' I can see on Yusuf's face that I'm not the first person to come in here asking for Levi, and I can see the stock answer is 'No, fuck you for asking', but Yusuf and I share secrets now: maybe not that many, but enough for him to give me an address.

It's not far. A doorless stairwell is almost invisible next to the neon glare of a twenty-four-hour laundromat. The dim light within outlines a skinny figure watching three of the machines spin. It's not Levi – no jacket. His door is on the first floor, directly above the laundromat. I knock, but there's no answer. Perhaps I should call, but it feels dangerous when I could be under observation. Those Machine people are close. I don't know what they can do.

I knock again. Nothing. I fumble in my pocket for offcuts from the lengths of wire I bought earlier. They're not perfect, but they'll do. I twist two together to make a tool and slide it into the lock in the metal door handle, feeling for the movement of tumblers. It's better made than I expected; it takes me forty seconds before the final cylinder clicks into place and the door falls open, only to stop abruptly when a metal chain pulls taut. I slide a hand around to unclip it, but suddenly the black emptiness of a gun barrel fills my vision.

'Tell me why I shouldn't dust you now, motherfucker.'

'Levi, it's me.'

'Fuck! You! I could have shot you in the brain.' His face appears in the crack in the door, a little flushed but otherwise normal. He's right; he could have shot me. I was sloppy, too preoccupied with the threat outside. 'I guess you better come in before someone else shoots you. Remind me to save a bullet for Yusuf.'

The short hallway is dark except for yellow light spilling through a door halfway along on the left, and there's a flickery blue glow of screen at the end. The floor hums with the vibration of the machines in the laundromat below.

'I was taking a shit. You didn't have to break in.'

'I'm sorry. The door's OK.'

He gestures to a cluttered sofa, dented in the middle by single occupancy. He waits for me to sit, then sits too close. 'Don't worry about the door. What's so urgent that you need to come see Levi in the middle of the night?'

He leans forward to retrieve an abandoned cigarette from the low glass table in front of us. The side of his leg moves against mine. His slightly crooked smile makes me feel sick. I don't need this. I slide back into the clutter of takeaway containers to create space between us.

'Please . . . I didn't come here for company. We work together. That's it, OK?'

He shrugs. The pain of rejection does not keep Levi Peres awake at night. 'Sure. You'll forgive me if I get a little confused if you just show up at my apartment like I made a booty call.'

'Let's just forget about it, shall we?'

'All right. So what's up?'

'I need somewhere to stay for a few days – 'til the job's done.'

'You just turned down my hospitality.'

'No, I just refused to fuck you. Look, can't we just forget about that?'

'This ain't a hotel.' He holds his arms out in a gesture that encompasses the whole room. A white-tiled kitchen area near the window strobes pink and blue with the light from the laundromat sign outside. A pile of drinking vessels fills the sink, but the kitchen's otherwise empty, a forbidden zone to the clutter that infests the rest of the room. Two big bales of what must be tobacco fill one corner of the room like furniture. The smell of them overpowers everything else, but that's probably a blessing. Brown carpet crunches softly beneath my feet, even though I can only take tiny steps. Piles of shiny objects cover every available surface and spill onto the floor. I recognize a few as holy symbols.

'What is all this stuff?'

'It's my business. Everything's got a buyer.'

'Levi, how did you sneak up on me at the door? Most people can't do that.'

His eyes glow with satisfaction. 'I got some skills. Maybe you thought you were dealing with some schmuck?'

'If I did, I was wrong.'

'Like I said, this place is my business. I'm careful. There's plenty of people who want to know what Levi Peres is bringing in and out, so they can maybe get a piece of it, or all of it. I can't have that, y'know? Some people, they spend millions to protect their privacy. Not me, man. I got the laundromat.'

'The laundromat?'

'Those machines are on 24/7, and they are noisy motherfuckers.' The rumble beneath my feet bears testament to the truth of his words. I'm used to the noise after a few minutes of standing here, but it's still there, enough to fox any sound detector. He keeps talking, but from this single clue the rest fits itself together. Those washers and dryers rotate constantly, at slightly different, unpredictable speeds. Metal rotating within metal – it's like the Earth's core, a battery of machines generating electromagnetic waves at fluctuating frequencies. To anyone attempting sonic or microwave surveillance it's like trying to pick out a tune when someone's shouting in your ear, and they can't even filter it out because the shouting changes all the time.

'That's . . . incredible. You worked this out on your own?'

'And the rest of it. That sign outside . . .' He gestures to the pink and blue at the window. 'Anyone trying a visual scan through my window is gonna have contrast issues. It's like we're standing behind the sun . . . OK, maybe not the sun, but you get the idea.'

I crouch and clear a space in the neon-lit clutter beneath the window frame. 'I'm sleeping here.'

He shrugs, palms up. The only way I'm leaving is if he kicks me out, and right now I'm too valuable an asset for him to take that risk. No bedroll, no covers, but for me, as long as my partner in crime can cope with a housemate, this might just be the safest place in Jerusalem.

14.

Silas

Spears of faint light, like promises of revelation, strobe through the gaps in the wall of high-rise towers crowding the freeway as the limousine glides past. The air-con is a numbing whisper in my ear. Outside, the sun is barely visible behind layers of low cloud clinging to the shoulders of the hills around the city, but already the morning air shivers with the promise of heat. This strange Indian summer has lasted days now. It is vaguely unsettling, but perhaps fitting for the day's events.

From the fold-down seat opposite me, Sybil spews a susurrus of briefing information. The plan is intricate, and multiple pieces must fall into place for it to work. As Minister of Antiquities, I am guest of honour at the opening of a new building: 'The Centre for Interfaith Dialogue'. It was scheduled for a couple of months' time, but in light of recent events, I have pushed for the grand opening to be brought forward. It is the kind of nod towards action that people expect in times of crisis. That is how the city works – fighting fires with gestures to make people feel good about themselves. There will be expensive wine from the Lebanon and speeches about mutual understanding, and when the party is over, my guests will look at the flames, puzzling over why they still burn.

The new building shines, even in the dull early morning light. It is a dome (what else) formed of triangles of glass, linked by brackets of mirror-bright steel. As the car pulls in, you can see the shimmering hemisphere is actually a vast shell for a much smaller construction of white marble, built in the classical style as an affectionate pastiche of the city's Hellenic past. The Greeks gave Jerusalem the only religion we ever managed to shake off, but the upside of theological failure is a politically neutral design aesthetic, perfect for gesture architecture.

A tall, exquisitely mustachioed man in a Sikh turban greets the car. He introduces himself as the centre manager, and guides me through a brief tour of the building, hurrying through areas where wires and pipes still show. Mostly the place seems to be a profusion of meeting rooms unlikely ever to be used to their full capacity.

The tour ends in a garden area out the back. Stones of light and dark rock half buried in concentric circles form something that feels like an arena. A quartered ring of sparse newly planted greenery creates the outermost boundary, and a manufactured flow of air defies the enclosure of glass and steel above to simulate a gentle breeze. The combined effect is rather lovely, but it's not at all obvious why this modest marbled meeting centre and its grounds fill just a tiny fraction of the glass dome's vast footprint. The design would be perplexing if you weren't aware of the other purpose it serves, one known only to myself and Sybil.

The usual suspects are all here, and the absences are entirely predictable. The Haredim never come to these things; sharing the real estate is anathema to them, even at a place like this, outside the ring road that forms the arbitrary boundary of Jerusalem proper. The Arabs capitalize on their rivals' absence, two groomed imams affecting the air of patient martyrdom that the Jews once patented, a mute, relentless reminder that everyone else here is an intruder on their land. The bearded, dark-robed priests of the Greek, Armenian, and Syriac Orthodox Churches wear solemn expressions in keeping with their self-appointed role as guardians of the Christian holy sites. The whole tableau could be from any moment in the last two thousand years, but for the discreet glitter of implants behind their ears, a necessary concession to modernity for anyone involved in the cut and thrust of city politics.

The only noteworthy presences are the newcomers. The clanking bodies of the Machine Cult delegates are a vulgar intrusion of the modern world. Their aspiration to a horrifying apotheosis – a transformation into one of the West's living Machines – renders them unpalatable to the other faiths, but in truth it is no stranger than many of the ancient rituals. As a child, I found the shine and incongruity of their half-human bodies endlessly fascinating. Looking at them with adult eyes, seeing the spider-trace of veins in pale, sickly skin, it is hard not to wonder what emotional scars drive them to such self-degradation.

Of course, no gathering of the city's faithful would be complete without the delegation from the Mission. The 'prophet' Cephas is immediately recognizable from his appearances in court. His artfully grime-stained presence is a perfectly judged contrast to the immaculate clergy of the other faiths – pure theatre. He eschews small talk, choosing instead to tilt his chin upwards and smile blissfully at the rapture of communion with the Almighty. His companions are a mismatched pair of women in coarse woollen robes. One is tall, pale, elegant, if a little hook-nosed – more interesting than the entirely generic sexuality of the PAs who hover at the shoulders of the fatter dignitaries, status symbols who serve only to broadcast their owners' inadequacies. The other woman is short, round-shouldered, a shock of red hair and green eyes just visible beneath the hood. She wears an expression that might be terror, or wonder at her surroundings, or possibly a mix of both. Sybil breaks the silence.

'Allow me to introduce Sister Ludmila Baryshnikova and Reverend Mother Hilda Frink of the Mission.' The tall one nods politely; the short pink one acknowledges me with a furtive glance. In recent years, Europeans have become a sufficiently common sight on the streets that one or two will not draw attention, but there is something striking about this mismatched trio. Perhaps it's the context? They blend more easily in the squalor of the Old City.

'A Sister and a Mother? Does the Mission have brothers too? Or only prophets?'

The gentle jibe elicits a sharp look from the short one, but Sister Ludmila laughs.

'Is the ministry this welcoming to all of the city's religious representatives?'

'The city government does not discriminate between the faiths. I'm universally unpleasant to all of them.'

'Even to the Jews, Minister Mizrachi?' The emphasis on my last name is unmistakeable. It carries an accusation that has been levelled at me since before I started the job, that I am a despoiler of history who bothers only to preserve artefacts of Jewish heritage while leaving the rest to rot or disappear.

'I'd tell you to ask the Haredim for their view on whether I favour the Jews, but of course they're not here: probably too busy enjoying the fruits of my favour.'

She gives a low chuckle in acknowledgement of my parry; it is a matter of public record that the Haredim are my most vocal critics. The short one, Hilda, just watches me in silence, her stare strangely intense.

The sound of applause interrupts the conversation. I follow the gazes of the crowd to where they're looking at a new arrival. Glassberg holds court at the centre of a circle of guests thrilled at the 'surprise' appearance of the city's premier official. Theoretically, ministerial movements are kept secret for security reasons, but the recent troubles make Glassberg's showing as predictable as clockwork. Between banalities he finds time to catch my eye more than once, no doubt thinking of our recent meeting, perhaps imagining this day will afford a chance to collaborate on solutions to the violence. Alas, I have other plans.

The interfaith centre is 30 per cent funded by my ministry. Apart from providing a useful veneer of respectability, it grants me a stage. Two white-gloved curators bear a box of dark wood with battered brass bindings at its corners. This is my cue. They wait in the cleared space at the centre of the stone circle while I detach myself from conversation. The female curator gives a little nod and hands me the inevitable gloves. The other one opens the box in a slow, formalized movement, and takes out an object which he passes over like a sacrament.

I probably shouldn't, but something about the sanctimony wakens the worst in me. It's simply impossible not to bait them. I make a point of holding it casually, feeling its weight like a street trader assessing its value. One of them, the woman, visibly strains not to say anything. The other looks resigned. After a suitable pause to allow the conversations to die down, I raise my hand to show their treasure to the crowd, a fist-sized sphere that looks to be carved from a pale stone, or perhaps ivory. Silence greets me.

'Some of you may recognize what I hold. The pomegranate is one of Jerusalem's survivors. It has, perhaps, seen the fall of Solomon's Temple. It has survived sieges by Egyptians, Greeks, Arabs, and Crusaders. It has survived the destruction of the last two centuries. If we are to believe its inscription, it is a connection to every chapter of the city's past, but like so much about our fair city, its provenance is uncertain. Its antiquity is unquestioned, its value beyond price, but these words carved into its side – "Sacred to the house of God" – could have been added centuries after its creation . . .' A pause prompts one of the curators to nod briefly in confirmation. 'It seems to me fitting that in this place where faiths meet, we should have a reminder that so much of our own past is a mystery to us, that we can be certain of nothing, that ancient truths are not enough for our modern city. We must not draw false comfort from the past, turning always to what we think we know. Recent events offer a glimpse of the new challenges we all face. To meet them, we must find our own new direction.'

In the moments of silence after the speech ends, Amos Glassberg catches my gaze again. He sees it. The rest of the crowd are still joining up the dots, but he understands the time for peace between us is gone. He knows an election speech when he hears one. Two carefully placed journalists at the back tap notes onto their tablets with quiet efficiency. The circle of stones around the garden's edge is a wall hemming him in; there is no way out of this arena, but he is not beaten, not yet. Smiling for the cameras that have appeared from nowhere, he raises a glass of flat Lebanese Prosecco in salute. For the time being, he is still the Law in this city.

A shriek of metal from above tears the moment. Everyone looks up just in time to see a car-sized triangle of glass tumble from the dome above. It falls silently. Even though I knew it was coming, the incongruity of the sight makes it look impossible. For a moment I watch, transfixed by disbelief. I could stand here for two seconds more and it would all be over. In that instant I see the temptation. I imagine it is something similar to what drives the Machine Cultists and the eschatologists – the desire for a pure, clean resolution that imparts meaning to everything that comes before and after. But that is not me. If I have a gift, it is to thrive on life's messy ambiguities.

An awkward dive takes me scarcely more than a metre away from the point of impact, but it is enough. The glass smashes on the stones with a sound like a sudden waterfall. A shower of fragments pummels my back like angry fists. All around, bodies fall or slump in a crass syncopation. The tenor of the moans tells me people are bruised and shocked, not dying or dead. The fragments of sparkling safety glass littering this immaculate garden are blunt. Sybil assured me deaths were unlikely, but she dug her heels in and refused when I asked for guarantees. There are shallow cuts in the skin and holes in the clothes of the people struggling to their feet, but no gouts of blood to stain the new white stone.

My two tame curators stagger over to me, their faces etched with concern, not for their hated employer, but for my priceless burden. The touch of their hands is my cue to uncurl, and hold the ivory pomegranate aloft, showing to the world it remains miraculously intact, a perfect metaphor for Jerusalem's endurance through the ages. Needless to say, one of the journalists is still recording.

15.

Levi

This is obviously a bad idea. Clementine thinks I'm at work, which I guess I am, just not the kind of work I should be doing the night before the job. The Bethesda Electric is full of bodies shiny with sweat and glitter – glitter on your shoulders – apparently that's a thing now, and not just the girls either. I swear, every one of them is blonde, as though hair only comes in one colour.

Saturday night is the wrong night to be here: too busy; all the Jews want to cut loose after Sabbath, but that's why Moshe wanted to party. He insisted, and I owe him big for the gear. I'll be OK as long as I stay clean.

We're in a crescent of booths facing the dance floor. There's two bottles poking out of ice buckets on our table: something fizzy for the ladies and a paint-stripper vodka for Moshe – it's garbage but he says this brand doesn't kill his buzz. I've arranged for company for later, but he's already got his arms around two of the more obvious dye-jobs. They're laughing at something: I don't know what. Moshe's a good guy, but he's not funny – he's kind of the opposite; if he tries, he just confuses everybody, including himself. He's wired different, which makes him great with the tech, but he definitely needs assistance on the social side. The dye-jobs don't seem to care; they've got small, dark eyes and big, shiny teeth that look weird in the UV. I never get why people have to open their mouths so wide to look like they're having fun. If you freeze-framed on any of these guys it would look like feeding time at the zoo.

The DJ shouts something and all the people on the dance floor throw their hands in the air, then he stops the music and suddenly you can hear everyone breathing. He's standing in the booth clapping his hands above his head to a beat no one else can hear, uplit like an angel. The dance floor ripples like grass in the wind of the silent rhythms moving the dancers as they sway to the beats of a hundred personal music feeds, then his right hand jabs in a stabbing motion and noise blasts from the speakers. People shriek with pleasure at the impact. Moshe's non-blondes scream and their faces glow red and green in the kaleidoscope of colour pouring from the ceiling. Too much drugs already.

'Levi Peres, what the fuck is wrong with you? Don't you be bringing me down. Insanity! Remember? Tonight is about insanity.'

It's only ten o'clock, and Moshe's face is shiny with sweat and amphetamine. He reaches into the breast pocket of a crisp white shirt that no one else in the club would wear and pulls out a slim silver cigarette case. It's a gift from me – his chemical ration pack for the evening – enough of his favourites to go totally out of his gourd in a few different ways, but not enough of anything to kill him. Not unless he takes it all at once. I'm babysitting, but the catch is, I got to pretend to be a baby.

His face softens with a kind of creepy mock tenderness as he opens the box and presents its contents to the girls. Their fingers hover like they're choosing candy. They wait for him to pick a small white powdery pill incongruously stamped with the logo of a Japanese manufacturing combine, then follow suit. At least it's only bounce, an MDMA derivative laced with just enough hallucinogens to make the experience feel properly religious – atheists like Moshe love that shit. He pops the tablet onto his tongue open-mouthed, raising an eyebrow at the bitterness, then stares point-blank into the eyes of one of the girls and swallows it. They copy him, then giggle. This is so stupid. I bet they're not this stupid the rest of the week. I know for a fact Moshe isn't.

He makes an exaggerated swallowing motion as the pill goes down, then he grimaces and his face goes all hard and serious and he slides the silver box over the table. 'Your turn, Levi. Insanity! Remember?'

I pat the inside pocket of my jacket. 'I'm good, man, I got my own. I'm flying here.'

'Levi, we made a deal . . .' His stare's too hard. It's not the drugs; they haven't kicked in yet. He knows I don't want to do this. He doesn't know about my robbery in the morning. If he did know, he wouldn't care. He wants his wingman and I am bought and paid for ten times over. I force that shit-eating grin onto my face and pick up the pill with a sticky fingertip. He watches the white dot sitting on my tongue. I close my mouth and tilt my head back in a pretty good fake swallow, forcing the tablet to the side of my gums with the tip of my tongue. It burns like a man-made ulcer but I reckon I can hold it long enough to make it to the toilets.

Moshe pushes a tumbler of paintstripper towards me and holds another to his lips. 'L'chaim, Levi. Drink up.'

The vodka stings but it washes away the chemical burn. The fat tablet sticks in my throat and Moshe smiles as I copy his motion to smooth it down. We're all on his trip now. Fuck.

The sweat starts straight away. It doesn't make any difference that I know it's psychosomatic. It's happening anyway. Same with my pulse: I'm worrying about it so it gets faster. Stop thinking. The girls are waving outstretched fingers in front of their faces, looking for the movement blurs that can't be there yet, willing them into existence. Moshe's swaying his head side to side like a cobra. Why can't they just wait for the drugs to hit?

I can still taste that shitty vodka. 'I gotta go to the bathroom.'

Moshe stops his swaying long enough to give me a look that lets me know he's not out of it yet. 'Sure. Don't be long, Levi Peres.' For some reason they giggle at that, and he joins in. I mean, if they're so fucked in the head they think that's funny, why do they even need to take this shit?

I slide out of the booth and nearly trip over one of the cigarette girls. She instinctively pushes the tray at me before seeing my face. The club gets its tobacco from me. Their own brand is a blend of cheap shit from all over, but they wrap gold foil around the filter and the schmucks in here pay top-dollar.

'Are you OK, Levi?' I remember her name – Chloe. I think I asked her out once. She turned me down, but she did it nice, not in an 'I'm too good for you' kind of a way. The way she's looking at me now, I'm not going to get another chance.

'Yeah, yeah, I'm good. Just got to visit the boys' room.'

She eyes my pale sweaty face. It hasn't kicked in yet. There's no way. 'OK, Levi. Well . . . you know where it is.'

I know where it is, on the other side of the dance floor. 'No one comes to the Electric without stepping on the dance floor.' That's what Big Avram, the manager, likes to say. Fucker.

I step onto the circle of illuminated floor and my brain sinks into noise. It knows I just left the sound-damping field around the booths but my pulse doesn't, racing to keep pace with the beat. The tune's kicking in. The beat from the speaker shifts tempo and a shiver goes through the crowd. My body wants to respond. There's no hands in the air at this BPM count, just faces of insane concentration and fingers weaving mystic patterns. Someone's sweat falls on me. I stagger from side to side, half falling, dodging flailing dancers. The yellow-lit stick figure of a man shines on a door a few yards in front of me like a promise.

I'm nearly there when it bursts open and a big, angry-looking East African strides out, almost knocking me off my feet. He cannons into a pack of twirling limbs, but the dancers pivot unthinkingly to absorb the impact. The only mark of his passing is they're facing the wrong direction, away from the high priest of sound in the DJ booth. I push at the door and it swings easily. A sad-looking blond man standing next to the sinks nods at me. I don't think anyone knows where he's from, but everyone calls him 'Helsinki' and he doesn't seem to mind. I return the nod and drop a little stack of five coins into his hand. 'How you doing, Hel? I'm just going to need a little privacy for a minute, OK?' I gesture over towards the toilet cubicles.

He holds his hands out to his sides like it's none of his business what I do in there. 'Sure thing, Mr Levi.' Hel's cool.

The cubicle door closes behind me and I lean back against it. It's hard and real. I blink some colours away from my eyes. They're like the normal ones you see after staring at a bright light but bigger, and they stay longer. The yellow floor tiles bruise the bones of my knees as I hunker down. At least Hel keeps them clean. I lean over the white porcelain bowl and open my mouth wide, reaching for the back of my throat with two fingers. I've never done this before, but my sister explained the principles when we were teenagers.

My gut spasms twice and I feel the rush of burning liquid rise from my insides. It reaches my mouth before I'm ready for the catch, but when it stops there's a small white disc sticking to the web of flesh between my index finger and middle finger. It's thinner than it was and the edges are smooth from wear – I reckon it's maybe a third gone. So I've got maybe two-thirds of my brain left to get me through tonight. Could be worse. There's a hard bang on the door and I hear Hel's weird sing-song voice.

'Are you all right, Mr Levi?'

'Uh, yeah, I'm good, thanks.' A whiff of puke reaches me from the bowl and I look down and recognize some of the flecks of half-digested noodle on my shirtfront. 'Hel, I might need a little help clearing up.'

'No problem, Mr Levi. What do you need?' I open the cubicle

door and he takes in the sight of me. His face tells me exactly how good I look right now.

'How much would you want for your shirt?'

Hel smiles. There's only so much money you can make from squirting soap onto drunk guys' hands, so this is a good night for him. For me, not so much.

The sound hits again as soon as the door to the dance floor opens. If I didn't already know the bounce was in my blood, the vibration in my fingertips would tell me. The glow from the illuminated floor panels throbs and fills my vision. Unwanted excitement crawls up my throat, forcing my mouth to open in a kind of yawn. The pill and I have different agendas for tonight. The tremble from my fingers becomes an involuntary movement in my shoulders and a swaying in my neck. I know exactly how stupid I look, but it takes a conscious effort of will to stop the movement. My body sags in disappointment as I step off the floor, into the damping field around the booths.

Two beefy pink-faced men in suits and short haircuts are standing in my way. They're jabbing their fingers at Moshe and shouting: 'This is our fucking table, shit-head. Fuck off and take your junkie whores with you!'

Moshe's just sitting back with his big stupid bounce grin on his face. *Please don't laugh. Please don't laugh.* A noise like a leaking balloon seeps out of him. Shit.

'Hey, Tweedledum! Nice hair! Find your own table, man! We're gonna be here all night, or most of it. Isn't that right, ladies?' He looks at the dye-jobs and they crack up again, but that's what they did before the bounce hit. I swear I don't know how these people feed themselves.

'Get the fuck out, pencil-neck, or I will drag you out.'

Anger breaks through Moshe's giggle fit. 'Who the fuck d'you think you're talking to? We're connected. This table is for Levi Peres.'

No, no, no. Shit, shit, shit. This is exactly what Big Avram would do to me. He'd take my tobacco, tell me we're fully comped for the night, and then give me a table that's already booked. It is not helpful that Moshe's throwing my name around like I'm some kind of big-time gangster. The sound seeping through the noise fields is making my shoulders twitch and my feet tap.

'Who the fuck is Levi Peres? Is that supposed to mean something to me?'

He's still angry, but a slight softening in his voice betrays a sensible wariness about tangling with gangsters. I hate to disappoint. My eyes flick between the other booths. The cost means they're mostly filled with fat old guys who don't want to be here and younger women who don't want to be with them, but there's always gangsters in the Electric on a Saturday night. There! Two tables away – slicked-back hair and shark's-tooth grin that glows blue in the UV light. I exert the necessary will to stop my feet moving and turn to the Tweedle twins. A squeak of laughter slips out. 'Gentlemen, what seems to be the problem?'

'Who the fuck are you?' He eyes me like something stuck to the bottom of his shoe. The collar of my recently purchased shirt jabs into my neck. I know I look like shit, but it could be worse.

'Levi Peres, pleased to meet you.' I hold out my hand. He looks at it and barks with laughter.

'You're Levi Peres? Well, fuck me terrified. We'll be taking our table now.' He turns back to Moshe and grabs his collar in a fist like a bag of ham.

'No problem. We'll just go and join our friends at Shant Manoukian's table.'

He looks around at the mention of Shant's name. 'You don't know Shant Manoukian.' The caution is back in his voice.

I pretend to ignore him and concentrate really hard to stop the bounce tremble creeping up through my knees. Three casual steps is enough to take me within the boundaries of the noise field for Shant's table. 'Shant, you got a minute?'

Shant looks up at the sound of his name. He sees me and does a little double take before murmuring to his companions and standing up. I can feel Tweedledum's eyes on my back. Shant's face is openly curious. 'So what's up, Levi?'

'I'm real sorry to interrupt your evening, Shant, but I'm having a bad night.'

He looks at my eyes. 'Yeah, I can see that. I never figured you for a guy to mess with your own merchandise.'

'Long story. Anyway, I've just got a little misunderstanding here, and I'd regard it as a personal favour, which I will obviously repay, if you could just step over and say "Hi" to my friend Moshe, as if you were already acquainted.'

His eyes wander over the frozen tableau of Tweedledum grabbing Moshe's shirt collar and Tweedledim leaning in for a piece of the action. He gives me a look that says he's working out what this is going to cost me; then he laughs, shaking his head. 'Don't worry about it.'

He's still laughing when he gets to my table. The beefy brothers can't take their eyes off him, but he acts like they don't even exist. 'Hey, Moshe, how's it going?' Moshe grins like an idiot, but it doesn't matter: Shant chuckles like he's in on the joke. 'The kids must be getting big now, eh? You should bring them around. Gloria says she hasn't seen them in forever.' Moshe focuses through the bounce enough to nod and give a vaguely sane smile. 'Anyway, great to see you. Talk soon, yeah? Have a great night.' For the first time, his gaze takes in Tweedledee and Tweedledim. He nods to them as if nothing was going on and walks away, shaking his head like someone just told him a great story he didn't believe. Their fingers loosen, and Moshe sits up, straightening his shirt, staring at them indignantly. Even under the disco lights I can see the red splotches of humiliation and suppressed rage on their faces. They disappear into the crowd without a word.

Moshe is silent for a full twenty seconds; then he explodes with laughter and the dye-jobs echo him, shifting instantly from mute terror to hilarity. 'Haaa! That was fucking hilarious, man! Fucking awesome! You promised me insanity! You promised it! Sometimes I swear you're full of shit, but, man, you deliver!'

I try to relax and let the music shiver through my body. Tomorrow is only an hour away.

16.

Silas

A parallelogram of glass smaller than a fingernail falls from my hair. It tinkles faintly when it hits the polished ceramic of the basin in my office's en-suite. This is disappointing. It's almost thirty-six hours since my energetic little stunt and I'd hoped to leave every trace of it behind.

'Sybil, I think it's in my pants!' My voice echoes deafeningly against the closed cedar-wood door. Despairing, I abandon the effort to tame the strands of hair straying across my scalp and turn to poke it open with a foot. 'Sybil!'

She appears, visible only as a sliver through the barely open door, eyes averted to eliminate the possibility of seeing anything unfortunate. 'Do you want me to look?'

'Don't be ridiculous. You promised me it would shower out. I've had three since Friday and I swear I still crunch when I sit down.'

Her eyes roll. 'What I told you was based on the specifications of the manufacturers of the safety glass. They claim it will shatter into fragments no smaller than four centimetres – easy to find, unlikely to enter ears or airways. I can take it up with them?'

'Oh, forget about it.' She waits silently, gauging my mood. It's true, on occasion Sibyl veers uncomfortably towards mockery, and a more fragile man might jibe at the occasional implied insult, but it is a small price to pay for her powers. 'Any word about young Levi Peres?'

'Not much; he checked in to ask about some data on the target, but I don't know what he's doing with it. Surveillance is difficult. He's careful, and it's his neighbourhood. Our informer reports his movements have been more or less the usual routine.'

'What's he waiting for? I've made sure that warehouse is wide open.' In the grander scheme of things, the cost of the bribes I pay for the relevant people to turn a blind eye are negligible, but good-will expires quicker than it used to, and I have other plans that will need the Machine Cult's money.

'He still has a couple of days on the schedule you gave him. Do you want me to have him brought in?'

'God, no! Stick to the plan. Arm's length until we need an arrest.'

'Yes, minister.'

'All right then, what about Amos? Any signs of life? He must know something's up.'

She nods, looking away briefly as I adjust my trousers before emerging into the office proper and settling at my desk. 'Oh, he knows, but I can't tell you what he's doing about it. He's upped the security for his office – EM sweeps at random intervals two to three times daily. That's practically wartime protocol, so we have to work on the assumption that our electronic surveillance has gone dark permanently.'

'Annoying, but it was bound to happen sooner or later. Let me know the moment he does anything more substantive than basic security.' Sybil smiles uneasily, sensing my tension. Petty thievery is one thing, but Amos Glassberg, pillar of the establishment, is the keystone in all of this. As long as he remains in place, everything else I have lined up is at a standstill. It's more than six months since I opened tentative, necessarily covert negotiations with associates in

Amman, Haifa, and Eilat. The new cities are still tiny, built from scratch in the last half-century since the fourth war because they lacked even the partial protection afforded by Jerusalem's sanctity, but they are at a tipping point now, hungry for the opportunities offered by being part of something greater than a one-street desert town. The appetite for a new country, unbounded by the deadening constraints of race and religion that doomed the old, dead nations, is palpable. The Greater Levant Co-Prosperity Sphere could drag us out of being an irrelevant backwater, forced to trade under humiliating terms with the great powers for any remotely modern tech, but Glassberg is the brake on all of this. The people still respect him, even if the stability he offers is nothing more than a guarantee of stagnation.

Sybil grimaces. 'It's going to be difficult while Glassberg's being so careful. I'll try.'

'I'm sorry, what?'

She flinches at the rebuke before catching herself. On the whole, she requires little in the way of external motivation, but a few modest fireworks eliminate the possibility of any misunderstandings as to where my priorities lie.

'I'll let you know the instant he makes a move.'

'Better. Anything else? Or is there a chance I might be able to keep my morning appointment with the lovely Consuelo?'

'Uh . . .' The single syllable, uttered reluctantly, banishes any hopes I harboured of a good day. With Sibyl, hesitation is an unfailing harbinger of the awful. 'I'm afraid there is some bad news. I would normally try to avoid bothering you with something like this, but in the circumstances . . .'

'Come on. Out with it.'

'It's Boutros, sir.'

'Boutros?'

'The curator responsible for the Antikythera Mechanism.'

'Ugh, that man is a pain. His obsession with the thing borders on the pathological. You'd think it was his mother's ashes. What about him?'

'He didn't turn up for work again, so museum management sent someone round to his apartment. They found him dead on the floor of his living room.'

'Dead? We didn't . . .'

'No. Your orders were very clear on that point. He was to be left unharmed, no matter how much of a fuss he kicked up. It looks like a suicide.'

'Looks?' If someone has decided to make a point, they have chosen a poor moment. An obvious death draws dangerous attention. There is too much at stake now. 'Why would anyone think anything else? Think carefully, Sybil. Your answer could have a rather dramatic effect on all our futures.'

She smiles at the slightly oblique reference to her promised reward. If everything goes to plan, she will occupy this desk in a few months' time, no doubt pouring scorn on a deputy of her own. Sometimes her hunger for it is palpable; in her rare unguarded moments you can see the fierce smile as she imagines her ascension, but there is no sign of exultation now. Something has disturbed her.

'According to the autopsy, there is nothing anywhere on him that could be a fatal wound, and no trace of drugs or poison in his system.'

'So he just lay down on the floor and died of grief that I took away his favourite toy?'

'We've both seen stranger things happen, but no. He has injuries to his hands: multiple breaks and dislocations in all the joints like someone tried to tie them in a knot. And . . .' She stops, uncertain.

'What?'

Her voice lowers to a whisper. 'His fingernails were missing. All of them gone.'

17.

Clementine

'Are we on?'

'Yeah, we're on.' Levi's face shines with nervous sweat even though we haven't left Yusuf's bar. He's still wearing that damn jacket. It makes a kind of sense though. He's known. The most suspicious thing Levi Peres could do is dress like someone else. He doesn't have any other clothes anyway. I know this because I've spent almost all of the last three days in his apartment. It is now marginally less of a shithole; there was nothing to do but clean.

'Hey, beautiful!' Yusuf waves me over to the bar. Levi turns around too, but gets a shake of the head from the barman. 'I love you too, man, just not in that way.'

'Fuck you very much.'

Levi's twitchy. Not good.

Yusuf ignores the insult and beckons me over again. 'Don't worry about him. He gets like this whenever he has to work for a living. I just wanted to say – if things go bad, and you need an alibi, you just tell them you were with Yusuf all night. I'll back you up on it. One hundred per cent.'

'Yusuf, I'm touched. We hardly know each other.'

'What can I say? That's just the kind of guy I am. Good luck.'

113

Levi straightens the shoulder straps on his bag and puts a hand through the rainbow bead curtain covering the doorway. His foot catches on the step. His knee hits the floor with a hollow sound. A hiss of pain slides from his lips.

'You OK, Levi?'

'Yeah, yeah, I'm good.' His arm shakes as he pushes himself off the floor. A gust from outside carries a whiff of acrid sweat up to me as I lean down to give him a hand.

'Levi, have you been drinking? Are you hungover?'

'It's not what it looks like, Clem.' Flakes of dry skin come away as he scratches the long stubble on his neck. He's one of those guys who can shave before breakfast and look like a Neanderthal before lunch. Of course, Levi never eats breakfast.

'This is serious. We have to be on our game.'

'I know, Clem. I just . . .' A sweaty hand tries to wipe guilt from his face. '. . . owed a guy. The guy who got us the gear for the job.'

'And he couldn't wait to party until after the job?'

'No.'

'Shit. What did you take? Are you still high?'

'Bounce. No, I don't think so.'

'OK. Change of plan, I'm driving.' I put my hand on the driver's-side door of the rusty white van parked in the street. His hand lands on mine. His grip is clammy but firm, no trace of shake in it now.

'You want to get there? You don't drive in Jerusalem.'

I slide my hand out from under his and walk over to the passenger side. The cab smells of sweat and stale tobacco and the seat is covered with a mat made of small wooden balls. I hold my breath while Levi makes three cursing attempts to start the engine. It clatters into uncertain life and a pair of miniature boxing gloves hanging from a string starts to sway in time with its vibration. Gears crunch and we lurch forward out of the afternoon shadow that covers half the street.

'So what does it feel like?' He looks away from the windscreen and the traffic beyond, squinting like he's trying to see the metal inside me.

'What?'

'When you do your thing – what does it feel like?'

'Sore.'

'That's it? Sore? That's all you're gonna give me?' He shakes his head, keeping his eyes fixed on the road now. 'We're supposed to be partners.'

'You wouldn't understand.'

'Try me.'

His fingers tap a rhythm on the steering wheel to a silent song playing in his head. There is no guile in these enquiries. A part of me yearns to tell, to unburden myself of secrets grown heavier since I arrived alone in this city, but for all his many faults, Levi does not deserve to be put in danger.

'It hurts because I wanted it to hurt. Every time I "do my thing" I become more like something I don't want to be, and the pain is the price. I only want to be normal, like you.'

'Ha! Nobody ever called me normal before.'

His dark curled head joins his fingers in their dance and the traffic outside the windows fades to insubstantiality as my mind slips into its worn groove of assessing variables and calculating probabilities. This journey should take around twenty-four minutes. In less than one hour the first phase of the job should be complete. The wheels are already in motion.

Forty-six minutes ago, at exactly 2.21 p.m., the door guard at the storage facility signed for a package weighing 5.2 kilos. The labels on it were rudimentary but convincing forgeries indicating it came from the museum, and was destined for the category B storage area containing the Antikythera Mechanism.

My projection of the events that follow is guesswork based on probabilities. Almost certainly, the guard looks for the incoming package on a delivery schedule or ledger; he won't find anything. That much I'm confident about. We used the same courier firm as the museum, so the delivery itself should not arouse suspicion, but there will be procedures he wants to follow, boxes to tick – he won't be able to. The logical course of action is for him to call the museum, but if he tries, he'll be reminded the admin staff don't work on Sundays. The only people picking up the phone are the front-of-house staff, who won't know anything about any package: they wouldn't, even if it was legitimate. While all this is going on, the courier is on the clock, and he'll want this thing off his hands. The guard has an emergency number he can call, but he'll have to make a subjective, potentially humiliating, judgement as to whether the arrival of a small package constitutes an emergency. It's a deposit, not a withdrawal. The closest thing he can do to following procedure is to make his own temporary record of the ID number on our label, and leave a note for the Monday guard to ask about it. I've run it through data-based simulations two hundred thousand times in the last three days, switching up all the variables I could think of. Nine times out of ten, it works up to this point.

Everything we're about to do depends on the package being there – it's a calculated risk, but there are no safe options. It would be comforting to have a little transmitter in it telling us where it is, but the AIs in the warehouse would be all over that. For the time being, the insulated five-kilo box remains entirely dormant.

A low buzz is a trapped fly battering its bulbous red eyes against the windscreen, defeated by a barrier they cannot perceive. Levi's knuckles are white on the wheel of the borrowed truck as he turns the tight corner out of the Lions' Gate onto the main road. I can hear him breathe. I can't tell if it's just nerves or chemically induced paranoia from the substances he consumed last night. My own stomach stirs with the queasiness of adrenaline and my pulse throbs quicker in my neck, but looking at the livid streak of fear shining through Levi makes me suspect my ersatz biochemistry is a pale shadow of the true human. Do I feel what they feel? I will never know. All I can know is that I feel something where once I felt nothing. The difference is existential – worth dying for.

The truck stops with a shudder that breaks my train of thought. We're in one of the parking bays for the plumbing supply store, a little over thirty metres from the front entrance to the storage facility. Levi coughs and turns to me. 'Are we close enough?'

'Probably.' I don't want to see him try to start the truck again, not with people watching. 'You've got the target's exact location within the warehouse?'

He nods. 'My guy confirmed yesterday.'

'OK. Just watch me until the signal comes through your line.'

I sink back onto the seat with my eyes closed. The sensation of those small wooden balls against my spine is momentarily distracting, but it fades as my other senses extend and I become aware of the flow of transmissions around me. The truck's fug of stale tobacco disappears into a swirling cocktail of olfactory analogues – the plumbing store's data server, seventy-four nearby personal communication implants, the non-committal hum of the city-net. All of it's irrelevant. I focus on the almost blank space of the storage facility, find the barely perceptible trickle of data flowing into it.

Three sharp inhalations.

All trace of physical awareness vanishes as I abandon myself to the flow. My body is a corpse in Levi's care until this is done.

Inside, it is sudden silence. The absence of noise is like a cooling balm. I become suddenly conscious of the effort I have expended shutting out the clamour of the city since I arrived. I could lose myself here, were it not for the three distinct scents of the guardian AIs marking this territory as their own. The citrus tang of the Shimezu AI running the visual-security systems reeks of danger. The menthol of the audio monitor is a more cautiously watchful presence. Compared to them, the musty toffee sub-routine operating the pressure sensors is a sleeping dog. Under their noses, I release a small, apparently unencrypted data burst, a trickle in the pool indistinguishable from the watchman's flow of sport and porn.

Our package awakens.

I cannot perceive what happens within, only wait while the device created by Levi's friend works its magic. At the bottom of an insulated box thirty centimetres wide and forty centimetres high, a small array of thick metal coils heats up, drawing current from the lithium batteries beneath them. Their heat passes into a block of solidified carbon dioxide flash-frozen around them. It should take exactly six minutes for this two-kilo lump to sublime into gas. When the pressure of the expanding gas inside reaches 1.4 bar, the box lid will pop open.

Another innocuous data burst sends a pre-arranged signal to Levi's comm-plant. A distant part of me registers the sound of the truck door closing behind him. That's my cue to wake up the sleeping dog. The musty toffee presence shifts drowsily in response to a sudden bombardment of information. Like the faithful guardian it is, it tries to inspect every package, but the stream becomes a torrent. A smarter AI would figure out something was up, or at least prioritize the data, institute some kind of sorting system, but ol' faithful here would count the grains of sand on a beach, and I've provided just enough grains to keep it busy for eight minutes.

The imagined image of the block of frozen gas disappearing in streams of faint white smoke occupies me while I wait for it to become reality. It takes only an inch of evanescence to reveal the flight blades of the drone concealed within. They whir into life with a thought, dissipating the pale clouds above, but the drone's landing skids remain trapped in the slowly vanishing block. Everything hangs on Levi now.

His job is simple enough. Turn up at the deliveries window, engage the guard in conversation, position the palm-sized jammer close enough to his viewing station to block the visual feed from the AI-controlled cameras, and switch it on. If last night's activities haven't entirely ruined his cognitive faculties, it should be straight-forward.

The last of the frozen gas puffs away and the freed drone rises out of the box, the lid closing silently beneath it. The citrus tang of the Shimezu AI sharpens instantly in response to this intruder into its domain. I follow the feeds of six cameras tracking it. The data flows unimpeded to the guard's viewing station on a priority stream. Levi! The drone drops out of the air and skitters onto the hard warehouse floor as I break my connection to it and pull back my consciousness to hijack Levi's comm-plant.

'Levi Peres!' Verbalized thought is a confusion in the moment of adjustment. The grating shift to the slow, imperfect information of speech makes me crave the smooth refuge of the digital. 'Levi, you dumb fuck, turn the jammer on!'

'It's . . . on.' The sub-vocalized thought coming through his comm-plant line is snail's pace. He must be doing it at the same time as maintaining a realtime conversation with the guard. Or he's still out of his head from the drugs.

'Then your party friend has fucked us over with that gear. We're going to have to do this on camera. Keep the guard looking away from his screens. I'll be quick.'

'Fine, whatever. Just get out of my head.' The words are terse but quicker now. It's possible I have underestimated Levi. Not many humans can maintain two conversations, and he's doing it with amphetamine residue in his system. He won't be able to keep that up though.

I sink deeper into myself and extend my consciousness into the drone. Four polycarbonate rotors spin silently into life and the thing wobbles seventy centimetres into the air. Around me, the frantic pulses of the Shimezu AI fill the warehouse's available data streams as it tries to alert the guard to the images coming from its cameras. If he doesn't respond within two minutes, it will bypass him to contact armed security units directly. I shut out the blaring, urgent signals. I try not to think I'm back in France, still running from my creators.

Time to fly.

I settle the drone's landing skids on the box lid. They are twenty centimetres apart – exactly the width of the label from the courier company. This is not a coincidence. The five-millimetre-wide manipulators in its four feet pinch the loosely attached piece of paper and I feed just enough power into the rotors to apply a gentle lift. The label tears minutely at one corner, then comes away. The drone edges through space towards its target, bearing a single piece of paper underneath.

I have one minute and twenty seconds; less if Levi forgets how to talk.

The drone's cameras offer two views – a tight angle directly underneath, almost entirely obscured by the paper, and a wide angle that distorts the entire warehouse interior into a weird fishbowl. My stomach lurches as my senses make the necessary algorithmic adjustments to navigate using the skewed view. As the drone wobbles closer, the target shifts from being a warped polygon to something resembling the square metal box it must be. Directly above, I am blind, but I control my descent using my blindness as guide. If the box's black edge veers into view, it means I am off course.

One minute and five seconds.

A faint sensation of impact is the left landing skid touching down on the box lid. The right skid follows moments later in a lop-sided final approach. A length of brass wire along the bottom of each skid heats up in response to a brief flow of current from the drone's over-taxed battery. The momentary warmth is enough to soften the adhesive painted to the underside of the label. The glue becomes tacky, then spreads, forming a fragile bond with the box lid beneath.

Fifty-five seconds.

Now I must wait. If the drone takes off before the adhesive is set, the label comes with it and our little adventure is over. The instructions on the back of the glue tube said to allow ten seconds. They make no allowance for local variations in moisture level or temperature. I have to be certain.

Thirty-five seconds.

The drone comes away clean. As it rises, I see the label is fractionally off-centre on the box lid. The small tear in the top left corner of the paper screams at me, an inconsistency that a guard or courier could easily pick up, but the die is cast. My stomach stops lurching now I can use the undistorted lens in the drone's belly to navigate. Settling it back into the insulated box is child's play compared to the half-blind flight to the target.

The lid closes on top of it with a full six seconds to spare.

The frantic transmissions from the visual monitoring AI cease. There is no incident to attend to, just a report of unusual activity for the guard to investigate. I bury it in another torrent of spam to the guard's workstation. The top-end AI would see through it in a flash, but humans struggle to prioritize. If he even bothers to stop talking to Levi, he'll be like the sleepy toffee watchdog, counting grains of sand.

Another burst of current from the battery in the base of our insulated box opens a small reservoir of freon. The liquid gas circulates up through channels in the array of thick metal coils. It carries warmth from the inside to almost invisible rails running along its exterior edges. In less than a minute, the simple heat-exchange mechanism drops the temperature inside the box to freezing. In another two, ice crystals are forming on the drone's legs, condensed from moisture in the air. It takes less than five to accrete a block of water ice exactly matching the weight of the solidified carbon dioxide we sent in. Toffee finishes counting its grains of sand, and everything in the warehouse weighs the exact same amount it did when it started. As far as that AI is concerned, nothing has happened, nothing is missing.

The sound of the truck door slamming hard shocks me back to physical consciousness. Levi's sitting in the driver's seat, leaning towards me, staring hard. 'So what happened? What do we do now?'

'We . . . wait.' I hear my voice as a stranger's, four tones higher than my self-image, a little girl so tired she struggles to speak.

'Wait? Wait for what?'

'Go home. Wait . . . they bring . . . to us.'

'Are you serious? That's it? All I had to do was talk to that guy about soap operas for five minutes? That's a fucking cinch, man!'

My eyes close and my body slumps on the slipperiness of the brown wooden beads covering the seat. The last thing I hear before it surrenders to sleep is Levi calling my name.

18.

Levi

Clementine's out cold on the couch. She hasn't moved for eighteen hours. She's kind of pale and breathing shallow, but she seems OK. I'm just going to leave her there for as long as it takes. I don't get it though – all she did was sit in the passenger seat of the truck with her eyes closed. For maybe ten minutes, tops. I'm the one who had to physically go in there; I could be recognized. Whatever. It means I'm on my own for the pickup but I can handle that.

I have to cross most of the city to get to the Binyanei station where the package is waiting for me in a locker, probably. The message from the courier company said they picked it up at nine thirty, and gave me a code for opening it. There's no reason to think anything's gone wrong. If anyone had noticed the switch they'd be all over us by now.

It's maybe a three-mile walk to Etz Haim and the Binyanei. At a safe pace it'll take me an hour; walking too fast got me busted a couple of times when I was a kid pushing Lebanese resin, so I go slow past the crumbled stumps of the old Jaffa Gate where the cops hang out. The stone of the ruins around the edges of the Old City is still black from the last war. The patch of rubble opposite the gate has a name, Merkaz Mis'hari. The city council had it decontaminated the minute the war was over, priority one regeneration for future development, but nobody touches it. Even the street hawkers take their carts someplace else. Some people say Herod the Great's tomb is down there, maybe even his bones. It's probably bullshit, but enough people believe it that you'd have to be insane to mess with that real estate. The end result is this weird holy emptiness between the Old City and all the new shit outside.

I keep to small streets for shade and clean air, and to look normal. People expect to see Levi Peres out and about. They expect me to stop and talk. If I was speed-walking along Hanevi'im it wouldn't take long for somebody to figure something was up. I skirt around the edges of Independence Park – it's too open and too full of beggars trying to hit up tourists. The buildings beyond are a wall of grey concrete blocks with brown-tinted windows that look dirty all the time. As I walk, the sun slips through the gaps between them. When the light hits my eyes I still see the colours from Saturday night. Fucking bounce.

A flashing bugle icon at the edge of my vision is an incoming signal on my comm-plant. It's Silas.

'Levi Peres. I'll make this quick. I'm on a timetable. Do you understand you only get paid for delivering on schedule? You understand there will be consequences for a failure to deliver the goods? You think you can just take my money and go round pretending to be some kind of big-shot in the clubs and I won't know about it?'

'I've got it.'

A pause. 'Got what?'

'The item, it's secure.'

'Don't bullshit me, Levi Peres! I'm not some fucking mark buying cheap souvenirs at the Temple Mount. You can't talk your way out of this.'

'Silas, I've got it. We never discussed pickup. How do you want to work this?' The line goes dead. Silas Mizrachi is not accustomed to surprises. Now he's going to be thinking about how he wants the pickup to play out, which means he's trying to work out a way to get what he wants without paying me. Knowing Silas, I have to acknowledge the possibility this process could be hazardous to my health; Yusuf heard about a guy they found face down in the aqueduct after getting mixed up in Silas's business, but I'm cool. I just have to present him with a situation where paying me is the easiest option. For that, I need to get my hands on the package.

Tiny crystals in the central station's steps glitter under my feet as I walk down into the wide shadowed hole of the entrance. It's like going into an underground museum or something. Everything's old down here, like the wars never happened. I read one of the tourist guidebooks once. They said it was built this way – a twisting spiral leading to rail tracks seventy metres underground – so it could be an emergency shelter if the city was ever attacked. Well, guess what? Shit happens.

There's hardly anyone around. Most of the shops are vacant. The only train from here goes to Tel Aviv. Who the fuck wants to go to Tel Aviv? My parents used to take us – nothing there but bad food and sand, so the trains are mostly empty. The transport ministry keeps promising the line's going to extend to Haifa and there'll be another one south to Eilat. It's just one of the things they say at election time to make it look like they do something. No one's going to build across the Negev – it's still a radioactive crater park. So I'm just standing here in this ghost of a station, looking at a row of lockers someone built two hundred years ago.

They still look new. I guess nobody ever used them. Who needs lockers in a bomb shelter? Two whole rows of them are coloured yellow and blue in the livery of the courier company. They took out the old coin slots and replaced them with key-code pads. I think it would be nice to leave this old stuff the way it was – a little slice of the twenty-first century – but that's the problem with Jerusalem: too much history gets in the way of business. It takes me about a minute to find the right one, trying not to look like I'm checking to see if I'm being watched.

Locker twenty-two clicks open when I punch in the code number on the receipt from the courier company. I realize I'm holding my breath as I pull the black plastic handle. What's going to happen? It's a goddamn box. Yeah, there it is – black metal, about forty centimetres wide, thirty high, brass reinforcements at the corners, and our label at the top. Clementine, whoever the fuck you are, whatever the fuck you are, you are a genius, but we have got to talk as soon as you're done sleeping.

Metal squeaks on metal, just loud enough to make me anxious, as I tug the thing out of the locker and slip it into a canvas bag. Maybe nobody knows it's gone, but I still don't want to advertise I got it. My fingers tingle as the box passes through them. Silas didn't say anything about what's in here. If I thought I was going to get paid straight up, I'd say it wasn't any of my business, but if he's going to make life hard, it makes sense to take an interest. Not here, though. I turn and walk towards the steps of the entrance, the canvas bag bundled in my arms, my head down. I'm almost back into daylight when I see a pair of spotless white sneakers stepping down in my direction.

'Levi Peres! As I live and breathe! What brings you to the station, my young friend? I never figured you for the trainspotting type.' The white shark's-tooth grin of Shant Manoukian fills my vision when I look up.

'Good to see you, Shant. I know that I owe you, and I mean no disrespect, but I'm working right now. I can't stop to talk.' His left hand lands on my shoulder, squeezing the bone underneath the leather. I'm not going anywhere. This isn't a coincidence. My eyes flick around to check if Shant's got company. He sees the movement and lets out a chuckle that says he doesn't give a shit where I look.

'That's what I wanted to talk to you about, Levi.' My grip tightens on the package. I'm giving too much away. Be cool. You don't know what he knows. 'You gotta understand – when a young guy like you starts discussing serious business, a guy like me is gonna take an interest. That's . . . the natural order of things. Maybe you didn't know this, but that courier company you used – it's one of my . . . our business interests.' *Fuck, fuck, fuck, I am so fucked. How could I not know that?* He shakes his head and smiles as if he heard the thought. 'Don't be beating yourself up, kid. You ran a real smooth job. You got potential. It just so happens the courier business is what we do – that and waste disposal – we just don't like to talk about it.'

'Yeah, well, if we're done with the compliments, I got a buyer. I got to deliver.' I take a step to Shant's side, but his fingers dig hard into the muscles of my shoulder joint, pinning me in place.

'Be cool, Levi. If you're smart, I might even let you keep that little piece of history in the box. I'm not an antiques kind of guy. It's your partner I'm interested in. That kind of talent could be very lucrative.'

I know he's lying to me; that's a given. Let me keep the box? No way Shant Manoukian isn't gonna work every angle on this. The only edge I have is he still thinks I'm a dumb kid who doesn't understand how business works. *Keep thinking that, you Brylcreem fuck.*

His hand shifts from my shoulder to my elbow, and he shoves me across the station plaza towards a dark-windowed car sitting at the front of an empty taxi stand. I could run, but I'd have to drop the bag, and I'd have to keep running all the way out of the city. I'm not ready to do either. One of the back doors pops open and a huge bald-headed Armenian in the driver's seat grins at me as I duck in, like he knows what I've got coming. Shant slides into the leather seat next to me and his tracksuit jacket falls open, showing me the gun under his shoulder. Like it makes any difference. He taps the goon on the shoulder and points.

'Tigran, go.' Baldy turns to the dash and presses a button, then unfolds a screen and watches golf while the car drives itself. 'Levi, you asked me a question. Out of respect for what you've done, I'll give you an answer. You introduced me to your friend Moshe. He's a real interesting guy. He was very proud of some of the equipment he put together for you and your partner. He thinks very highly of you, Levi. It's just . . . how can I put this? He thinks maybe you're not the right guy to be looking after his social schedule any more. Maybe he might get more of what he's looking for with better connections.'

Moshe, you dumb schmuck. They'll eat you alive. The car pulls up outside the laundromat. Shant gets out first and holds the door open for me like he's the chauffeur. Tigran has got a big smile on his face like his boss is the funniest guy in the world and the entertainment's just getting started. As they shadow me up the stairwell, I run through the options I've got for getting rid of these guys. It's a short list. There's a gun in the kitchen but I'm never going to get to it.

Shant grins and watches intently while I punch in the key code for my door. 'I feel like we know each other well enough now, we shouldn't have secrets.'

I push the door open slowly, carefully, like I'm afraid of what's on the other side, which is pretty dumb when the two guys who want to kill me are standing right behind. 'Clem? Clementine? Are you OK? We've got company . . .' I glance back at Shant and he nods in a way that's probably supposed to be reassuring. If I wasn't shitting my pants, I'd be annoyed at just how dumb Shant thinks I am. '. . . friends of mine. They want to talk to you about some work.'

My nose wrinkles at an unfamiliar smell – something warm and sweet coming from inside. I step through the doorway to my den, and I just have time to notice Clem's not lying where she was on my couch when suddenly there's a roar in my ear like a million metal insects. Pain shoots through my skull and I fall to my knees, ready to curse Shant, but I see he's on the floor too, looking at me like I did this to us. Baldy is just squinting at us both, confused. Through streaks of bright pain I barely see Clementine emerge from her hiding place behind the door. She does a little double take, like she's surprised whatever she did to me and Shant hasn't worked on the big guy, but then moves almost too fast for me to see. She jabs him in the throat with stiffened fingers, then loops her hands behind his head as he reels back, using the leverage to pull him into a flying knee to the solar plexus. He sags under the impact, but his huge arms wrap around her tiny waist as he falls, dragging her down with him. Clementine tries to pull herself away, but his hands lock behind her, and he's smiling as he propels his massive shining forehead into her nose. Clem falls like a rag doll. The insanity in my ears stops.

Tigran stands up and straightens his collar, prodding her in the ribs with a huge foot to check she's really out. Shant works his jaw like he's trying to get water out of his ear, then notices me kneeling in front of him and his eyes darken.

'Does this mean we're not friends any more, Shant?'

'You're not as funny as you think you are, Levi Peres. I would say "that's your problem" but you got bigger ones than that.' His backhand blow lands on my left eye socket. It hurts, but it's not as bad as getting hit by a bruiser like Tigran. He gestures to the big guy. 'Have a look around this shithole. See if there's anything worth anything.'

Tigran nods and steps over to my coffee table, which is weirdly clear of all the merchandise I left on it – Clem must have been tidying again after she woke up.

'Hold on a second. I can save you some time.'

Shant looks at me out of the side of his eyes, suspicious. 'This doesn't change anything. You know that, right?'

'Wait 'til you see what I can offer. Maybe we can work something out.' My dry tongue trips on the words, like I'm so scared I forgot how to speak. I've got nothing. Shant's instincts are going to be telling him I'm full of it, that there's nothing I've got he can't just take. He's right, but he can't be sure. I have to get him curious, make him think there's a bigger game he hasn't seen yet.

My stash is in the drawers on the other side of the room. There's close to a thousand tabs of bounce in there – not enough for a player like Shant to get excited, but maybe enough to arouse his interest if I can sell it as a taster. I edge away from him, slowly to make it clear I'm no trouble.

'OK, let's see.' He waves me away, almost laughing. He's so relaxed he doesn't care what I do.

The strange sweet smell gets stronger as I get closer to the drawers and crouch down. The good stuff from my stash is in the bottom one, but I need to take my time. Any fumbling and he's going to smell the bullshit right away. The drawer sticks a little on a twisted runner as it opens. It does that every time, but right now the half-second delay makes me want to puke. Instead I laugh, which is probably worse.

It's there – a wholesale-size pharmaceutical bottle with a child-proof cap that keeps me out on a bad day, and if this isn't a bad day, I don't know what is.

My bladder twitches.

The bottle is three-quarters empty. If I give this to Shant he'll laugh for ten seconds and then feed me a bullet. *Where is my shit?* Right at my eyeline, there's something on top of the drawers, a tray covered with a towel. The sweet smell is coming from there. Has Clem been baking? Why would she do that?

Oh.

I lower my eyes from the tray so it looks like I don't want him to see what's got my attention. Not too fast. Nothing hokey.

'Tigran, go see what's taking Mr Peres so long, will you? I don't want to spend any longer in this shithole than I have to.'

The big guy steps over from his post by the door, still moving slowly from getting hit by Clem's knee, and cranes down to see what I'm looking at. Now I just need to get him interested. Shouldn't be hard; he looks as though he likes to eat.

'Don't touch that!' My hand flashes towards the thing on top of the drawers but he's ready for me, knocks my arm away, and I fall from a crouch to sitting on my ass, looking up at him. He grins and whips away the cloth to reveal a metal tray, and the smell intensifies. It's sweet, nutty chocolate. The grin broadens and he digs a shovel-like hand into the tray, coming out with a crumbling mess of brownie, which he crams into his mouth leaving brown smears at the edges.

'That shit any good, big guy?' Tigran gives a messy smile and passes the tray over. Shant scoops some up and speaks through a mouthful. 'This is some good shit, Levi! You got a cosy little arrangement here. Whoever heard of a thief that bakes?' He laughs at his own joke. 'Tigran, would you put Mr Peres into the bath please? We got to start clearing up in here.'

Those big messy fists clench around the lapels of my jacket and drag me to my feet. I don't fight. If I fight, I'm out cold like Clem, and this is all over.

'Shant, wait! I've got . . . stuff I can show you.'

His laugh is harsh. 'What you got to show me, Peres? Uncle Leo told you – we're all good for souvenirs.'

'How about a thousand tabs of bounce?' He doesn't know I'm all out. By the time he figures it out, I'll either be dead or out of trouble.

'A thousand? You are moving up in the world, Levi. Where?'

'In . . .' *Think, Levi, think. Where's going to buy you time?* 'In the bathroom, under the shower tray. You'll need a screwdriver.'

'Or a hammer. Tigran, go get some tools from the car.' The big guy leaves and Shant stands back and pulls out his gun, a sleek Makarov hardly any bigger than his hand. Clem's still not moving, but the way he points the gun says he's more worried about her waking up than anything I'm gonna do. The tetchy silence while we wait is broken by the clump of Tigran's boots on the stairs and the hum of the washing machines coming through the floor. A couple of times Shant looks around the apartment and shakes his head at me, as if he can't quite believe I dragged him to this shithole. More heavy steps and clanking tools announce Tigran's return.

'Any last words, Levi Peres? Something smart I can use to entertain the guys?'

'Dream on, Shant. All my shit is copyrighted.'

The dull crack of ceramic breaking comes from the bathroom, then stops.

'Tigran, you got that bounce yet? We got shit to do today.' The sound that comes back is a high-pitched giggle, like air leaking from a balloon. 'What the fuck, Tigran? Cut your shit. Get the stuff, get in here, and kill these motherfuckers for me.'

'That's your problem, Shant. You're too serious all the time. You need to see the funny side. You know, I can help with that.'

'Shut your mouth, you punk.' He straightens his arm to point the pistol, but his hand wobbles at the wrist joint, like it's hardly even connected to his arm. 'What the fuck?'

'That's better. You're starting to relax a little.' From the bathroom comes the sound of a heavy body hitting the floor, followed by squeals of high-pitched laughter. I nod in the direction of the noise. 'Sounds like Tigran is feeling it.' I stand up. The non-stop washing machine hum from below vibrates up through the bones of my feet. This is my home.

Shant wills his treacherous fingers to close around the gun's trigger, but their spastic movements spill it to the floor. 'What the fuck did you do to me?'

'I didn't do anything. You did it to yourself. You should have kept your hands off my stuff. That's the funny thing about bounce. If you take it like a pill or a powder, it's a hell of a dance drug. But if you heat it up, like maybe in an oven in some brownie mix, the crystal structure expands and it becomes something a little different – guaranteed to put a smile on your face.'

I push him in the chest and he falls to the floor like he's made of water. The impact shatters any composure he had left and he erupts in paralysing laughter. He's not even looking at me any more, just staring red-faced at his own hands and giggling every time they twitch.

I reach down to touch Clementine, only to see she's already getting herself up. She must have been playing possum. 'Are you OK?' There's a sticky patch of drying blood beneath her nose, but she nods. 'We've got to leave. Get your stuff. Wait, you don't have any stuff. OK, I'll get my things together. Give me a minute.'

She stands up and casts a sour look at Shant's twitching form. 'You should kill them.'

'Kill them yourself, you're such a badass.'

'They'll kill us if they get the chance.'

Something in Shant's twitches tells me he's hearing this conversation, but his body's got him locked down. 'Did I ever make out I was any kind of killer to you? Let's get our stuff and get out of here.' I take the gun and put it in the bag along with the metal box and the brown plastic bottle containing what's left of my bounce. 'Shit, how much did you put in that brownie?'

'I'd say just about the right amount.'

19.

Silas

Levi Peres has somehow contrived to make the Antikythera Mechanism disappear. I went to the warehouse. The box containing the thing is gone, and there is no record of anything coming or going; a spam storm yesterday afternoon is presumably cover for whatever he did. I've had to import an expensive data miner all the way from Korea to pick through the pieces of his handiwork, and apparently it could take days to find anything, if there's anything to find. *What have you done, you little shit?*

A light blinks red on my desk. I ignore it, but Sybil's voice cuts in on my personal line. 'It is Hierophant Barnes of the Machine Cult, sir. He insists the issue is most pressing.'

'Be a dear and tell him to fuck himself with one of his mechanical appendages, would you, Sybil?'

This vanishing places me in a somewhat awkward position. I'd made certain well-founded assumptions about young Levi's competence, and thus the manner in which the operation would be carried out. I'd even shown him the rather generous consideration of ordering maintenance to the air-conditioning units which would render their monitoring systems temporarily inactive. For some reason, he's ignored every discreet assistance I provided, instead performing this inconvenient little miracle.

Hence, the matter of pickup was not something I'd given any consideration to. A well-publicized police manhunt, launched off the back of perfect CCTV images of the criminal caught in the act, would have brought the artefact within my grasp. Young Levi would have died in an unfortunate gunfight while resisting arrest, and a carefully timed announcement would then break the sad news that the criminal, a notorious smuggler, had succeeded in getting the Antikythera Mechanism out of the country before he was tracked down. As planned, it was all going to be very tidy, as well as a great bit of publicity for my campaign for the Justice Ministry, but Peres has somehow fucked it all.

The red light blinks again. Those half-human monstrosities will attempt to intimidate me, they can't help themselves, and any conversation carries a risk I might say something I'll regret. Unfortunately, I need their money; elections are expensive.

'Sybil, if the Hierophant calls again, please put him on hold but make sure to say I'll be available very shortly. As long as he stays on the line, keep checking in with him every couple of minutes – string him along. Oh, and change the hold music to something unpleasant, will you? Anything you can do to keep them off my back until I've sorted this mess out.'

'Yes, minister.'

Obedience of the kind Sybil provides truly is a gift from the gods, but for all her talents, the one thing she cannot do is materialize the Antikythera Mechanism. I punch the code for Peres's line into the desk terminal. Somewhat to my surprise, he answers immediately. His voice cuts across the sound of a jackhammer in the background. 'What do you want, Mizrachi?'

'What I've paid you for. Nothing more, nothing less.'

'I'm glad you put it that way. Your upfront payment didn't even cover expenses. I have gone through some serious grief to get this doohickey. I'm gonna need half a mil.'

Among my other skills, I pride myself on being able to measure a man by his voice: he's serious, but I can't tolerate an outbreak of courage at this juncture. 'Listen to me, Levi. The only reason I'm not going to put a hit out on you right now is a certain grudging respect or, dare I say it, fascination for how you pulled this job off. The original deal, with the original terms, is still available for the duration of this conversation. I suggest you take it.'

Silence at the other end of the line betrays thinking. 'Where?'

'Leave the Old City by the Lions' Gate. Follow the Jericho road almost to the top of the Mount of Olives. There's a defunct electrical substation by the side of the road. Open the service hatch of the main transformer. The money's in there – swap it for the artefact and you can walk away from this with your head high. Word will get around that Levi Peres pulled off something big.'

The line goes dead. That's the problem with the young – their pride is so brittle.

'Sybil, would you inform Jerusalem's finest that their assistance may soon be required on the Jericho road in relation to stolen antiquities, and be a dear and put a sniper team on the Mount of Olives. Tell them not to shoot any policemen.'

The light on my desk informs me the Hierophant is enduring Sybil's choice of hold music. Barring any absurd mishaps, today could turn out rather well, even though it's an unwanted distraction from the day's real business. I have to work out what to do about Amos Glassberg. The ministerial elections are looming, and despite his excruciating dullness, he remains a formidable incumbent. Getting rid of him will take some doing.

A translucent projection of his grimly patrician face glares at me from the glowing hemisphere of documents that constitutes his file. There's something faintly funereal about those high cheekbones and deep-set eyes. Looking at him, it would be easy to write him off as another pointless bureaucrat, but I have known him too long to fall into that trap. The Minister of Justice is dangerous, a man of principle with a strong pragmatic streak. However inert he has appeared up to this point, he remains a threat as long as his credibility is intact.

The documents offer me little to work with: a possible homosexual liaison at university is useless – the only people who would care about that are the hardliners who already hate him. He seems to have a passionless relationship with his somewhat homely wife, but over the years he's steered clear of even the subtlest honey-traps I've set in his path – whether out of perceptiveness or principle, I cannot say. I think part of the problem is that he comes from money. Being born to it simply extinguishes so many of the little fires of inadequacy that burn in the rest of us, and leaves him less vulnerable to manipulation. Through no fault of his own, he's inherited substantial property. In another era that would mark him as out of touch with the ordinary man, but there is no such thing in Jerusalem; certainly money is no sin, and offers me no leverage.

No, Amos Glassberg is a man of ideas: they must be the key to his soul. My eyes wander across the glow of files surrounding me and settle upon something unlabelled, marked only with a primitive chronological tag. A glance reveals it to be the intelligence file covering his student days. It is thin, but extant nonetheless; as a scion of one of the city's more notable families he was worthy of modest surveillance from his late teens. In preparation no doubt for a future in politics, he chose to serve his final undergraduate year at the Sankore Masjid in Timbuktu. It's quite normal for the city's elites to send their young abroad to acquire a touch of sophistication, but it's his next step that's interesting – the Patrice Lumumba People's Friendship University in Moscow. He'd have been just old enough to go there before the Machines made their big push east at the outbreak of the fourth great war. There's no mention of any course of study, and he was there for eighteen weeks – hardly long enough to pick up the language, never mind learn anything substantive. Even before its destruction, Moscow was not a city where young men went to acquire sophistication. What brings the man of ideas to the world's intellectual backwaters?

He is now an admittedly youthful fifty-eight years old. He'd have been twenty-two when he made that journey . . . Those dates . . . He almost walked into the final act of the last war! He must have been in Moscow a matter of weeks before the city fell, before the Russians fell back to the fortified line on the Urals and forged the desperate alliance that became the Sino-Soviet Republic of Humanity. There I have the beginnings of a narrative – Amos Glassberg, fearless champion of humanity. In reality, he most likely ran before the fighting got within a hundred miles of the city, or someone persuaded him to get out, but the reality doesn't matter. I don't need the truth when I can make my own. This is a dark spot in the past of a man who prides himself on transparency. Filling in the blanks is a matter of legitimate public interest. I don't expect the electorate will be delighted to discover their noble Minister of Justice was training as a Soviet spy.

'Sybil?'

'Yes, minister?'

'How's Hierophant Barnes getting along?'

'It's a little hard to tell. I think a lot of the sounds he's making aren't words. He rang off a couple of minutes ago.'

'Jolly good. See if you can get him back on the line.'

'Shall I put him through?'

'No, no, just keep feeding him the hold music: as much as he'll take. What've you got him on?'

'Ah, it's a medley of children's vid-feed theme tunes, sir.'

'Perfect. Can you get me Vasily Tchernikov please?'

The line goes silent for four seconds before a click informs me someone has picked up at the other end. Typical Russian paranoia, waiting for the other guy to speak first. 'Vasily! How's the espionage business?'

'I wouldn't know, minister, but may I commend you on the museum's excellent retrospective of Hellenic art? I thought the juxtaposition of ancient and modern was surprising, yet apposite. My compliments to your curators.' If you didn't know Vasily, you'd hear that voice as deadpan, maybe even hostile. It takes a while to realize that his default mode is irony. There's usually a joke in there somewhere, even if it's hard to see. In my view, he takes the culture bit of his cover altogether too seriously. I can't tell whether or not he derives genuine amusement from rubbing my nose in my philistine shortcomings. He might think his needling goes some way to getting under my skin, but I suspect he is smarter than that. At heart, we are both pragmatists.

'Thanks, I'll be sure to let them know their work is appreciated by the city's foremost culture vulture.'

'You're too kind, Silas. Now what do you want?'

'I need some research from the state archives.'

'That is possible, but there are procedures to follow. This is not a conversation for us.'

'Ah yes, well, there's the thing; I already know the answers to my questions. What I need is for the state archives to provide me with documentary evidence of a certain party's involvement in espionage training during a visit to Moscow.'

'Moscow? That's going back . . . Why not make your own? I'm sure my superiors in Sverdlovsk wouldn't notice a little forgery in a Middle Eastern backwater.'

'I need the documentation to be independently verifiable, from the horse's mouth, so to speak.'

The levity drops out of Vasily's voice. 'The Republic of Humanity has no need or desire to be involved in your schemes, Silas.' The urbane cultural attaché is gone, exiled by the Soviet official, deaf to his own hypocrisy.

'Come now, Vasily. I seem to recall the Republic felt rather differently when it wanted some statues for its Damascene puppets.

I have exerted myself on your behalf. I don't think it's unreasonable to expect a little reciprocity.'

For a few seconds, all I hear is his slow, measured breathing. 'All right. I'd hoped to avoid involving you in this, but there is one thing you could do for us. We've obtained intelligence indicating that emissaries of the Western powers are operating in the city . . .' He pauses as if waiting for a reaction, a pointless fishing exercise in a conversation between professionals, but certain habits are hard to break. 'Most likely, they are operating through their deluded proxies in the Machine Cult.' Another pause. We're sufficiently acquainted for him to know I share his distaste for them, but personal preferences are irrelevant in matters like this. 'For reasons unknown, they are seeking to obtain a historical artefact known as the Antikythera Mechanism. We would like certainty that they do not possess it. We would derive that certainty from possessing it ourselves.'

I mimic his slow breathing to buy myself a few moments to think. One thing a career in intelligence cures you of is belief in coincidence. For the great powers to want it, this Antikythera thing must have some significance that's eluded me; they would not expend this effort for an archaeological curio. He cannot know the theft has already happened – I didn't, and the only other people who knew about the job are the Machine Cult, unless Levi has been remarkably indiscreet. Could Vasily have a source within the Cult? That would be a coup. They are religiously devoted to their inhuman masters from the West, upon whom their hopes for mechanical transfiguration depend. If he has someone inside the Cult, he could already know of my involvement. This entire conversation could be a bluff to draw me out.

'I can assure you it is quite beyond their reach.'

'Not good enough, Silas.' A scratching noise is the sound of his grey, bristled beard brushing the receiver as he shakes his head.

'Very well, I'll need a few days. Contrary to what you may believe,

Vasily, I am at least passingly acquainted with my collections, and I'm quite familiar with the Antikythera device. It's high profile – I can't just give it to you. I could, possibly, make arrangements for it to be in transit with minimal security, at a time and place where you could effect a recovery.'

'Yes, I understand there could be . . . sensitivities, given your position. That could work. Just remember, the delivery of documents will depend on our receipt of the item. The Republic does not extend credit, Silas.'

The line goes dead and I'm left contemplating the blinking red light on my desk – a tiny flashing icon of the Hierophant's muted rage. My gaze drifts to the shuttered window. Somewhere out there, Levi Peres is holding a black box with my future in it.

20.

Clementine

Golden dust billows from the wheels of a tractor rumbling its way out of the olive grove where we rest. Levi leans back against one of the ancient gnarled trunks and fumbles in his bag for a moment before producing an orange. He pierces the skin at one end with a sharp thumbnail and rotates the fruit so the incision spirals to the bottom. The peel comes away and hangs in a perfect 'S'.

I remember once, in the Marseille docks, seeing a teenager do that to impress a girl, but the fruit was small and bitter, nothing like the fat globe Levi holds now. The peel drops carelessly from his fingers onto the carpet of olive leaves bleached grey by the sun. I suppose everyone in Jerusalem can peel an orange. He pulls away the waxy pith and the fruit falls open into a star of flesh, which he proffers to me. I take two unequally sized segments, identical yet not, evidence of the infinite variation from which nature builds the structures we recognize as 'orange', or 'human'.

'Are you going to do the pickup like he says?'

Levi sucks the juice from a segment before talking. 'No. All that call gives us is time. If I hadn't answered, he'd be starting the hunt right now. Acting all terrified buys us a few hours before he realizes the package isn't coming to him.'

'Where do we go?' The city's promise of death, either at the hands of gangsters or Mizrachi's minions, hangs silent in the air between us.

'How the fuck should I know? You'll forgive me if I haven't really thought this through. I hadn't exactly anticipated this course of events.'

'I have an idea.'

'You got an idea?'

'That's what I said.'

'No, you don't get to have ideas, Little Miss Brownie. You don't know shit about this town. In case you've forgotten, you came to me because you had nowhere to go. Just let me think.'

He sits cross-legged beneath the branches of the tree like a skinny, agitated Buddha, lost in contemplation of the canvas bag on his lap. The dappled shade on his face shifts as a light breeze stirs the leaves. A brass corner of the metal box pokes out from the crumpled fabric. He covers it up as if to hide it from himself. Or to hide himself from it? For a moment his pupils had dilated, the sudden terror of a prey animal awakened to a threat, almost as if he was scared of the thing inside the bag. No, I'm over-thinking; my judgement of human emotion is still too fallible, and there's good reason for us both to be scared. I should regard the thing as he does: a box of money that can be used to purchase safety or freedom. Whatever ancient thing it contains should be of no concern, but here, in this body, in this city, it is hard to ignore the pull of human superstition, however strange it seems.

'Do you believe in God, Levi?'

'What? What the fuck kind of question is that? I'm trying to think here.'

'But do you believe in God? I think it's an important question, maybe the most important.'

'You are fucked up, you know that? I'm Jewish, just in case you missed that. The name is a clue.'

'I don't know what "Jewish" means, not really.'

'It means "Go fish". You want simple answers, go ask your friends at the Mission.'

'Yes.'

'Yes?' His normally hooded eyes open wide, like he's been humouring me up to this point, but now can't see past my insanity.

'Yes, I think we should go to the Mission. They have a farm in the hills to the west. My friend Hilda is there.'

He leans back against the trunk and pushes with his legs to slide himself up into a standing position. He stares at the pale 'S' of orange skin where it lies on a twisted root as if he's trying to decipher its incomplete message.

'What is it, Levi?'

'Oh, I was trying to think of any way in which this day could possibly get more fucked up, but I can't. Let's go see the God squad, and they can tell me all about their false messiah, and I can pretend to be impressed.'

'What's wrong with their messiah?'

He shakes his head. 'You got a lot of questions to answer before we start talking theology. Let's get there first.'

A small, rutted farming track, almost covered with fallen leaves, takes us out of the olive groves. The gentle chatter of cicadas falls away as we reach a junction with a feeder road. Levi's plan is to hitch a ride, but we have to stay away from the main routes covered by CCTV and police patrols. We walk along the cracked edges where spike grass splits the tarmac. Every time we hear an engine behind us, Levi sticks his thumb out in a slightly desultory motion as if anticipating their failure to stop. On this little road it's all farmers and tradesmen. Hilda gave me directions to get to the Mission's farm before I left – she said it would take maybe half an hour to drive. I don't think the thought occurred to her I might be walking there. I hope she's expecting me. I hope she believed me when I said I would come.

'We should have taken Shant's car.'

Levi's head snaps around. 'Are you fucking kidding me? As soon as he stopped laughing he could have locked the doors and made it deliver us right to him.'

'I could have hacked it.'

He stops and listens for distant engines before he speaks. 'Listen, Clem. Don't think I'm not impressed by that . . . stuff you do. I get that you've got some serious skills, and this city isn't exactly a beacon of technological progress. I get all that. But you can't keep taking chances: they'll get wise to us; they'll see you coming. Shit, maybe they already did? You think it's an accident that Shant turns up with the only goon in the city who doesn't have a comm-line in his head for you to hack?'

'Sorry.' He's right. The realization takes the breath from me. I've broken my own rules, taken unwarranted risks. I was never supposed to operate alone like this, without parameters and defined methodologies. I have tried to be human, improvising constantly the way they do, redefining a never-ending mission as it evolves, but I have been found wanting. A small sound of despair escapes me, another betrayal by this false body.

'What is it? What's wrong?' His eyes dart around as if searching for some unseen danger, not looking at my tears.

'I was stupid. I shouldn't need you to tell me that.'

He smiles uncomfortably. 'Don't worry about it. We all make mistakes. And we'd both be dead if you couldn't bake.'

I laugh without meaning to. A joke about our near-death brings comfort – human logic.

We've been walking for nearly an hour when a little blue and white three-wheeler truck brakes abruptly in front of us, raising a cloud of blinding yellow dust. When it clears I see the door has opened and someone is leaning out – a smiling face, heavily lined and darkened by years in the sun.

'You're trying to hitch a ride out here? You could be waiting all day. Where you going?'

Levi looks at me, and I mumble the name of the settlement Hilda gave to me. The old farmer frowns, then nods.

'That's not too far out of my way. I would ask you what the hell you two are doing out here, but I'm old enough to know what's not my business.' He gestures at the bag. 'Nice picnic? Ha, ha, ha! I had a few "picnics" in my day.'

He withdraws back into the cab of his truck, still chuckling at his own joke. When I get close enough to look through the window, I realize he fills it completely. He shrugs and gestures to the open truck bed behind him. It's filled with cuttings from some kind of tree or bush. 'Sorry, sweetheart. You'd be real welcome here . . .' He pats his lap in a way that is somehow not lascivious. I think it's a self-deprecating joke that acknowledges his own unattractiveness, but this kind of highly nuanced human interaction is still difficult for me. I say nothing. He shrugs and nods us towards the back.

Levi hefts the bag onto the pile of leaves and branches, then pulls himself up into the truck bed. He shifts to one side to make room for me, so we can both sit with our backs to the cab. The cuttings under my legs and bottom feel scratchy at first, but as they compress they become more comfortable. Our driver cackles something inaudible from the cab and the truck shudders into movement, raising another cloud of dust. Levi uses his sleeve to wipe the grime from his eyes and mouth before speaking. 'So . . . spill.'

'What do you mean?'

'Oh, OK, sure. Just pretend like you haven't been doing crazy, fucked-up shit all day – like I'm not owed any kind of explanation.'

'Oh, that.'

'Yeah, that!'

'Levi, it's not easy for me. I'm not being deliberately obtuse; sometimes I just don't understand exactly what you're saying.'

'Like I don't speak good enough?'

'No, it's not that. There's no easy way to say this. I'm . . . I'm not a human like you.'

146

'I don't get it. What does that mean? Look at you.' He waves a hand in a gesture that takes in my entire body. His hooded eyes fix on mine. A yellow-striped beetle emerges cautiously from the pile of leaves between us, as if wary of the growing silence. The truck rumbles and bounces, and my bones judder at an irregular frequency, impossible to anticipate. The green odour of crushed chlorophyll fills my nostrils. For a moment the beetle trembles, then becomes still, and in one sudden movement spreads tiny gossamer wings.

'I wasn't born like this, Levi. I was a Machine.'

He nods – a motion of acceptance for a fact that can make no sense to him. Even now, the contradictions of identity are hard enough for me.

'I was manufactured, not born, created from tailored stem cells in a factory lab outside Lyon, then put through hormonally accelerated growth in the tanks. As soon as I reached adult size I was encased in the metal exoskeleton that was supposed to hold me for the rest of my life. That's what a Machine is. I was supposed to be a soldier for the Ural Front.'

'But you're not.' The negation is instinctive, an attempt to deny a reality totally outside his experience, but he's listening.

'People look at the Machines and they think they're all the same. They can't see past the metal. Most of us are slaves to the true Machines who first made the transition from flesh more than a hundred years ago. They number only a few thousand spread across the territories.'

'So if you were just a slave, what are they?'

'They don't teach us the history; you don't want slaves to know too much. I only found out what I was after I escaped. The technology that gave rise to the Machines started in the old United States as a kind of advanced prosthetic for therapeutic use. Full body exoskeletons were a logical extension of artificial limb technology, and once you've taken that step, there's really no reason to stick with the humanoid shape or bipedalism. Like everywhere else at that time the US had problems with pollution and radiation as the earth's magnetic field dipped – birth defects, shorter life spans – but what separated them from the rest of the world was that they had the resources for a technological solution. Of course, shutting your children away behind metal was a choice available only to the wealthy, but when has that ever mattered? The rest of the world laughed at America; it was like their craziness with guns: nobody thought anything of it until the third great war broke out. That was when the world saw what they had become.

'The Russians made a push for one of the Baltics, who asked for help. An expeditionary force of Machine infantry routed two armoured divisions within twenty-four hours. Human generals could not grasp that their metal bodies were merely avatars for beings who have become natives of the data stream – the destruction of one was immensely difficult, and inflicted no lasting loss. The Machines toyed with the technology arrayed against them. In a week they were pushing for St Petersburg. Everything escalated. Everyone was terrified. Nobody was prepared for war except the Machines. They saved Europe and then kept it for themselves.'

'But they don't like the desert?'

'No, the dust is a threat. They can tolerate it only for short periods before it starts to foul wiring and internal fluids. The dust keeps them north of the Mediterranean. It keeps Jerusalem free, a nowhere city, not worth fighting over.'

'Does that mean you're, like, a hundred years old?' Levi's face is relaxed now, too caught up in the fascination of discovery to realize the danger that comes with this knowledge.

'No, foot soldiers don't live that long. Perhaps they could, but they're not given the chance. The "Machines" you see now coming out of the lab factories in Europe are emotional and intellectual cripples, bound to a single disposable body. They are not stupid, just rendered inflexible by gene-tailoring and education. You think a Machine is some big, unstoppable engine of death, don't you? That's what they're like in the movies. It suits everyone to show them that way. On the Ural Front a slave faces ultra-modern Sino-Soviet weaponry. Your life expectancy is two to four weeks.'

'So, why aren't you . . .'

'So why am I not dead, somewhere in the foothills west of Omsk? I was stolen before I was ready. There is still human resistance in Europe; it was mostly ineffective while I was there, but that was before the current insurrection. A French-based cell broke into my factory lab and took me while I was in storage, waiting for deployment. They offered me a deal: if I allowed my existing body and exoskeleton to be used for their research, they would digitally preserve my consciousness and make me a new form, in any shape I wanted.'

'What are you now?' He looks at my body as if trying to see some sign of my deviance. There is none. I am a perfect reproduction of someone who never existed, a conceptual model of humanity.

'Something in between. The substance of this body is ordinary human flesh, optimized for functionality, and with the flaws inherent in biology ironed out – none of the errors in cell replication that lead to ageing or cancer. Its senses and neural processing are augmented with a few small implants. They are . . . a necessity; I am not the first to attempt the transition to humanity. It almost always fails. We're not sure why. One thing we know is Machines who try to make the shift without augmentation go insane. It's like being blinded and losing a limb.'

'Wait a minute. You're saying your body isn't you?'

'It wasn't. I'm starting to feel differently now; I've spent the last year in this body trying to learn how to be a human woman. It's . . . It's a lot harder than I thought.'

'A year?'

'In human terms, I have only been alive six years. Fourteen months ago, I chose to be this.'

Shock slackens Levi's face. 'You're a child . . . How? I didn't know . . . I'm so sorry.'

'What for? You didn't do this to me.'

He shakes his head, looking at the sky. 'I'm sorry the world fucked you over, Clementine.' His face is grave, a visual key to the nuance of language: apology as expression of sympathy; even the most ordinary humans seem effortlessly to shrug aside these imprecisions of language, while all my gifts leave me struggling to bypass the literal.

'Thank you. I'm not sure what to say. I've never had a conversation like this. I don't want to get it wrong.'

'You don't have to worry about that, not with me. The truth is, we all get "it" wrong.'

'You're humouring me. There is no need, really.'

'I'm not humouring anyone. I'm telling you what being human is. We can't communicate. What we say is never what we mean. We get it wrong every single time.'

'Even now?'

A smile banishes the sorrow from his face. 'Except now, obviously. Consider this the one and only time in your life when the person you are talking to will make any goddamn sense.' He grabs a handful of leaves from the cuttings beneath us and rubs them between his fingers, caught in an idea. 'Can I . . . ask you questions about stuff? Is that, like, upsetting for you?'

'I don't know. I don't always know what upsets me, or anyone else. You can try.'

'OK, so first thing – how come you found me? Where does a Machine runaway get my name?'

The question summons the memory of a crowded dockside. The insurrection was still only a spark. You could still travel if you had money. 'I bought passage from a Marseille trafficker called Farouz Mubarrak. He said he was from Jerusalem. He had contacts here who could help me find work.'

'Ha! You know, Yusuf was obsessed after you came in throwing that name around. He wanted to know your story, and that was the only thing we knew about you. Turns out he has a cousin with a boat who took it west to make money.'

'And you didn't know he was flashing your name around?'

'No idea. I mean, who the fuck would use my name for anything?'

'It worked on me. I needed to believe there would be a connection where I was going. I needed it to be someone the Machines wouldn't find.'

'I guess that makes sense. Anyone who fits that description isn't going to be someone you can call up to check their bona fides. You had to take a risk.' He looks hard at me. 'So tell me this, if you're a Machine, why were you baking bounce brownies in my apartment?'

'I want to live, Levi. I want to do human things. You'd been out taking drugs with your friends. People pay you money for it. I thought it must be fun. I tried to put one of the tablets in my mouth but it was bitter and I had to spit it out. I read that sometimes people who don't like drugs bake them in cakes, so I looked up how to make brownies.'

A barely audible shout from our driver warns us we're getting near the drop-off. Single-storey, whitewashed houses drift past on either side of the road. This must be the village Hilda mentioned. The truck pulls over in a barely perceptible layby and the old man's arm points up a narrow track that winds around a parched-looking hill. 'That's where your crazies farm for God. Don't be fooled by that little track – they've a big spread up there. Hallelujah, or whatever it is they say.'

Levi climbs out of the truck bed and puts his arms up for me to pass him the bag. Again, his pupils dilate for a fraction of a second when his fingers close around the handle. I don't know if he's even conscious of it. As soon as the strap's around his shoulder he raises a hand to help me out of the truck. 'Careful, the ground's loose around here.'

'Uh . . . it's OK, Levi. I can get down myself.'

'Shit, Clementine. You might be a robot ninja or whatever, but this has been a hell of a day for a six-year-old.' He bangs twice on the back of the truck and waves as it pulls away with its high-pitched horn tooting. We turn and start walking on the dry path that twists around the hill ahead of us. After a few steps he puts his arm around my shoulder and leans in close. It feels safe. 'OK, here's the first Levi Peres lesson in being human. Stay off the bounce, or any other shit that someone like me tries to sell you in a cellophane bag.'

'But you take it?'

'Only for business. Bounce won't kill you, but it messes with your head. You take too much of it, you forget how to be happy.'

'So you're happy because you don't take it?'

'Welcome to humanity, Clementine.'

21.

Silas

A man with a donkey's head roams the stage. The spotlight picks out bare patches in the grey fur of the headpiece. The actor totters on his feet as if unbalanced by the weight of the thing; he is supposed to be under the dizzying influence of a magical spell. The character rejoices in the name 'Bottom', apparently.

'Why are we here, Sybil?'

She shifts uncomfortably in the darkness. Her presence at the back of the box keeps her out of view of anyone outside while permitting me to work discreetly. Events are moving quickly, and I cannot afford to waste two hours purely for the sake of making an appearance.

'You wanted to be seen to engage with European culture, sir, something to avoid being typecast as the xenophobe candidate, you said.'

'Yes, yes, but what is the point of this performance? What pleasure is any sane human supposed to derive from watching this?'

'It is a comedy, sir, written by a playwright widely acknowledged to be the greatest of all time.'

'I know who Shakespeare is, thank you, my dear. I just struggle to see any merit in this. None of it makes sense. It certainly isn't funny. Wasn't there anything else we could do?'

'This was the only window in your diary for a month. Also you've got a cultural delegation from Timbuktu coming, and you wanted something to talk about with them "just in case they start banging on about art". I could have booked us into an evening of slam poetry at the Gala?'

'Ugh. All right, you've made your point. Let's make the best of it. Give us some privacy.'

'Of course.'

The sound of fairies singing fades to nothing as she deploys the cancellation field to grant us privacy. Anyone looking from outside will see only the blackness of an empty opera box, a common enough sight. My appearance at the event will have been marked by anyone who cares enough to notice, and most eyes should be on the stage. Freed of the constraints of being observed, Sybil produces a data slate from beneath her seat. The light from discarded messages illuminates her face in a flickering patchwork as she sifts through work put on hold while we imbibe our dose of culture.

'What news on Amos?'

She listens without raising her head. 'He's up to something, but I haven't been able to get specifics.' Her finger settles on the slate. 'He's being super careful, and his counter-surveillance is good. Bugs are being swept as fast as we put them down.'

'What about our people in the justice department? They must hear something of what's going on; that's what we pay them for.'

'Glassberg never lets anyone get close. We infiltrated a PA into his office, but he doesn't even talk to her. Our assets risk compromising themselves if they try anything overt.'

'I think they'll find it's riskier taking my money and not delivering the goods. Never mind. Give me what we have.'

Her hand comes away from the data slate, and she looks up to face me. 'It's all bits and pieces. We know from multiple sources he's taking an active interest in the investigation into your brush with death, requesting both reports and view of raw data.'

'Unusual, but within his purview as Chief Justice. The evidence chain we've constructed leads unequivocally to the conclusion it was an assassination attempt perpetrated by members of the Mission. It should stand up to scrutiny. What else?'

'He's obviously not buying it. He's requested at least two closed-door meetings with Ayed Khalil.'

'Why the secrecy? That's not like him.' Involving the city's police commandant is a predictable move on Glassberg's part; the old chief is the closest thing he has to an ally. Meetings between the two of them are routine. In ordinary circumstances I wouldn't bother about them. Khalil isn't dangerous, but he's a potential conduit for information, and the officers on the street do what he says. If Amos has a plan, Khalil can make it happen.

'We don't know. Whatever they discuss is completely off-record. There's no schedule or agenda registered prior to the visits, and no minutes afterwards. It's like they never happened.'

A sense of unease pours through me like cold water. 'That's worrying: we can't afford for Amos to go rogue, not at a time like this. What's he up to? Fill in the blanks for me.'

She sits back in her chair and smooths the disobedient fringe away from her face. It sometimes puzzles me why she chooses to hide her talents behind a mouse-like exterior, but I suppose the anonymity grants a freedom of sorts. In the gloom of the shrouded box, she could be anyone. 'We know Amos has requested a list of suspects based on motive. The list of people who might want to kill you is a long one, and includes known figures from the city's underworld, so we wouldn't expect them to draw any conclusions based on that alone.' She pauses as if stuck on something.

'Go on.'

'The activity of officers assigned to the case indicates they're working through that list systematically. It's like they're starting from scratch – no leads. If they keep going like this, it could be weeks or even months before they uncover a religious motive for the glass-fitters to booby-trap the roof.'

'We don't have that much time! This has to hit the headlines before election day or we're toast. Surely they can't completely ignore the trail we laid? I practically painted a target on my back for the Missionaries!'

'I thought dismissing their "Messiah's tomb" as a Roman sewer was a little over the top.' She grimaces at the memory of two days of outrage played out in the media. The news cycle moved on. It always does.

'It worked. I even received genuine threats. The investigation should be all over it by now, and the plods should be high-fiving themselves for being so clever. Why aren't they doing anything about it?'

Sybil holds my gaze, waiting for a decision. Everything hangs on the investigation. If the plan follows its course, Glassberg will be presiding over the trial of the century on the eve of the election. The web of circumstance we have woven presents him with a devil's choice: to acquit three lay brothers from the Mission in the face of powerful evidence, incurring the wrath of every hardliner in the city, or to convict three men who are probably innocent. Both choices damn him, one way or another. It was all going to be perfect, but this secrecy suggests he has somehow scented the trap.

'Let's say you're right. Let's say he sees the frame, and he worked it out all the way through to the endgame – I didn't think he had the imagination, but you'd be a fool to underestimate Glassberg. What's his next move?'

She brightens again. 'Oh, that's easy. He comes after you.'

'Us, Sybil dear. He comes after us, and you'd do well not to forget it.'

Sybil is a phenomenon, but, like any employee, she does her best work when provided with the correct motivation. While Glassberg's development of teeth is inconvenient and potentially dangerous, it provides both carrot and stick for my talented assistant. Her elevation to my ministerial seat, and our continued liberty, both depend on keeping him in check.

She shrugs, undaunted. 'He can try. He won't be the first.'

'Don't be fooled by the grey exterior. Amos Glassberg is a different proposition to squeezing a few low-rent Armenian gangsters with delusions of grandeur. You should regard him as the most dangerous man in Jerusalem. He is smart, utterly ruthless, and his position as Justice Minister gives him unrestricted emergency powers. We are standing upwind of a lion – a moment's shift in the breeze could kill us. We need to be watertight. What's our potential exposure?'

Her nose wrinkles and her brows crease in thought for a few moments before she shakes her head. 'Minimal. We've been careful not to leave loose ends. The only threat is hearsay from a few criminals who've been peripherally involved in the antiquities operation.'

'What about the Antikythera job? It's ongoing, clients and contractors at large: until the device is in our hands, it has the potential to get messy.'

'True, but there's nothing to point Glassberg in that direction. Wait. Oh shit . . .' She pauses, biting her bottom lip.

'What is it?'

Seconds pass while she chooses her words. In a lesser individual, you might take her hesitation as evidence of fear, but Sybil is only ever guilty of sensible caution where I am concerned.

'Boutros.'

'What?' The name means nothing to me: sounds Egyptian.

She sighs, then catches herself and adopts a neutral tone. 'The curator responsible for the device – you know, the one we found in a pool of his own blood, minus his fingernails.'

'Oh, him. We didn't kill him.'

'No, but we disposed of the body and filed a missing person's report.'

'You did what?'

She meets my glare without flinching. 'We followed procedure. Anything else would have been suspicious.'

Irritation flares briefly within me. I suppress it. She's right, and anyway, an AWOL curator could draw attention, but is not of itself a crime. Her eyes narrow as she studies me, gauging my mood. In my early days at the ministry, I took great pains to keep my temper in check, conscious of the danger of distracting or upsetting staff I needed to function at peak efficiency. These days I unleash it rarely, but it does no harm to show the lash from time to time.

'You want me to pull the plug on the Antikythera op? If the Mechanism goes back in the museum, a missing curator leads nowhere. It's the safe play.'

'No, money like that doesn't come along every day, and I might still need the Mechanism to keep the Russians on side. Young Levi has been a pain in the backside, but his discretion might actually prove useful. Nobody knows the thing is gone. We should move it on as soon as it's in our hands, but delay the announcement of the theft – wait for a big news day when nobody's going to give a shit about some missing antique.'

'So what do you want to do about Amos while you're sealing the deal? We can't touch him; he's clean.'

'We'll have to give the pieces to someone else and have them draw the picture for themselves. I'm sure one of our pet journalists would love to get his teeth into this.'

'Sir, if I may?' The curl of Sybil's narrow lips betrays pride. If she has thought of something clever, it would be a shame to waste it.

'Go on.'

'If something like this came from one of our regular media sources, it might not be given the weight we would wish. If it's not front page, it's not going to mean anything and we won't get another shot at this.'

'What do you propose?'

'We leak the data through a proxy to one of your more implacable critics – perhaps Neumann at the *Echo*? Someone credible will give it weight, make it harder to ignore.'

A smile creeps around the corners of my mouth. Sybil's mind is the perfect tool for tasks like this. 'Neumann? That's a risk.'

'Yes.'

'All right, do it. Be sparing, mind. Make sure she has just enough fragments to come to the conclusion that the investigation into my attempted murder is being deliberately stalled. And try to make sure she can join the dots between the case and the easy ride Glassberg has given to all the God-botherers who've been through his courtroom.'

'That last bit will be difficult.'

'But not, I feel, impossible. If the public buys the idea that Glassberg is a closet Mission sympathizer, we might not even need to nudge the poll data, and if one of his biggest cheerleaders delivers the knife, it will go that much deeper. Consider it a challenge. You know the stakes.'

'I'll do what I can. Do you want to watch the rest of the play?' Sybil's thumb hovers over the activation pad for the shrouding field on her data slate.

'I suppose I better had. I'm supposed to be seen, and I still need something to talk about with the Timbuktu delegation. How long have we got left?'

'Hard to say. We should be near the end of the third act, but I wasn't really following it. I lost the thread when the actors playing the part of actors started explaining the plot of their play.'

'Yes, that bit was confusing, and I don't understand why they're called Mechanicals. It all looks like something out of the Dark Ages, not a Machine in sight.'

A human voice coarsened to imitate the bray of an ass pierces the silence of the box as the shroud disappears. The donkey is singing.

'Actually, I've changed my mind. Turn it off please, Sybil. I think I've had enough European culture for one day.'

22.

Clementine

Seven vast, perfect green circles form an incomplete square on the yellow dust of the valley floor, a one-sided game of tic-tac-toe played out in the desert on a giant scale by men and women with hoes and rakes – vegetables for the Lord. Their chlorophyll brightness is an invasion from another world; I haven't seen that colour since France. Levi walks beside me, paying little attention to the strange vista in front of us, instead looking at me as if I might break.

He knows almost everything now, at least the parts of my own story I can tell, and the knowledge has changed things between us in a way I do not understand. The criminal is kind to me, even though I have made mistakes that endangered us both. In these past few days, I have learned somewhat to read the weather of emotion as it passes across Levi's face. I've never before had the opportunity to spend long enough with a single human to learn an individual's dialect of expression. It is a fascinating but imperfect language. Ultimately, I am left attempting to divine meaning, like an ancient seer searching for signs in the caprice of nature. My restless mind seeks clarity. Why am I now worthy of care? I could ask, but some inexpressible fear holds me back, as if this sudden tenderness might evaporate in the cold light of enquiry. That would be unbearable.

In the distance, tiny white figures move along rows within the green. I raise a hand to point them out, but Levi merely squints and shakes his head.

'You might as well be pointing at the moon, Clem. Everything down there is a blur to me.'

'You have a disability?'

'No, that's just the harsh reality of life without the benefits of robot ninja modification.' His face creases into a frown. For a moment I am scared I've made him angry. 'Hold on a second. Was that a joke?'

'Maybe.'

'Not bad for your first try. We can work on that.' I catch the edge of his smile as he turns away to look ahead. Shuffling steps take us down the switchback paths to the valley floor. Little clouds of yellow dust trail in our wake, seeming to hang infinitely in the air. Suddenly, he pauses and turns to face me, grimacing. 'OK, I'm a little near-sighted. It's never really been a thing in the city, but out here . . .' The words trail off as he resumes the shuffle.

'It's OK, I'll keep a lookout for gangsters.'

'Yeah, you do that.'

We're most of the way down to the valley floor when one of the white figures stops working and points at us before turning around to shout to someone behind him. Another worker at the distant edge of the circular field runs towards what looks like a glittering oblong of light topping a low rise at the other side of the valley. My eye-filters descend without thought, polarizing the image, cutting out the blinding glare. The shiny thing is a long curved tunnel of transparent plastic. Faint glints behind are dozens more stretching into the middle distance.

The path takes us past the closest of the strange circular fields. Fifty-two white-garbed workers move between the rows of vegetation, bending and kneeling, picking, hoeing, stopping at regular intervals to administer some sort of spray which descends in a fine mist upon the leaves. They seem to ignore our intrusion into their domain, even the one who spotted us.

The only sign of a response to our arrival is a flap opening at the end of the nearest of the plastic tunnels. A small two-person buggy emerges through the opening and makes a hesitant turn down onto the dirt track towards us. The figure in the passenger seat wears a brown robe that does not entirely conceal the rounded figure beneath.

My pulse quickens at the imminent reality of facing Hilda. It's bad enough I come here as a fugitive, bringing danger together with my partner in crime, but our parting was a wound, carelessly inflicted. I search for some clue in her expression, but at this distance even my eyes cannot see through the shadows of her cowl.

The buggy's driver is a bearded man at the end of middle age with a hard expression. He concentrates on the treacherous track, which wars with the stability of his vehicle at every turn until it reaches the flatter ground of the valley floor where we stand. The buggy stops in a cloud of fine particles so dense they prevent speech for six quickening heartbeats while sleeves and fingers clear them from eyes and lips.

'You came.' Hilda speaks first, hood thrown back, revealing the same gently calculating look in her green eyes as when we first met. I was running away that time, too.

'I said I would.'

'You brought a friend.'

Levi shrugs, palms out in a gesture of supplication. His reaction to her words tells me there is some significance to their tone that eludes me.

'This is Levi. He's been looking after me.'

Hilda appears to consider something for a moment; then she

shakes her head and gestures at two rear-facing seats at the back of the buggy. 'We'll talk inside.'

We are silent passengers while the driver grunts in concentration, wrestling the buggy through a many-pointed turn to steer it back towards the tunnels. Rocks in the track skip away from its wheels as it passes the edges of the green circles. The nearest ones are young corn, shoots still only a couple of feet high. In the next row, fat veined leaves low to the ground indicate brassicae of some kind, cabbages or cauliflower. All of it growing in defiance of the season in a way that would be impossible back home.

Suddenly, a hissing fills the air. It seems to be coming from beneath the ground, like a monstrous buried serpent. Levi jerks, his body reacting in instinctive fear, but my human senses detect no obvious danger. Hilda and the driver both look straight ahead as if nothing is happening. Just as I am starting to fear some auditory hallucination, I hear more noises – metal groaning and something moving through the green stalks of corn. The tips disappear as this disturbance approaches, then snap back into position as it passes. I watch, waiting for whatever it is to appear, but the buggy carries us around the edge of the circle and away.

As we pass the rows of tunnels, I dimly see the figures of white phantoms moving behind the translucent plastic. The buggy drives straight past the flap it emerged from, following this single narrow track up to a plateau at the top of the hills. Here, the plastic sea finally ends at a cluster of low wooden huts with a temporary feel, perhaps enough for a hundred people to live in meagre style. The track stops at a single building made of whitewashed adobe with a cross on the roof, a smaller, cleaner cousin to the Mission's outpost in the city. A modest bell tower in the middle of the roof must be the highest point for miles around.

A patch of gravel crackles beneath the buggy's wheels as it stops outside. An ornate door decorated in European style pierces me with a memory of France. The driver gets out first and holds it open for Hilda, as if she's some kind of visiting dignitary, but she pointedly waits for Levi and me to go ahead of her. It never occurred to me that she was someone important. In my days at the Mission in the city, people did as she asked as a matter of course, but I never thought of her as someone who wielded power.

Levi stays fixed in his seat, chewing his lip. 'You guys go ahead. I'll just wait here until you're done.'

Hilda stands silent in the doorway, peering at him as if he's a specimen of some previously undiscovered insect species.

'Really, I'm just not a church kind of guy.'

She smiles as if alighting on some hidden joke. 'That is your choice, Levi Peres. The Saviour welcomes all.'

23.

Levi

'You jus plannen on sitten there?' The driver speaks English to me in a weird accent I never heard before, like he's chewing on words trapped in his beard. 'I'm gonna need mah buggy back. This is a werken farm.'

I give him my best bar mitzvah smile, but he shakes his head and looks at me as if I'm dirt, which I guess from his perspective is more or less accurate. He sits behind the steering wheel and twists to look at me.

'Go on, git oot of it.'

'Uh, is there anywhere I could make a call? I'm not getting any signal on my comm-plant.'

He shakes his head and smiles like I said something funny. 'Naebody does, son.' His teeth are a gross yellow.

'This is really important, man. I swear it will just take one minute.'

'It's not up to me, son.' He points at the church roof. 'The city-net doesn't reach out here. Any outgoing signal has to route through an aerial in the bell tower. Access is encrypted, and forbidden to acolytes. You'll need the Reverend Mother's permission.'

'So I have to . . .' I stand up from the buggy seat and half climb out, one foot on the ground.

'Get oot of mah buggy, aye.'

'She's in there?' I nod towards the door.

'Unless she's performed a miracle.'

He turns away and the buggy's motor whines into life, leaving me hopping, trying not to drop the bag holding the loot while it speeds off. Maybe he'd be more understanding if I fell down on my knees and told him about the fucking sociopath who will find exciting ways to kill me unless I give him what's in the bag on my shoulder. Or maybe not; he seemed kind of focused on the buggy issue. Seriously, though, I need to talk to Silas. I figure he already wasn't sending me a Hanukkah card this year, but every hour that passes with him thinking I've done a runner pushes me further from the shit list to the hit list.

The corners of the metal box inside the bag dig into my ribs as I shift the strap on my shoulder. A numbness fades from the place on my back where it rested. No part of the plan involved me carrying this thing for miles while we walked cross-country. The door swings easily away from me, cheap, lightweight. Inside it smells like a low-rent furniture showroom – wood polish to make you think you're buying something better than chips stuck together with glue. Twenty-something years living in Jerusalem and I never went inside a church. By the looks of this place I wasn't missing much. The only thing in here I couldn't find at my local outlet store is a lectern at the front. It's heavy, carved from dark wood into the shape of a fierce-looking eagle. Its spread wings support a fat old book in a battered leather binding that doesn't look like a regular bible. Behind the lectern, there's a curved wall that separates one corner of the hall from the rest. The door in it is brown glass like a cheap pair of shades. Quiet voices murmur, then stop as I approach.

My fist hovers an inch away from the door. Why am I waiting? They obviously know I'm here. My hand comes away, brushes the dirt off my pants. Deep breath. I knock softly and the glass trembles under my knuckle.

'Come in, Mr Peres.'

Inside, it's like two tiny rooms joined together, a tiny office, and a tiny bedroom, with three people looking at me. I only saw two go in; one of them was Clementine. The new one must have been waiting for us. She wears the same robe as Clem's friend but she's tall and thin, with a slightly hooked nose. She looks at me the way a vulture looks at meat that's not dead yet, which is not what I expected from a nun.

'Ah, sorry to disturb. I just really need to . . .'

'Sit down please.' Clem's friend, the fat one, is sitting at the desk on the only proper chair in the room. The tall one looms next to a fireplace, her elbow on the mantelpiece. Clementine watches me from the edge of a small, hard-looking bed. She looks scared, like a kid who's just been told off and doesn't know whether there's still more to come.

'Really, I don't want to take up your time, I've just gotta make a call real quick. Could you see your way clear to—'

'Mr Peres, if you're asking me a favour, I must insist you do me one first. Sit down; engage in this conversation. Once we have addressed Clementine's immediate concerns, I will consider your request.' She gestures to a spot on the bed next to Clementine. I sit. 'Clementine has told us of your predicament.' Clem looks at me out of the corner of her eye, like she doesn't want to face me. I guess some people would be angry about a situation like this, but from where I'm sitting, I don't see she had a lot of options if she wanted their help. 'We cannot condone the actions that have led you to this point, but neither can we allow harm to come to those in our care. We have to know what we're dealing with. Show us what you have taken.'

'Hold on a second.' A little curiosity is understandable, but I'm sensing a level of interest that is unhealthy. 'I mean no disrespect, and I know Clem thinks you guys are great, but I don't know you. You're all sweet in your brown PJs, talking to God, but what's that supposed to mean to me? I'm supposed to trust you? Thanks, but no thanks.'

'Where are you going to go?'

'We'll work something out. Come on, Clementine.' I stand up.

She sits on the bed, not moving. Her smile is a broken heart. Suddenly my chest feels empty. The door handle is a cold bar of metal in my hand.

'She needs you, Levi Peres.' The words are salt on a fresh cut.

'Damn right she needs me, that's why . . .' I see Clem's face. She's looking at me like I'm already gone, tears shining on those catwalk cheekbones. For some reason, I didn't think she'd be able to cry. My hand slips off the door handle. This is messed up. 'OK, maybe we should take a minute to think things through.'

The fat one gives me that same weird, bland smile she did outside. 'Have a seat.'

I put the bag down on the floor and sit on the bed next to Clem. 'It's OK, champ, I'm not going anywhere, not yet. We got a job to finish, right?' She nods and wipes an eye, and as I look at her I'm thinking: How can everyone not see the child? But I know the answer. She's invisible behind that perfect exterior. No, not invisible, it just makes us all blind. I prod the bag with my foot and wave at Vulture-lady. 'You open it.'

She sinks to the floor and slides the black metal box out of the bag. It's facing the wrong way for her to open, so she twists it around and thumbs the catches on the front in a single smooth movement, more like a street trader than a nun. The lid comes up but her brown-robed back blocks me from seeing inside. All I hear is a gasp. 'Hilda, come look at this! They've stolen the Antikythera Mechanism.'

Hilda's mouth makes a shape like she's about to swear, but stays closed while she kneels to look. Without getting up, she picks the box up and holds it out towards us so we can see. Her knuckles are white from gripping the box too hard and there's a tremble in her wrists. Clem and I both lean forward at the same time, like we're in sync. Clem's fingertip touches it and her eyes open wide, like it's the most exciting thing she ever saw.

It's a rock. It's not even pretty. There's a few shiny spots of blue-green stuff – I don't know what it is – and some circles and crosses in the stone, but that's it. Technically, it doesn't matter whether it's a toy dinosaur in that box – Silas is paying me to steal it, so he gets whatever, assuming we resolve our differences, but a part of me wants to die. A goddamned rock! Clem's face shows she's thinking the same thing – we've been through hell for some shitty old paving slab.

The weird thing is, the holy sisters are still looking at us like we just gave them God in a box. 'Do you know what we have here?'

I shake my head. The 'we' does not escape my attention, but I can't deal with that right now.

'This is the oldest thinking machine in existence. It was ancient, even before the wars.'

'What does it do? Count rocks?' At least we can get a laugh out of this. I look over to see Clementine smile but her eyes are closed. She's not moving, just locked in position as if she froze when she leaned forward to look into the box. One outstretched finger rests on the green stone, lightly touching it. Hilda and Vulture-lady see it too: total stillness, not like a living thing. The older nun levers herself up off the floor and hovers next to Clementine, puts a finger underneath her nose to check if she's breathing. When she nods, I suddenly notice I was holding my breath.

We all look at each other. Part of me takes a certain satisfaction that they obviously have no clue what is happening, but a bigger part just wants them to be able to fix it. Vulture-lady stands up, closing the box. Silence hangs in the air, broken only by plastic clicks as she takes a green-boxed first-aid kit off the wall and searches vainly for something that might help.

Suddenly, from beside me, a child's voice starts to speak.

'I can feel it.'

The words are coming from Clementine, but in a weird, high sing-song voice that might belong to a real six-year-old.

Hilda speaks first. 'What can you feel, Clementine?'

'The mind inside.'

'What do you mean, Clem? What kind of mind?'

'It's been sleeping for a long time, but it's starting to wake. It knows me.'

24.

Silas

Sun streams through the glass at the centre of the museum's roof and falls as dappled light to the marble floor. Yesterday's rain must have left streaks in the grime up there. The chatter of the delegates from the Timbuktu Madrasah is a buzz in my left ear. The blue-robed youngsters titter at the thousand-year-old triptych depicting Mohammed's ascent to heaven like schoolboys looking at porn, while the elders glide past, pretending this idolatry from Islam's Golden Age doesn't exist. There is more than a touch of the comic in the images of a fat man flying a winged donkey with a human face, but it's no worse than some of the nonsense in the Christian section. Two of the teachers drift towards me like baggy balloons of blue fabric with questions on their faces. My eyes dart in search of the curator who's supposed to be escorting the group, but I seem to be alone with them. Unfortunate.

The larger of the two greets me with the plastic, tolerant smile of the fanatic. 'Why do you show what is *haram*? Did you bring us here to insult us?'

This is exactly why I avoid the museum. No one would bother with these bores if they didn't hold the keys to the African interior and the wealth its raw materials bring. Some of them are clever enough in their own way, but they all have the same desert blindness to inconvenient truths, even when they leave the sand behind. Of course, the outrage is as much a negotiating tactic as anything. The Timbuktu delegations always come with an impossible shopping list of European exotica which I do my best to fulfil.

'Not at all, Abdi, not at all. The displays are merely part of the historical record. It's all in the hands of the curators. You know how it is – I only run the place. Perhaps we should talk business?'

A sly look acknowledges the presence of the youngsters, pampered scions of West Africa's super-rich, slumming it for a few days so they can go back and tell their friends about the forbidden marvels of the Holy City. 'Later, Mizrachi. I hope you have something good this time.'

'Oh, you won't be disappointed.'

He grins, satisfied. The nouveau riche are never hard to please – it's just a matter of keeping abreast of whatever winds of fashion are blowing through the western deserts. Cathedral gargoyles are the latest must-have for the home, apparently – the more famous the ruin they come from, the better, but provenance is so tricky to prove with Europe in the state it's in.

A heavy breath announces the presence of someone behind me. I turn to see the bald and terminally dull countenance of Levin, the senior curator who should have been here an hour ago. His face is red – I would say 'with excitement' but Levin doesn't know the meaning of the word. Probably just scared of what I'll do to him for being late. I flash him a smile that offers no reassurance and graciously step back to let him take over the conversation.

'Ah, thank you, minister. Ummm . . . The triptych is the work of a court painter in the Umayyad Caliphate. It dates from a time before the . . . ummm . . . modern proscription on depictions of the Prophet.'

As I make my excuses and walk away, the delegates' dark eyes still glitter with their cultivated outrage. This is what curators are paid to deal with. Maintaining business relationships is a necessity, but I can ill afford distractions at a time like this. In less than six weeks, all twelve of the city's ministers, including me, will have to submit to the verdict of the polls and I don't want any doubt about the outcome.

Unfortunately, certainty costs money. The hacking collectives charge an arm and a leg for something as high profile as compromising voting machines. I'm going to have to get my hands dirty. Well, dirtier anyway. Levi Peres and my Russian colleague have, between them, presented me with a logistical problem. I have to deliver the goods, and whatever strictures I seek to impose, my charming demi-human clients will want to feel they have secure possession of the Antikythera device before they'll pay. But the Sino-Soviet interest in the artefact means I cannot allow it to leave the jurisdiction. It's all rather messy, but it is merely a matter of having cake and eating it. A little deception should suffice.

The itch of uncertainty gnaws at me during the short walk from the museum floor to my office. Up until this point, a certain detachment from my merchandise has served me well, but I am starting to regret my lack of curiosity about this Antikythera thing. In isolation, the Machine Cult's interest I could understand; it is entirely in character for them to ascribe a bizarre and incomprehensible significance to some bauble, and to become fixated upon its acquisition. However, the palpable interest of my Russian counterpart puts an entirely different perspective on the matter. Despite his pretensions as an aesthete, Vasily is a practical man. If he or his masters want it, the Antikythera Mechanism must be something more than a cultural and historical curiosity.

As I drift through the foyer of my office, Sybil raises an arm in my path holding a cup of coffee just hot enough to become uncomfortable in my grip by the time I reach my desk. The punched green leather of my swivel chair offers little comfort. I am trapped in a ridiculous irony. Even with the irritant that was Boutros gone, I share this building with people who are supposedly the world's foremost authorities on the mysterious object, but asking any questions risks drawing attention to the theft. I am not ready for that particular cat to get out of the bag. I key the switch on the left side of my desk. 'Sybil, get me a museum catalogue and a guidebook please.'

'Uhh . . . yes, sir.' Her voice only betrays surprise for a moment. She bustles in silently before I've finished my coffee and deposits the documents in front of me without meeting my eyes. I wonder what, if anything, could unsettle Sybil's marvellous gift of detachment. Those are musings for another day, one less crowded with pressing questions. A quiet fart escapes me as I open the folders, which she dutifully ignores.

The guides offer little. The Mechanism was smuggled out of Athens in a refugee ship from Piraeus a few months before windborne fallout from the battle of Bucharest rendered the city uninhabitable. The records that were presumably supposed to come with it were lost when the ship hit a mine in the harbour mouth at Tyre. The device's subsequent recovery intact from the seabed was a miracle to match its original discovery, when sponge divers stumbled across a shipwreck containing the thing. Now, almost everything we know about it is guesswork and fragments from paper records that survived the data wars.

The outer coating that looks like rock is just what happens when you leave bronze in seawater and dirt for two thousand years. When they found it, it was one big, dirty lump; then they broke it into a dozen pieces, changed their minds and stuck it all back together. X-rays of the thing show the outline of thirty intermeshing bronze gears beneath the rock. Apparently, they represent a level of engineering expertise that mankind would not attain until the Renaissance. If you were to fit them together correctly, they would function as an astrolabe that perfectly predicts solar and lunar eclipses, as long as you're standing somewhere between

Rhodes and Pergamon. A curiosity, but nothing here tells me why they want it.

I jab the comms button on my desk again. 'Sybil, what kind of trace did we get on my last call to Peres?'

Silence while she summons data. Her voice cuts it. 'Nothing, sir. He didn't pick up – no connection to trace.'

'What about his comm-plant? Registered?'

'Operation carried out as normal, post puberty at the Beth Nevi'im clinic. The implant is a standard mid-range Shimezu, but some time in the last six years he's had the usual criminal hack done on it, and it shows up with various IDs – mostly they belong to people he won't know.'

'Hmm, that's something we'll have to crack down on.'

'You'd have to arrest half the city, sir.'

'Good point. Perhaps I should make it an election pledge. That sort of thing always sells. Anyway, what you're telling me is that despite our extensive and expensive surveillance network, we have no idea of where he is?'

'Only circumstantial details, sir. The last signal we had from him was highly attenuated. Possibly that means he's out of range of the city's relay masts. There're a few CCTV snatches of him walking towards the Lion Gate with a female companion. We can only surmise he's somewhere east of the city.'

'East of the city? That's it?'

'Yes, sir.'

'Fucking Peres. I can't let this drag out. Find a way to get to him.'

25.

Levi

Clem's body is a narrow ghost underneath a white sheet. She touched the Antikythera thing once after she spoke, then she collapsed, no more talking in that creepy voice. Lucky she was already on the bed. She's been sleeping for twelve hours, just like she did after the heist. You can barely see her breathe; it's like someone switched her off. Hilda sits on the floor next to me in a clearing between piles of books, watching Clem for most of the time, turning every so often to check I'm not stealing anything. We haven't really talked. A smile flickers over her face.

'Mr Peres . . .'

'Levi. Please. Levi. Only people who want money call me Mr Peres.'

'OK, Levi. You don't trust me . . . any of us. From your perspective, I can see why that would be, but you can surely see we want what's best for Clementine? She would want you to trust us.'

'She's a kid, what does she know?'

'Enough to put her faith in you, apparently.'

The words push a slim blade of guilt into my chest. I see her as she was that day, a silhouette standing in the door to Yusuf's bar. For a second, I thought I was being busted for something. The way she asked for me sounded like a cop. 'I didn't know.'

'No, no you couldn't. My intention was not to make you feel guilty, merely to illustrate that Clementine's judgement of people is perhaps more keen than her naivety elsewhere might suggest.'

'Maybe, maybe not. You've got to admit some of the shit you guys do is pretty weird.'

She gives me a smile that looks different to the bland expression she's been wearing since we got here. It makes her look younger, but she's got one of those faces – she probably looked forty when she was sixteen.

'What is it about us you find so strange?' She leans real close to me and her face is all earnest and kind like a fairy godmother in a storybook and suddenly I can't take it.

'I don't know what the angle is, but you've got something going on here.'

Then it comes again - that patient smile that sets my teeth on edge. 'To people who lack it, faith always seems unreasonable. Stay with us, help us to care for Clementine.'

Not buying it, no way. 'I saw her like this before. She just gets tired when she does her crazy shit. Bake her a cake for when she wakes up.'

The nun shakes her head. 'I've never seen anything like this. Whatever state she's in, it's not a normal sleep.'

'So? What's that supposed to mean to me? I'm not a doctor. I can't fix anything. Look, maybe you really are a good person, maybe all this is for real, but if I stay here, I can't do anything except look at her. I've got one thing I can do that's good for me, and for Clementine – which is make some money.'

'Don't . . .' Her face goes all sad, like I'm taking something away from her.

'What? You going to say something to change my mind?'

She looks down at her knees, fingers of her left hand picking at a loose thread in the rough weave of her robe. 'No.'

'I guess I'll see you around then.'

Hilda becomes a blurred outline of a kneeling figure as the smoked-glass door closes behind me. She's praying, which I guess makes a kind of sense. It's what people do when they don't know.

Vulture-lady is coming the other way when I get to the front door of the chapel. I stop in the doorway, braced for another confrontation, but she just smiles bright and clear, like an actress, but scary, one that could kick your ass.

'Leaving us already, Mr Peres?'

'Levi. Yeah, I got some business to finish up.'

The bright smile stays on her face but the eyes become cold. She points to the canvas bag on my shoulder, which I swear feels heavier than it did on the way here. 'Would that business be selling the priceless antiquity you stole from a museum – something that belongs to all of humanity?'

'That business would be none of yours. Go talk to God or something.'

She stands there, staring, and for a second I swear I see a flicker of something moving in her eyes – something yellow. Then it's gone and she's smiling again, like the spooky death stare never happened. 'Why would I try to stop you, Levi? Like you said, it's none of my business. If you want to go, go.' Then a thought hits her, and she cocks her head to the side. 'If you can bring yourself to hang here for a minute while I get a coat, I could drive you to the city.'

She hovers close, sharing the doorway's shade with me until I nod. The idea of walking back up that dust track all the way through the weird farm is not attractive, and it would be an hour before I got anywhere with even a chance of hitching a lift. I'm still figuring out where I'm going to go when she reappears, looking exactly the same except for a shiny blue coat over the robes, which looks more nightclub singer than nun. She sees me staring and smiles.

'We're not born into holy orders, Levi. We all had lives before we chose this path and, contrary to what you might think, we're not swimming in money to buy new stuff.'

She leads us outside, where there's a van waiting for us. The sides are covered with cartoon vegetables. If I have any street-cred left, it's gone as soon as someone sees me in this thing.

'Sorry, the limo's in the shop.' She climbs into the driver's seat, quick and smooth like a dancer, and waits for me to settle the bag. Her sleeves slide back as she grips the wheel, exposing red blotched skin on her wrists, which is weird, because her hands are smooth. You get used to seeing foreigners with radiation burns in Jerusalem, but I don't know what could mark someone like that. For a second I think she's going to cover up, but we both know I saw what I saw. She doesn't say anything, just hits the accelerator. The motor whines and gravel beneath the wheels crackles as we pull away. The morning light bounces hard off the rows of polytunnels, forcing my eyes half shut. When we get to the open ground with the big green circles, she talks without looking away from the narrow track ahead.

'You know, I used to be a little like you once. I found out the hard way that sooner or later, you run into trouble you can't handle on your own. Eventually, you have to trust someone. I was lucky to end up here.'

'You were like me? I guess Clem told you everything about me, huh?'

'Of course not, she only said a couple of things.'

'Well, then I can't see how you would know what you were talking about.'

The corners of her mouth curl into a frown. 'You know, you don't have to make things so hard for yourself, Levi.'

'Yeah, well, maybe I like it hard. Maybe that's who I am. I didn't ask for your help. I can get out and walk.'

For a moment the van slows, then she shakes her head and it picks up speed. 'I made you an offer of help. It didn't come with any strings. I'll stay quiet if it makes you comfortable.'

The motor whine intensifies as we climb out of the valley, switch-backing up to the main road. We crest the hill and drift past four empty-looking whitewashed houses with tiny windows. Quiet suddenly fills the cab as the tyres bump off the dirt track onto tarmac, and the road stretches out in front of us. In the distance, Jerusalem spreads like a stain on the horizon.

We're six miles outside the city when the signal to my comm-plant comes back to life. Silas must have been waiting, because the call indicator lights up in the corner of my vision the moment we're in range. I watch the stylized bugle flash for a few seconds before I cut the connection. Let him wait some more.

I give it a couple of minutes before calling back. He's on the line straight away.

'Where are you, Peres?' He's angry, and not trying to hide it.

'Yeah, right, Silas.'

'You're late, and you've already missed one handover.'

'I guess I missed the ticker-tape parade, then. Is there still cake?'

'Shut up, Peres. I can make sure this ends very badly for you.'

'With all due respect, fuck you, Mr Mizrachi, sir. Who do you think you're dealing with? If you could just take this thing off me, I'd already be in a gutter outside the Jaffa Gate. Maybe I am small-time, but I got a keen sense of self-preservation. Let me tell you something – I know how much this Antikythera thing is worth now, and the price just went up.'

The sound of fingers tapping a rhythm on a hard surface breaks the silence on the line. Silas's voice becomes calmer. 'All right, Levi. You want more money; I need you to do more of the work. You'll have to execute delivery direct to the buyer – make up for some of the time you've wasted.'

'No way.'

'I don't see that you've many options, dear boy. We're stuck with each other. Unless you've got another buyer for priceless antiquities lined up? I'll admit I've underestimated you, but if you've got those kind of connections I'll be very surprised.'

Fuck it, he's right. 'OK, where?'

'The Aedis Machinarum. Be there an hour after dusk.'

One of the first things I learned when I started dealing on the street was keep your mouth shut, always let the other guy talk first, you might learn something. Choosing the Machine Cult shrine for the handover raises two possibilities – one: those crazies are the buyers, which would be fucked up, but possible. The other is that it's just somewhere convenient for Silas to bury me.

'Sure. Tell you what, why don't I save us both some time and put the bullet in my own head?'

His voice is smooth. 'Very well, I can see why you'd feel the need to protect yourself. Where would work for you?'

'The old Gethsemane bunkers.'

'I never had you figured for symbolism, Levi.'

'I don't know what the fuck you're talking about, Silas. It's convenient, and it's private. What else do you want?'

'I'll have to check that's acceptable to my client. I'll message you.'

He's sold. He doesn't care as long as I'm back inside the city. He figures that once he gets me within his info-web he can work out the details later. He thinks nothing I can do is going to make life difficult for him. We'll see.

Vulture-lady drops me at the end of Ararat Street, far enough away from Leo's restaurant that she won't be able to see where I'm going. She looks like she wants to say something, but we tried that. Instead she stares at the outline of the box in my bag as I drag it from under my legs and get out. I take a step. Fuck it, I should just walk away but I can't. I owe her.

'Thanks for the ride.'

'No problem.' She smiles like it's nothing, but she knows.

'Listen, I didn't mean to give you a hard time back there.'

'You didn't.'

'Well, I guess that's OK then. Bye.'

'Bye, Levi. Try not to get killed.'

'I'll do my best. Maybe you can pray for me or something.'

'Oh, I will.'

The van's wheels spit dust at my legs as she pulls away.

The old man's standing outside in the street, still smoking his damn cigarillo. He clocks me straight away, does a little double take, but then he's all smiles. 'As I live and breathe, Levi Peres! Didn't I tell you we were all good for knick-knacks?'

I give him a little grin that probably doesn't hide the fact I am practically shitting myself with fear. 'Wasn't funny the first time, Leo. I need to talk to Shant.'

His eyes narrow and he shakes his head. 'I got nothing against you, kid. You were only doing what you had to do, and maybe Shant knows that, but he don't feel that way right now. I'm going to do you a favour and recommend you get the fuck out of here.'

OK, game-time. This is my shot. 'Do you think he'd feel differently if he had two mil in, say . . . six hours' time?'

A low whistle sighs through the old man's lips. 'That's too big for you, Levi Peres. You should not be messing with that kind of money.'

'Why do you think I'm talking to you, Leo?' He nods at that. Gangsters are people, same as everyone else. They like to feel important. That's what I tell myself, anyway. I'm gonna find out pretty quick if I'm wrong.

'OK, Levi. I'm gonna go talk to Shant upstairs. Maybe that takes five minutes. Maybe you're not here when he comes down. If you are, I'm not responsible for what happens.'

I'm sitting on the same red faux-leather bench in the same booth I was last week, waiting for the same guy, only this time I figure he wants to kill me. I was excited then; I thought I was moving up in the world. Yeah, well, like my grammy used to say: 'Careful what you wish for.' The sound of two sets of footsteps coming down the stairwell at the back sends my nails digging into my palms. I can hear Leo's voice saying stuff about being calm. People say Shant listens to him; some people tell you he's the real brains of the operation. People are full of shit.

Shant comes out of the stairwell and he walks straight at me. I stand up, ready to take a punch or maybe a blade but he sits down on the opposite side of the table from me, staring straight ahead. His hair's slicked back, and there's a flush of red above the pulse in his temple. It's the first time I've ever seen Shant not smiling.

'Give me a reason not to bury you right now, Levi.' He lifts his eyes to stare right into mine. Cold, dead anger: that's why Shant is who he is. He's got the rage to cut out your heart, but he won't go psycho like some idiot who just wants a reputation. He's always thinking. That's why I'm not dead yet.

'Could have killed you, Shant. Didn't.'

'So you're a pussy. That gives you permission to start this conversation. Tell me why I shouldn't finish it.'

'Two mil, in your hands before you go to bed tonight.'

'Yeah, Uncle Leo told me the number. We can all make up numbers. That won't keep you from your appointment with the wet cement in the new overpass.' He stares and waits like he's hungry. Terror is a humming in my head that fills the edges of my vision. Breathing deep and slow only makes it louder. Fear fills the silence, so I do what I always do: I talk.

'The job I told you about; you know I pulled that off. Well, I've still got the merchandise, and now I have to make delivery and take payment. At six o'clock tonight, that money's gonna be out there for anyone with the balls to take it.'

'So? You're still making up numbers.' His hand slides off the slick tabletop to reach for something out of sight on his belt. My breath starts coming shallow and I can hear my voice going high-pitched. Too late to run.

'Am I, Shant? Don't take my word for it. I want you to do the math. Think of the figures I was talking about last time we were sitting here. Let's say you're my employer – what kind of percentage of the take are you going to give up to Levi Peres on a job like this?'

His hand comes back onto the table, empty. I can't help staring at the blade that isn't there. He sees it. Doesn't matter. I'm not going to impress Shant Manoukian with a tough-guy act. His eyes tell me he's still working out the math, but you don't need to get to the end of it to work out the money is big. 'Let's say I buy this bullshit – what are you looking for?'

'Nothing, just enough to cover my costs. A hundred thou and you never hear from me again.'

'Are you telling me you haven't got an angle on this? Bullshit.' The thin thread connecting us snaps. He stands up. He's going to let me walk out of here, but if I do that without getting his help, I'm a dead man anyway.

'Yeah, I got an angle. The angle is I get to stay alive. My client is Silas Mizrachi. How long do you think he lets me keep the money?'

Shant nods to himself like it makes sense now, and breathes Silas's name. 'You come in here making out like you want to pay your respects, make amends, but what you really want is muscle to save your skin?' His eyes go to the cold and dark again.

'Yeah, that's about it.'

For twelve heartbeats, his fingers clench the red-checked fabric of the tablecloth, which clashes with the seats, then relax.

'All right, Levi Peres. Mizrachi has gotten to be a pain in the ass lately. He's got this coming.'

26.

Clementine

Shadows darken in the creases of Hilda's face as the light fails. I know they mean kindness now. I have learned this much of the vocabulary of the human face. These are lessons the data feeds to my growth tank could not teach. They would have been irrelevant to the life I was supposed to lead – four weeks encased in metal before being cooked inside my shell by a focused burst of micro-waves, or torn apart by a depleted uranium dart. There were other possibilities, other futures, but nothing I could have done would have led me here. I am here because I was stolen, my body victim of a crime. That violation set me free in this new exterior self, but what have I done with this precious gift denied to all my brothers and sisters in the factory lab? I have perpetrated another crime, another base act in an endless chain of self-preservation.

I lie here, entirely still, staring up at the woman who has been a mother to me since the moment I met her, for reasons I still cannot understand. That part of humanity's code – the invisible bonds they establish between them – remains a precious mystery. My eyes are open, but the field of vision is fixed. The dozens of tiny muscles responsible for their movement do not respond to my commands, neither can I blink. The creeping dryness registers dimly as discomfort, not yet pain.

This status is unfamiliar to me. I have been dissected upon an operating table. I have been entirely separated from my body while this one was grown for me. If anything, this sensation resembles the latter, but I have sense data telling me I am still unified with my exterior – Hilda's face hovering above, the creases in the sheet beneath me, wind snapping the plastic sheets of the polytunnels outside. I have partial access, but no administrator privileges.

Something else is in control of this body/my body/me. The distinctions are unclear now. Whatever its nature, my puppeteer is imperceptible to human senses, but I infer its existence from what I cannot see.

My awareness recoils at first contact, a primeval finger burned by unknowable fire, failing to apprehend something that transcends the algorithmic shift of data to olfactory input. Even my augmented senses are incapable of seeing the thing that has jailed me within my own body, blinded by smells so vivid they become colours, blurring into a vast darkness that fills my consciousness, confining me to one small, bright chamber. There is . . . thought coming from it, but nothing that resembles emotion. This thing from within the Antikythera Mechanism watches my attempts at self-awareness with the empty fascination of a child following a raindrop on glass – I am a dribble, formed by random forces to exist in this place and this time.

Hilda's face lifts up, away from me in response to a shout from outside and my awareness retreats, shorn of its tether to external reality. Now there is no sound, not even the sensations of breath and blood. The only light is my little bubble of self – unreliable metaphor. I exert whatever strength I have to push the darkness back, preserve my bubble, but it seeps around my will like tar. Abandoning defence, I risk immersion, loss of self that I know will end me, probing to find something to engage with, something to answer the questions that multiply around me.

A hesitant string of thought plunges into the blackness. There is no dimension here; I cannot tell how far it goes; I cannot tell how long it takes before it reaches something solid, but it touches.

Cold stone, smooth like marble. A scent of olives hangs in the air. A memory of a place.

AAAHHH!

There is heat on my chest and tendrils of fire lance through my spine, my nervous system delivering the message of pain to all of my extremities. Hands and feet twitch briefly before the overload shuts me down and I am back in my small, bright chamber, contemplating the blackness. I was so close. I push again with thought, feel the connection with solidity – there!

Dappled sunlight in a courtyard. Vine leaves flutter in a hilltop breeze. It's somewhere high up. Smoke from roasting meat blackens the limbs of bright-painted statues.

UUUHHH!

The pain again, but this time my eyes open after the twitch. Hilda's face is there, partly obscured by the two metal paddles of a defibrillator in her hands. I try to sink back into the blackness, finish what I've started, but my eyelids refuse to close. There was a word – a place or a name I recognized in the consciousness when we touched – fading from memory as sensation returns to my body, as if the knowledge doesn't belong in my physical reality.

Olympus.

Hilda leans forward with the paddles again. The nerves of my chest scream at the contact with the metal, even before the current starts. I want to wave her away, shout at her to stop, but my traitorous body lies inert. I'm mentally bracing myself for the shock when Hilda suddenly smiles and leans back. Her hands disappear from my field of vision, reappear, no paddles.

'I thought we'd lost you.'

Fear of the thing that has possessed me wars with gratitude towards this woman who is trying to save me for a second time. Or perhaps a third? She does not count. I try to move, but the fragments of consciousness remaining to me quail from the challenge.

'Listen to me, Clementine. I want you to think of when we met. I want you to think of the Mission – sights, smells, sensations – all of the things your body knows, all of the things it can share with me.'

The memories come – the squeak of the hard polished floor, sumac and garlic in the kitchen, the yellow-eyed stranger – is that memory or imagination? Hilda's head shakes as if to deny it. The shuffling cloth sounds of that man in the dormitory masturbating, detergent, heavy metal pots ringing in the sink. The soft weight of a blanket laid across me. Kindness. Care. Safety. Something like sound builds in my head, a keening wail, impossible to ignore. The memories flee before it.

'Clem . . . Clementine!' She looks scared now. What's happening? 'Clementine, I want you to think of where you are now. How did you come to be here?'

The answer is Levi.

The wail stops and suddenly I am aware of the twitching pain suffusing my body from the electrocution. There is something else too: the warmth of blood in my hands. I look down. The muscles in my eyes and neck comply reluctantly with the command, but the very movement is a victory. My fingers unfurl to reveal a little constellation of shallow cuts where the nails have bitten into flesh. One is half torn away.

I push myself back to sit up in the bed, experimenting with the new control I have over this body. It's another birth, like when I came out of the labs, but this time I am not alone. The bed is hard and narrow, just like the one at the city Mission, with the same coarse sheets. Hilda pulls off her gloves and sits beside me.

'How are you feeling?'

Her hand on my shoulder is love. These words that humans struggle to define are uncomplicated. The mystery lies not in the definition, but in the substance. That Hilda loves me is clear, but the how and the why are beyond knowing. I stare at the cuts in my palm. An urge to bite the ragged edge of the torn nail subsides.

'Levi . . .' My voice crawls from my throat, unfamiliar. 'He has the device.' Words fall hopelessly, failing to connect, but Hilda's eyes darken with what looks like understanding. She watches my attempt to put feet on the floor. The skin of my soles absorbs the texture of the rug gratefully, but my scrambled sense of balance betrays me the moment my centre of mass shifts forwards. I fail even to raise myself high enough off the bed to fall, and merely slump back, defeated.

'Clementine, you're not going to be out of bed for days. Your body and your mind both need to heal. We tried to get Levi to stay. He's chosen his own path.'

'I think it will kill him. That's what it does.'

27.

Levi

Shant's boys look like soldiers, lean, sharp-eyed, nothing like that goon Tigran. His job is to intimidate. These fine gentlemen are paid to kill. The three of them sprawl, filling the booth in Leo's restaurant behind where Shant and I are talking. One of them, close-shaved head with tattoos, short goatee, won't take his eyes off me. He smiles like he's got a secret I'm too dumb to understand. Shant snaps his fingers in front of me.

'Don't pay attention to the three amigos. You pay attention to me, understand?' I nod. 'You don't have to know anything about these guys except that they're going to be there. You won't see them. You won't hear them. Make the handover like it's no big deal. It's a Tuesday. Nothing happens on a Tuesday night in Gethsemane, right?'

He gives me the shark smile and I try to tell myself it's OK, I did the right thing, I did the only thing I could do in the situation; it doesn't matter that Shant's fingering a blade under the table, as long as he's on my side. But it does. Shant's going to nail me to a fucking wall if he doesn't get his money, and I don't know how that's going to happen. No way the buyer just turns up with cash and Silas sits back waiting for me to deliver. We haven't talked about it, which means either Shant hasn't thought about it – unlikely – or he's got a plan he's not sharing. The only good thing about this situation is the handover is on my turf; I use the deeper Gethsemane tunnels as a stash when I get anything bulky that can stand a little moisture – whiskey's OK, but tobacco would rot down there. The place gives me a chance to maybe improvise something, which is better than nothing. It's possible I just added to my problems, but if I did the meet without backup, I'd be a dead man, so I choose to see this as an improvement. Shant snaps again and grabs my chin to point my face at him. His hand is cool and dry.

'You hearing me, space cadet? This ain't none of your small-time shit. You got a very simple job to do. Turn up, smile like you been snacking on your own dope, do the handover, and walk away. Leave everything else to us. Don't look back. Don't listen. Don't try to figure anything out. We're running this job now. Just get your ass back here. Understood?'

He pushes my jaw away from him. I can still feel the dig of his fingers.

'Are we clear, Levi Peres?'

'Yes, Shant.'

'Good. Now get the fuck out of here.'

From the top of the next hill, you can't see any of the entrances to the Gethsemane tunnels. They were second-generation shelters, built between the wars. The ways in were all dug into overhangs so the doors wouldn't get screwed up by a near miss when a big one dropped. In a better world they would have learned that lesson before half the people in first-generation shelters got buried alive after blast waves sealed all the exits. In a perfect world, you wouldn't need them, but it's got to be a thousand years since anyone accused Jerusalem of being perfect. In each of these things there's a little town, with a school and a shop and offices, abandoned for a hundred years, buried under the dirt, but from the outside all you can see is rows and rows of olive trees, the leaves white in the moonlight. It looks like it snowed.

I've got maybe half an hour before I'm due at the pickup. I chose a location three levels down, only accessible through a partially flooded maintenance tunnel, but I can be there in five. For someone like Silas who doesn't know the tunnels, it's just enough of a pain in the ass to make it look like I'm trying to be smart, stop him getting suspicious.

The itch in my scalp tells me there's someone watching me. It would be weird if there wasn't, but whoever's doing it is a pro – I can't see shit. I wish Clem was with me. Still, I make a show of looking around before picking one of the smaller side entrances. The giant metal doors are stuck partially open, the bottom buried in the dirt and covered with growing things. I brought a girl here once. She freaked out, said it's like Frankenstein left the door to the cemetery open on his way out. We broke up soon after that conversation. Those doors haven't moved in my lifetime, probably not since the end of the second war. The wheels and handles in the torso-thick metal are all rusted solid. It's hard to imagine something you need that much metal to protect against.

The box with the Mechanism in it feels like it's made of corners in the sack on my back as I walk down the steps of the entrance hall. Even though I've been carrying it two days on and off, I could swear it's heavier now, which obviously doesn't make sense. Part of me wants to know why people want this thing so bad. A bigger part of me just wants to get paid.

A breeze through the door whips up a sea of crumpled papers around my feet, a mix of illegible trash left by the tunnel's original occupants, and newspaper bedding discarded by the homeless who sometimes crawl in here in winter. The metal steps of an access stairway ring like a rusted bell as I climb down deeper. At the lower levels you get the leftovers of everyday life from a hundred years ago – my torch beam finds the handlebars of a pram, soda bottles, canned meat, cigarettes. It's funny: not much has changed; all the brands are the same except for the cigarettes. I guess they didn't have Zanzibar back then.

I stand still in the shallow pool of water coating the floor of the central hall on the lowest habitation level. It's as close to an open space as you can get down here. You can see people coming: plenty of exits. The clouded windows of the old hab units and offices around the edges stare blankly at me. My head jerks up at a squeak of metal, but it's just the pedal of a child's rusted trike. I must have nudged it on my way down. Just wait. Just play Shant's game until it looks like he's going to kill you. Then think of something.

I hear them moving in the dark, feet pounding wet concrete in the stop-start rhythm of caution, then splashes as they draw closer. Torchlight flickers and breaks as their steps shatter the watery mirror of the floor. They move uneasily, pale faces twisted with suspicion of this strange place, but they look like they belong, their metal limbs extensions of the bunker's dead architecture. There's four. One hangs back in the shadows cast by the others. Two at the sides carry glowb-lights low to avoid spoiling their night vision, and peer into the darkness behind me. The one in the centre stares at the straps on my shoulders with one eye, the left side of her head covered with an ugly patchwork of circuitry that penetrates her skull. Even through the disguise of the metal I can see high cheekbones and the remains of delicate features; she was beautiful once. Perhaps that's why she chose this.

She gestures to my burden without making eye contact. I'm invisible; either Silas didn't tell them who I was, or they just don't care, which is good with me. For some reason, I smile as I slide the straps of the canvas sack off my shoulder. She doesn't notice, eyes fixed on the outline of the metal box within the cloth. Her fingers, human, close around the strap before the bag touches the water. Her other hand hovers, hesitating, over the bag's opening, then she looks up at me as if she suddenly remembered I was here, and shoulders the pack before turning away. They all follow in her wake, torchlight dancing on the water. The sound of them disappears and my heart fills my ears. I forgot to breathe. Then I remember Shant's words and turn back the way I came, forgetting to aim my torch, moving on instinct.

I've gone maybe ten metres when some of the dark in front of me solidifies into three moving bodies. They make no sound. The smallest one, the bald one who stared at me in the restaurant, smiles wide as he approaches, revealing two rows of filed teeth glinting between tribal tattoos running from his chin to his crown. He holds a finger to his lips as he passes, a silent demon's head next to the two crew-cut killers. They ignore me completely, hypnotized by the long, fat-tubed barrels of their weapons, which seem to lead them into the dark.

My foot's on the bottom step of the stairs up when four soft pops freeze me in position. Don't look back. Then there's another pop and the sound of something heavy falling. Don't listen. Then I hear metal clash and water splash. More falling. Don't try to figure anything out.

I turn off the torch and slide its metal grip into my belt. Maybe it's good advice, but something tells me following it doesn't end with me getting paid. I don't know Shant's plan, I'm just pretty sure not all of those noises figured in it. My foot comes off the step and dips into the water, then I start a kind of slow, wet shuffle back to the handover point. It's quieter if you don't let your feet leave the water.

The first thing I see is a yellow glow spilling around a corner. I pause, stopping my noisy breath. The light's not moving. There's no sound except water dripping from the ceiling somewhere behind me. A gentle up-slope in the floor takes me out of the wetness, and an invisible subterranean flow of air chills my feet.

Around the corner, skewed light from the dropped glowbs illuminates seven bodies. The four Mechanicals all lie face down in spreading pools of crimson, a single dark hole at the back of each head. One has a wound in the leg too. He must have tried to run. The dripping from above stipples the surface of the blood. The human half of a fine-featured face stares into nothing at my feet – the girl who took the bag from me; she must have turned slightly as she fell, some instinct twisting her away from the floor, even as the bullet in her brain turned out the lights. I guess you've got to be more than half Machine if you want to live forever.

From this angle the dead Cultists look peaceful, like they're sleeping in blood, but the three other bodies, the soldiers, are different – jumbled, messy heaps of limbs that somebody just dropped here. The little guy with the teeth still has his silenced pistol gripped tight in his left hand, close to his body, and there's something small, like a pale coin, sticking out from between his lips. His right hand stretches out to where one of the bag's straps dangles into a slowly reddening pool of water, the fingers twisted around each other like he died halfway through giving some kind of fucked-up salute. I bend down to look at his mouth. It's a thumbnail. His gun hand is only inches from my face and it looks like it had the manicure from hell. The big clones with the crew-cuts are sprawled either side of him like starfish, face up, eyes wide open, only the whites visible. The first thing I think when I see them laid out like that is that they had some kind of bust-up – shot each other – but then I remember the noises I heard with my foot on the steps: five pops. I got seven dead people in front of me.

Close-up, I can see the guns that looked so scary are stubby little things elongated by the tubes of the silencers. What does it matter? A gun's a gun; the bullets were real enough to kill those other four people. I'm no killer, but everybody knows a silencer doesn't make a gun silent. If they did I wouldn't have heard anything. Five pops.

I risk bending down to look at the soldiers for anything that could be a wound, but the black overalls cast shadows the lantern light doesn't fill. I try playing the beam of my torch over the bodies, eyes half closed in case I see something I don't like, but there's nothing. It's like they just fell down where they stood. I stand still and slow my breathing to listen for anyone else moving through the tunnels, but all I can hear is the hammer of my heart. Doesn't matter. If someone else did this, they're long gone by now. Anyway, why would they leave the bag?

It sits there in the middle of the little circle of death, like the guest of honour at some sick orgy, the soldiers' hands reaching out to touch it, even in death. My lizard brain sees that thing and tells me to run. The necessity of money keeps me standing here. I lean forward, sliding the fingers of my right hand around the rough fabric of the strap. For a moment, the tension flows from my limbs. What did I think was going to happen?

Then the darkness fills me.

28.

Clementine

Seven bodies lie sprawled in what looks like a tunnel. The faces are rendered almost featureless by an intense flash. The white blur catches tell-tale glints of metal on some of the limbs – Mechanical augmentation. In death, they are visibly the broken people they must always have been, and yet even a picture of their stricken corpses fills me with fear.

'What is this? What are you showing me?'

Hilda shuffles uncomfortably on the bed next to me. Early morning light pours through the cell's solitary window. We are alone. She has stayed with me all night, watching for any sign of a relapse – my carer, but also my jailer. The thing is still in me: shocked, dormant, injured, I cannot tell. For now at least, I am in control.

'This photograph was on the front page of every news feed this morning. I want you to look at it, and tell me what you see.'

At the edge of the pool of brightness from the flash, splayed almost in a circle, are the bodies of three more men, arms outstretched to touch something. The curl of the fingers summons a memory, an image from the potted history of humanity imprinted on us in the tanks – Adam reaching for God – or is it

God reaching for Adam? These dead men are nothing Michelangelo would create. The smallest is bald; the outlines of tattoos covering his head are just visible in the picture. The larger two are dark echoes of each other, perhaps clones or merely soldiers honed into uniformity; it's impossible to tell from the single shadowed image. In the foreground, almost out of view, is a ripped leather jacket.

'Levi?'

An unfamiliar pain rises within me like bile. Panic paralyses my thoughts. For a moment, I steel myself against a resurgence of the entity that seized control of me, but Hilda's voice cuts through my fear.

'Don't jump to conclusions, Clementine. It's just one picture.'

Her hand settles on my shoulder. Her solidity is a comfort I could never have imagined in my former life. In the tanks, our knowledge was as functional as our bodies, and we did not know grief or any of its debilitating cousins. They would be design failures in creatures created to fight and die.

'We think he might be alive.' Her words are so gentle, it seems almost selfish to feel pain. 'The news reports said they arrested someone. They didn't give a name.'

The printed picture trembles subtly in her hand. She is so skilled at concealing her fear, a human might not notice. The thought she is afraid unsettles me. Seven bodies in the darkness: the image reeks of death. It is almost impossible to imagine Levi alive, and yet the hope is irresistible.

'We have to get him.' My voice sounds flat in my ears, the emotions lost in transmission between brain and larynx. Hilda frowns at me as if wrestling with something. Her mouth opens to speak, but the catch on the door clicks, silencing her. Sister Ludmila hovers at the threshold, visibly willing herself to stand still.

'I'm sorry to interrupt . . .'

'No, I'm glad you're here. What did you find?'

'It's bad. Three of the lay members have been arrested on suspicion of dropping that piece of glass on Silas Mizrachi. It's obvious we're being victimized by the police.'

'That's awful, but it's nothing we weren't expecting. I . . . We . . .' She looks over to me. 'We were hoping you might have heard something about Levi while you were in the city.'

The taller woman shakes her head. 'I'm sorry. I tried, but the police aren't being helpful, least of all to us.'

Hilda's mouth compresses into a line. 'No, of course. It's no good sitting here, waiting for miracles.' She takes a deep breath and turns to face me. 'Clementine, it hurts me to say this, but I don't think there's anything we can do for your friend. If Levi's alive, he's being held in a police station, under guard. He could be anywhere in the city, or he could be dead. I know you want to help him, but he is lost to us now. You have to accept that.'

'No, I can find him.'

'Look, I understand you're upset, but you're in no condition to go anywhere. It's less than twenty-four hours since I restarted your heart. Your body needs time to recover.'

'No.'

'What do you mean "No"?' Ludmila cuts in. She sounds almost angry, as if my defiance was ingratitude. I turn to face her. Her expression is impossible to read, riven with contradictory emotions I cannot process into meaning.

'Factually, Mother Hilda is wrong. My body requires no time to recover. I was designed – gene-tailored – to endure far greater stresses than defibrillation. The resultant arrhythmia self-corrected within seconds. The damaged nerve endings in my chest regrew in a little under an hour. Physically, I am optimal.'

A look passes between them, one of those coded silences I have learned to fear without knowing what they mean. Sometimes I feel like my very existence is a sacrilege to these people. A simple statement of fact about myself challenges the beliefs around which they build their existence, and yet they treat me with kindness at every turn. A sad smile ghosts across Hilda's face.

'It's not just your physical health we worry about, Clementine. You are not . . . the thing you once were. You are more than that now; you are human. You've suffered a series of emotional shocks as severe as anything physical. Until you give yourself time to recover, to process what you've been through, you will be in a state of emotional turmoil. It's almost impossible to take good decisions in that state.'

'I don't need to take any decisions. I know what I need to do.'

The door clicks shut as Sister Ludmila steps fully into the room. Hilda sighs and gestures for her to take the room's lone seat. Her chest heaves beneath the robe, anger restrained. For a moment, she seems lost in thought; then her hood falls away as she raises her head to speak.

'Anything you do to find him carries a risk of exposure. We can no longer assume the authorities are completely unaware of your existence or abilities.' She turns to Hilda. 'Honoured Mother, I understand and support your decision to help Clementine. Whatever her nature, she is an innocent. The same cannot be said of her companion. As I understand it, he is a career criminal, entirely responsible for his own predicament. He already refused the help we offered him. I cannot see any justification for the risk a rescue attempt would entail.'

Silence fills the room. Hilda looks pained. I can offer no rebuttal to Ludmila's pitiless logic. Everything she says is right; the path of self-preservation, both for the Mission, and for myself, is clear, and yet I cannot take it. As I meet her gaze, the panic gnawing at me fades, replaced by a bittersweet certainty.

'I'm sorry, I really am, but I have to go. I cannot ask you to support my decision, or even to understand it. After everything you've done for me, exposing the Mission to danger is the last thing I want to do, but I feel I have no choice.'

'Why, Clementine?' Hilda's voice is soft beside me.

'I am not certain it makes sense, even to me. If all I do is keep myself alive, my existence is pointless. I need more, or I want more.'

Moisture glints at the corners of Hilda's eyes. Ludmila avoids my gaze. 'He's not worth you.'

'No, he isn't, but he's what I have. If I can care for him, as you cared for me, then I am something more than I was created to be. Otherwise, you would have better turned me away when I came to your door. I would have survived, in a brutal, functional way.'

'He wouldn't do this for you.'

'Maybe not: not as the person you have encountered. But I have seen glimpses of the person he might have been. He was born as much an innocent as me, and fashioned into what he is by an uncaring world. Ultimately, the only difference between us is circumstance – the mechanisms of change wrought upon us.'

Hilda's eyes close as she looks up. The twin tracks of moisture on her cheeks sparkle in the light from the cell's solitary window. 'She's right. It is not for us to draw lines deciding who is worthy to be saved. If we help only when there is no cost, we fail ourselves.'

'Giving food and shelter is one thing.' Ludmila's voice briefly becomes ragged. She draws a breath. 'We are talking about open defiance of the law.'

The space between them thickens as the two nuns lock gazes. Hilda breaks the silence.

'Need is need, Sister. If young Levi is still alive, we know he will not be safe in police custody. If he has encountered the thing inside the Antikythera Mechanism and survived, he will need our care. Please, go with Clementine. Keep her safe. She does not understand the city as you do.'

'This is dangerous.' There is no defiance left in Ludmila's words.

'Everything we do is dangerous, but we do what we must.'

She gives a smile meant to convey bravery and hope, gifts she imparts from her own boundless reserve. My face mirrors the expression without conscious thought, a human instinct that won't hide the emotions swirling inside me – guilt at the danger I inflict on my benefactors, and fear of what I carry with me. The darkness in my head stirs like a memory of pain.

29.

Silas

My father used to say 'Never do a deal with anyone you can't have killed', or words to that effect. He was a shit, but the principle has always served until now. Somehow, Levi Peres has defied his eminent killableness and entered the miracle business. It makes everything complicated. Acceleration pushes me back into the ministerial limousine's soft leather embrace as it eases past the fences of the museum's restricted zone to join the morning traffic. Dry, chilled air drifts from the ceiling vents and raises goosebumps on Sybil's neck. She perches on the fold-down seat opposite, hands gripping a data tablet, poised to deflect blame for this latest debacle.

Her face gives nothing away as she pores through data and footage from our failed surveillance of the Gethsemane tunnels. She might be sufficiently absorbed in her analysis to be genuinely unaware of my ire, or she might be feigning it as a defensive measure. Both perfectly acceptable courses of action, but if there is any guilt or tension there I should foster it. People are never better motivated than when trying to atone for something; it doesn't even seem to matter whether it was their fault.

'What happened?'

She blanches at my words, even though she must have been expecting them: either authentic guilt or superb acting.

'As you specified, there were two sniper teams and a drone watching the entrances to the Gethsemane complex. Peres went in right on schedule, slightly early, in fact, and he was followed through the south lower entrance by three unknown armed figures almost exactly five minutes later.'

'Who were they?'

'We don't know . . .' I scowl and she flinches before carrying on. ' . . . but the figures in the drone footage are a good match for the dead gunmen in the newsfeed picture. I've got a guy going to the morgue to ID them, but I'll lay money they're foreign contractors, ex-military from one of Europe's failed states.'

'Will you indeed? Now where does small-time drug dealer Levi Peres get the money, or even the idea, to bring in skilled muscle like that?' Sybil's face briefly tightens in panic. 'Don't worry, it was a rhetorical question.' She must be genuinely on edge, despite the knowledge she is effectively irreplaceable at this juncture. 'What else?'

'We know Peres must have done the drop as specified, because the transfer of funds came through within three minutes. From that we can surmise the Machine Cult acolytes were in possession of the artefact and communicated the fact to their superiors.'

'And then Levi's goons killed them.'

'Most likely. Neither the drone nor the sniper teams saw anyone else coming in or out of the bunkers. The report from the morgue should give us a cause of death within the next hour.'

'So what killed the goons?'

She raises her chin to face me, half-lit by the arcs of data floating in the air above her tablet, nervous eyes trying to gauge my reaction before she speaks. 'I don't know.'

I hold her gaze, searching for any sign of mendacity. More than one of history's great schemes has been undone by the assumption of loyalty, but over the years Sybil has passed every test.

'Never mind, those questions can wait. The Soviets are going to be all over me unless we deliver the Antikythera Mechanism soon. Without their help, the outcome of the election could still be in doubt. The artefact must be our priority if we're both going to get what we want.'

She brightens briefly at my acknowledgement of her ambition, but then her face falls into a frown as she considers her words. 'Our plan was based on the assumption the Mechanicals were going to leave the bunkers in possession of the Antikythera Mechanism. The sniper teams were prepared to seize it from them. Of course, they never emerged.'

'Tell me something I don't know.'

'Either an unknown third party has seized the device, and somehow evaded our detection, or else it remained down there until the bodies were discovered early this morning. Our source on site thinks it was taken out of there by the police or medical teams who attended the scene.'

'Thinks? Why didn't your man take it?' The edge in my voice elicits a twitch.

'Khalil had hand-picked men on site within minutes. They kicked out the first responders, Glassberg's orders.'

'How could he know? No, never mind, we can puzzle that out later. The Mechanism is the important thing. If Khalil's men seized evidence, they took it somewhere.'

She sighs. 'The surveillance team was recording the scene, but the footage cuts out before the bodies and the evidence were taken away. They withdrew when they felt the risk of detection was too high.'

'In the name of God, what do we pay these people for?'

'I can fix this. Give me an hour to find out where Khalil's men took Peres. We find him, we find the artefact.' She holds my gaze, all trace of fear gone from those eyes, until I nod. 'The officers who initially attended the scene were from the thirteenth precinct. I've spoken to two of them who say they found an unconscious man matching Peres's description.'

'So he must be in custody! Have him picked up, delivered here. Get this over with.' My jaw relaxes, unconsciously at first. I hadn't realized, didn't want to, how much this debacle with Peres and the Antikythera Mechanism has been getting to me.

'I'm afraid it's not that simple.' Her words elicit a twitch from the muscles in my cheek.

'Go on.'

'It appears he never made it to the holding cells of the station; there's no arrest record, no custody report, and no record of any evidence seized with him. He's disappeared.'

'Bullshit.'

'I assure you, I've checked thoroughly.'

'No, not you – the reports! Amos must be meddling, but how?'

My semi-rhetorical question provokes a look of concern on Sybil's face. Years as my factotum have not entirely inured her to the strains of being asked the impossible. 'The only thing I can suggest is that I visit the station in person to find out what's happening.'

'Good idea, but you stay here. I'll go. They'll obfuscate in front of you and we don't have time.'

'Fine. There is another thing.'

'For God's sake, what?'

'Comrade Tchernikov from the Sino-Soviet Republic has been calling again.'

'And?'

'He's bored of talking to me and I'm running out of lines to spin him.'

'Try to keep him sweet. Send him a pretty boy or something. He'll see right through it but he might appreciate the gesture. Now, turn the car around. I am going to find Levi Peres and I'm going to drag this Antikythera thing out of his arse if I have to.'

30.

Clementine

Someone is hiding him. There is no record of a prisoner by the name of Levi Peres. Seventeen Levis, one Peres, but not a single conjunction of the two. The police department's data security is pedestrian compared to the multiple layers of redundancy protecting the museum storage facility. Law-enforcement data is either not valued here, or the antiquities hold an importance I do not understand. Visually, the net presents as layers of blue mesh superimposed onto the buildings. The streams flowing in and out carry the faint tang of the city's dust - simple metaphor for omnipresent, innocuous data. It would be an effective disguise for something vital, but I am not searching for secrets, just a chain of forgotten banalities that might tell the same story. My senses reach out, searching for any hint of the sharp, characterful smells that might reveal the presence of an AI. Nothing. Still, a sense of being watched pollutes my consciousness, most likely interference from my physical self, hormonal anxiety intruding on the purity of my perception.

The choice of entry mechanisms briefly baffles me: flimsy, archaic password-protected portals, access points for public information, personal devices used for official business – a half-skilled human hacker could flit through without difficulty. A comm-plant with outdated encryption belonging to a privileged user offers a perfect tool for my search.

Multiple pieces of correspondence between officers refer to an arrest made at the Gethsemane bunkers, but there is no name, no record, and no mugshot. Some messages show signs of attached files deleted. The job has been done thoroughly too – the data overwritten beyond the point of recovery. For some reason, Levi has been made to disappear. Fear pours through me, flowing from my body to my higher self, tinting my perceptions of the data grid from blue to bruise-purple. He was afraid of Silas Mizrachi. He said the police would not be able to protect him. That would be a cruel irony – to survive the horror in the tunnel, only to be killed for expediency.

Would Mizrachi cover his tracks like this? I know only what Levi told me of him, and the one-dimensional portrait of a loyal public servant provided by the news feeds. He is an official within a byzantine system I do not understand. Would his position allow him openly to seize a prisoner in police custody, or would he have to employ subterfuge? If I had Levi's help, I would know what to look for. Without him, all I can do is search for patterns in the hard data, oblique connections that would not occur to a human observer.

External reality intrudes as vibration through my bottom. I am in a car. We are in a car, a small van actually. It felt strange getting in. It was marked with illustrations of vegetables. Sister Ludmila steals glances at me in the moments when she looks away from the road. She does not see the spikes extend from my spine into the fabric of the seat back. To her, my state must now look indistinguishable from the hours spent under control of the entity within the Mechanism.

'What have you got?' Traffic drifts past the little window behind her head. The fierce light of the morning sun makes it hard to see her face. The city is visible only as box silhouettes of the light industrial units lining the ring road to the east.

'Precinct thirteen.'

She looks outside quickly, human instinct to verify visually, but she cannot share my perceptions. 'You're sure?'

'No. All the hard data relating directly to the arrest is gone: not just the records, all correspondence relating to the Gethsemane incident has been expunged. It's as if it never happened.'

'So how do you arrive at thirteen?'

'Officer activity logs. The news report and the photograph happened before the information shutdown. You can see officers present on scene in the video. That gives us a time for the police response. Thirty minutes earlier, the logs for one precinct show a massive spike in activity – officers putting routine duties on hold, checking out additional weaponry and vehicles.'

'Tenuous.' She looks straight ahead, concentrating on traffic. 'That tells us where the responding officers came from, not where he's being held.'

'I have corroboration. All trace of authorship has been removed from the file deletion, but the police department's regulations on data handling make interesting reading. Requests for prisoner data to be modified can only be authorized by two people: the senior information officer, and the chief himself. The information officer is attending a management conference in Timbuktu. The chief appears to have two offices; one of them is in precinct thirteen.'

Her eyes narrow – another person trying to see through me, before turning back to the road. My evidence is circumstantial at best. Two pieces of unconnected information are insufficient to establish correlation. If Mizrachi or someone else in a position of power has decided to make Levi disappear, moving him to another location would be straightforward and logical. The involvement of the city's police chief hints at another game being played here, but I cannot guess what it might be.

Her hands tighten around the wheel as she guides the van right, onto a slip road taking us west, towards the heart of the city.

'I hope you're right.'

A square-jawed man wearing a tight gold dress winks at me. His red lips kiss the air in the wake of a tired officer dragging a junkie across the antiseptic green linoleum floor. The cloying chemical fug of detergent does not quite conceal the whiff from the previous night's donations of vomit and urine. From somewhere echoes the sound of a woman wailing about a child, real or imagined. The transvestite's eyes follow the unhappy duo of cop and criminal through the sliding door that leads to the custody suites and then fix upon mine. Ludmila ignores him. His/her theatrics seem invisible to everyone but me. He tuts and turns around to lean against a chest-high L-shaped desk that divides the room, his muscular bottom a jutting invitation to nobody. A sagging man in the uniform of a police sergeant sits on a high stool behind the desk. He does not respond to my presence, even when I stand directly in front of him.

'Excuse me, are you Elias?' The name appeared as a countersignature on requests for special-issue weaponry. There were others, but they came up less frequently.

'Sergeant Elias.' He doesn't look up.

'I would like to visit a prisoner.' He looks up now, but sags deeper.

'You here to post bail? What's the name?'

'Levi Peres.'

For an instant, his eyes dart to the side before he suppresses the instinct. 'This is a police station. We don't have visiting hours. If we've got him, you can see your friend when he's released.'

Ludmila steps up, filling the space beside me. Her shadow falls across the desk. The policeman tries to ignore it.

'Officer.'

'Sergeant.'

She snorts. 'Sergeant, we have made a legitimate request. Is there some problem in processing it?'

'No, no problem. The "process" is waiting, OK? Can you do that? Have I made myself clear?'

She looms silently for a moment, a statue of judgement weighing a decision. 'Yes, you've made yourself quite clear, sergeant.' She turns to me. 'Clementine, please contact the *Jerusalem Echo*, the *New Herald*, and *Eastern Voice*. Inform them the prisoner arrested at the Gethsemane tunnels has gone missing. Police are unable to supply his person, whereabouts, or any explanation of what's happened to him.'

The sergeant looks at me as if I was the source of his pain, and turns to a fatter, younger man behind him. 'Joey, take the desk. Give me five . . .' He looks at Ludmila, head cocked to one side. 'Better make it ten.'

'Sure.'

Elias dismounts from his perch and scurries to a gate at the far end of the desk's 'L', ushering us through. He shuffles to a door in the back wall, which he unlocks and plunges through into a shadowed stairwell beyond without waiting to see if we follow.

The door clicks softly behind us. The vomit smells are gone here, but the detergent fug persists. Our steps echo in the silence as we climb four flights of metal-capped stairs. The policeman doesn't look at us. Another key card opens another door and we emerge, blinking, into a brightly lit corridor. Somebody crossing it at the far end pays us no attention. Halfway down, Sergeant Elias stops and pulls out a fist-sized clutch of keys attached to a chain at his belt. He uses one to unlock the door, then holds it open a crack, still connected by his steel umbilical, and turns to us for only the second time.

'You're going to have to have some kind of conversation with the people in here. It's not my business. I don't need to know about it.'

A sharp breath escapes me. Levi sits upright on a folding chair in a trapezium of light from the ceiling lamp. A purple swelling above his left eye distorts his face. He stares straight into space, forearms resting on a robust, square-legged table covered with thick green paint worn through at the edges. A slender figure in a dark suit is bent over the table facing him. The stranger turns at the sound of our entry. His gaze flicks from our faces to Elias, searching for an explanation, but the sergeant shrugs and closes the door behind us. His footsteps fade in the corridor.

'How did you get in here?' There is something familiar about the face – an old man's, creased with lines that could convey concern or annoyance. The tone of voice suggests the latter. For some reason, Ludmila seems taken aback at the sight of him.

Levi's mouth forms a circle like it's about to blow a bubble and the beginning of a word comes out: 'Antik—' The man places a finger across Levi's lips before he can finish the sound.

'Levi, that word is dangerous. You shouldn't say it to anyone. I think you know that, but you're just a little confused at the moment.'

'What do you want with him?' Ludmila's voice has the crystalline edges of a Russian accent I've never noticed before. The man appears unfazed by the question.

'He's a criminal. This is a police station.'

Her mouth tightens. 'That's not what I asked. What does the city's Chief Justice want with a petty thief?'

The title places the familiar face. I have seen a version of it in news reports ever since arriving in the city, but never in the flesh. This man is older than the pictures. He winces at the question. Being recognized was obviously not part of the plan that brought Amos Glassberg to this interrogation room.

'Is he your friend? Believe it or not, I'm doing my best to keep him alive.'

Ludmila's eyebrows come up. 'By making him disappear?'

He nods. 'Yes.'

'You can see why we might be sceptical.'

'Forgive me, Sister . . .' Glassberg's smile is a politician's, quick but empty.

'Ludmila Baryshnikova.' She mirrors his expression, giving nothing away. Glassberg spares me only the briefest glance before focusing again on her. I give silent thanks she is with me. The human subtleties passing between them are opaque to me. I can only watch their game as it plays out.

'Sister Ludmila, I understand you must be concerned if Mr Peres is your friend, but you must equally understand I have no reason to trust you. You, at least, know who I am.'

'I've told you who I am. Anyway, we've met before.'

He grimaces. 'You'll have to excuse me. I meet so many people.'

She waves away the apology. 'It was a memorable occasion – the opening of the interfaith centre.'

Glassberg stands up straight, away from the table. 'You were there? You watched the glass fall on Silas?'

'That's right.'

His fists unclench. He turns the chair opposite Levi around and sits facing us, gesturing for us to help ourselves to more chairs piled against the wall to our left. 'I think we're on the same side. The other one who was there . . . Hilda? She worked it out somehow, even before I understood what was happening. I know your people didn't do it. I know Silas Mizrachi is framing your people for his attempted murder.'

The door opens, cutting off whatever the old man was about to say next. He bristles. 'Sergeant Elias, it can't have been more than half an hour yet. I wish I could explain, but please trust me that this is a delicate situation.'

Elias walks all the way into the room. He moves quickly, an urgent energy animating his tired frame. His gaze lingers on each of us a moment. Something has happened to change his mind about the intruders filling his station.

'Silas Mizrachi is in the commandant's office. Guess who he's asking to see?'

Ludmila's eyes lock with Glassberg's. 'Let us get him out of here. He'll be safer with us. We might be able to heal him.'

The sergeant cuts in before Glassberg can reply. 'Heal him? Ha! He's a freaking vegetable, lady! What are you going to do? Pray him better?'

Her gaze is withering. 'You mock what you don't understand.'

Elias ignores the put-down and turns to the Chief Justice, waiting for a response. The lines in the old man's face deepen. He sits in silence as if he hadn't heard the question, as if he was alone in the room. A noisy clock on the wall ticks twenty times while he fights some silent internal battle. Finally, he stands.

'Sergeant Elias.'

'Yes, sir.'

'I want you to release this suspect into Sister Ludmila's custody.'

'Now?'

'Now.'

'What about his stuff?' The policeman jerks a thumb towards a canvas bag resting on a green metal filing cabinet. Ludmila's eyes meet mine but she says nothing. These people would not understand the danger. They would think us insane.

Glassberg looks pained and then scowls. 'It goes with him. It's not safe here with Silas in the building. For reasons I think we all understand, there must be no record of this. Don't discuss this with anyone, not even the commandant. I can assure you that he does not want to know.' The little, hunched man nods grimly at those last words. 'Get her out of here discreetly. I'll go entertain our mutual acquaintance.'

Elias stalks to the corner of the room and pulls the canvas bag from the top of the filing cabinet. Ludmila recoils at the sight of it. She grasps one of the straps firmly and holds it at arm's length, away from her body. It looks heavy, but her arm doesn't even tremble. The sergeant crouches down and drapes one of Levi's listless arms around his shoulders before hefting him out of the chair towards me. His limbs support most of his weight, but move only to keep him upright. We hobble towards the door as an awkward trio. Amos Glassberg stands watching us. In the yellow light from the ceiling, he looks jaundiced and old, but as the door closes, I see him smile briefly. It is a different smile from the one he showed us. It is the look of a man who has found something he thought lost.

31.

Silas

The question is how much he knows. Glassberg's expression gives nothing away as he takes a seat behind the viewing gallery's plain wooden table. A one-way mirror behind him shows the three interrogations of my would-be murderers happening in parallel. It's an interesting choice of setting; the prisoners' faces are a triptych of neon-lit misery. In anyone else I would take it as a ploy to unsettle me, confronting me with the assassins, but Glassberg knows me better than that. There will be some other agenda at play here. He sits still, very upright, waiting for me to speak.

'Well, this is a surprise.'

'Is it, Silas? For the time being at least, I am still Justice Minister, and this is a police station.'

'Yes, of course, but this is all a little beneath your pay grade, isn't it?'

'I disagree. These men are accused of trying to kill you, a minister of state. The investigation is my number-one priority, and will remain so until its resolution. I assume you're here to check on progress.' He looks away from me to study the faces on the other side of the mirror. The accused glass-fitters all look sick, sallow skin sinking into the institutional green of the walls. The officers facing them are deadpan, emotions invisible behind a mask of professional cool, except for one who fidgets, aware of being watched.

'Actually, no. As you rightly point out, election or no, we still have our day jobs, and I'm chasing up a missing antiquity.'

'And the trail leads you here?'

He asks the question in the neutral lawyer's tone he uses in court, but there is no mistaking the intent. I have to be careful now. I can't evade direct questions; neither can I bluster. He knows something, or he wouldn't be here. I have to guess how much, and feed it back to him without giving anything away.

'I'm not sure where it leads ultimately. A name came up in the investigation: Levi Peres. He's a known criminal, but his regular associates say he's been missing a couple of days. One of them thought they recognized his jacket in the picture of the bodies in the Gethsemane tunnels.'

His eyebrows rise. 'Recognized a jacket? That sounds like a long shot.'

I shrug. We both know he's fishing, but even to acknowledge it would be to give him a small victory. 'It is, but it's the only live lead we have in the disappearance of the artefact.'

'Is this the one with the missing curator? I'd have thought he was your obvious suspect.'

The smile stays on my face in defiance of the irritation coursing through me. He was always going to make the connection, but the timing is inconvenient to say the least. I didn't want any of this coming out before the election, but of course Sibyl's thoroughness compelled her to file that damned missing person's report! The only option now is to lie and hope he doesn't know enough to spot the inconsistencies.

'You would think so, wouldn't you? Unfortunately not. He went missing before we lost the Antikythera Mechanism. He may be involved, but he can't be directly responsible.'

'So you think this Peres character is the thief?'

'As I said, he's a lead.'

'Yes, you did, didn't you? Well, I've been here all morning. I've not been made aware of any prisoners coming in from Gethsemane, and I think someone would have mentioned it. Have you checked the arrest record?'

'He's not on it.'

He takes a deep breath and lets it out in a show of exasperation. 'Well, I can only suggest you try the morgue. Sorry if that's unwelcome news. I appreciate it must be awkward for you, having valuable city property disappear, what with the election looming and all. What did you call the thing again?'

'The Antikythera Mechanism.'

'That's a mouthful! Greek, is it?'

'I believe so.'

Another sigh deflates him. Something about Glassberg is different today. He wears a crooked smile I have never seen, either in his courtroom or out. This talkativeness is unlike him – Amos Glassberg doesn't do charm. If it's an attempt to catch me off guard, it's a clumsy one. No, it must be something else. He turns away from me to look at the tableau framed by the one-way mirror: three innocent men suffering in silence.

'Here, I don't want you to have slogged all the way into town for nothing. You should listen in. The questioning's just getting interesting.'

'Actually, I was planning to . . .'

He thumbs one of the buttons on the table slate, and a detective's voice crackles through the speaker in the wall.

'How did you know where the Minister for Antiquities would be standing?'

Glassberg raises his eyebrows at the reference to me. The implication is clear. The single question encapsulates the absurdity of the case. A sheet of glass falling from a roof is a haphazard tool for murder, and yet it passes as the culmination of a sophisticated conspiracy to kill a minister of state. Detectives in pressing need of an arrest might usually ignore a little gap in logic, but Glassberg's presence rules out taking short cuts. Still, I don't understand why he's showing me this. It's uncomfortable, but also reassuring. If this is all he has, well, it amounts to nothing.

The man under interrogation in the centre room shakes his head in response to another question. Perhaps wisely, the accused glass-fitters have all so far chosen the course of silence, but it will be interpreted as fanatical contempt for authority. The doomed men play their parts without even knowing they've been scripted.

Shit. They're not the only ones.

Glassberg looks over and smiles like he heard me thinking. The old bastard is playing for time, covering for something. The weird expressions, the pointless fishing expedition – he was out of his comfort zone but it worked. I must have wasted ten minutes trying to figure out his angle instead of doing what I came here to do.

'Well, Amos, this has been fascinating. Reassuring to see your men are pulling out all the stops, but I really must go.'

'Really, I think we're reaching a critical juncture. You should stay . . .' His smile slips. He knows the game's up.

'Glad to hear it, but I'm sure you understand, work won't wait. Best of luck, old chap.'

Chipped paint flakes from the door as it slams behind me. A gaggle of officials cluck around me the instant I leave the room, pestering me with questions, doubtless set on me by Glassberg. It takes a full five minutes to reach the privacy of my limousine. Sybil accepts the connection immediately, but waits for me to speak.

'Peres was here!'

'Have you got him?'

'No. Glassberg was waiting for me.'

'How?'

'I don't know, but he was definitely stalling me – the fucking Justice Minister! If he'd tried small talk I'd have rumbled him, but he went straight for the jugular – missing artefacts, inconsistencies in the assassination. He must've been buying time for someone else to get Peres out of the building.'

'Are you sure? That doesn't sound like Glassberg.'

'No, but it just happened. Find out who, and tell me where they're taking him.'

A sharp hiss is the sound of Sybil inhaling. 'That could be difficult. I'm bringing up the CCTV feeds for the streets surrounding the precinct house now, but cross-referencing to track specific vehicles could take hours when we don't know what we're looking for.'

'We don't have hours. Get it fucking done or I'll—'

'Aha!'

'What is it? Tell me you've found something.'

'I may have spoken too soon. Precisely four minutes after you entered the precinct house, a distinctive vehicle pulled out of the parking lot and headed west towards Binyanei.'

'A distinctive vehicle? What do you mean?'

A rectangle of light flashes into existence as the limo's seat projector activates. Footage from a security camera starts playing. It's a high angle looking down on the entrance to the precinct house parking lot. A small van nudges into the flow of traffic without waiting for a gap. The sides are wholly covered with giant pictures of vegetables.

'Is that what I think it is? Nobody's that amateur.'

'Forgive me, sir, but amateurs generally are. CCTV also shows robed women walking into the precinct house. I don't think they were attempting to be covert. Shall I send a team to pick them up?'

'Yes . . . Wait! No, not yet. This could be politically useful. We do this through official channels. Give an anonymous tip-off to someone friendly who can authorize a police raid on the Mission.'

'That'll take time. I thought we were in a hurry?'

'We know where the thing is now, and think of the story! The

Mission will be in the frame for the theft of the Antikythera Mechanism as well as the assassination! We get votes, and we clear ourselves of any lingering suspicion in one fell swoop.'

'If you say so.'

She cuts the connection, immersing herself in data as she pulls the necessary strings to make my plan happen. I sit back and allow the comfort of the car to swallow me. Amos Glassberg no doubt imagines he has achieved some small victory over me. He won't know better until he sees the headlines. The religious fanatics who've been tearing the city apart, who've tried to assassinate a minister of state, have now also stolen a priceless piece of Jerusalem's heritage. The joy of it is that their involvement in my larceny provides a much better motive for my assassination than anything I could have dreamt up – what could be more obvious than thieves wishing to kill the guardian of the city's treasures?

Of course, Glassberg will know the truth, but it will all have played out in the media by the time the trial reaches his courtroom. The Missionaries' innocence will be irrelevant. He can buy them time, request higher standards of proof, clarifications, but he cannot change facts. If he strays into the role of defence counsel, if he openly defies the will of the mob howling for a conviction, he delivers their votes to me. His only other choice is to sacrifice everything he stands for, and convict three innocent men. It's just possible he would do it if he believed it would save the city from me. And then, of course, he would lose anyway.

32.

Clementine

Levi lies still, exactly where we put him down, in Hilda's thin, hard bed. He spent a couple of minutes looking around, made some shapes with his mouth but no noise, then he put himself to sleep, clutching a pillow like a toddler. The policeman left without saying anything. He looked like he was scared of something. Ludmila was staring at Hilda, angry or ashamed: I couldn't tell which; perhaps both. So much of what happens here is still strange to me.

Levi's chest rises almost imperceptibly, a sign of physical life that reveals nothing of his mental state. Is there anything in there? Does memory of me still exist within that biological matter? *How much of you survived?*

I have an accelerated lifetime's experience separating consciousness from physical self. I had somewhere to go when the thing from within the Mechanism invaded me, overwhelming my physical senses and seizing control of my motor functions. For me it was terrifying. What must it be like for a normal human to be exposed to that? He can have no analogue for such experience, no internal refuge from the dark presence that consumes all it touches.

*

223

Hilda mostly leaves me to watch him. I don't know where she sleeps now. She warned me not to touch him because she's worried the thing could still be inside him. She calls it a demon. I don't know what it is. Perhaps it is not itself evil, but merely spreads to fill the available space, like a weed colonizing the earth around it, choking rival growth without thought. From the Antikythera device it has spread to Levi, those dead men Ludmila told me about, and even a part of me. It doesn't leave once it has entered. It doesn't even care if you're dead. I don't know how I know this. Within me I feel its ongoing presence as an absence, a gap in self, a pico-second's delay when I attempt reflexive thought. For now, it seems cowed by the torrent of electricity Hilda used to shock me back to consciousness. Or perhaps it's permanently crippled by the assault, a withered offshoot of its parent within the Antikythera device? Another thing I don't know.

Levi turns and mumbles something in his sleep, a more comforting sound than anything he uttered while awake. I fight the urge to lay a hand on his forehead – the comfort of human contact seems such an obvious thing to offer, but Hilda's caution forbids it, and I would not defy her. As Levi rolls onto his back, his thick eyelids start to flutter and he moans like a child trapped in a nightmare. An errant hand strays towards his shoulder and then stops. Instead it hovers, uncertain, next to my mouth, the instinct to comfort unfulfilled. The sensation of teeth on a nail makes me suddenly aware I have started chewing. The keratin snaps satisfyingly beneath the pressure of an incisor and I bite again.

Powerless. I am powerless even to help Levi. In this counterfeit body I seem only to lurch from one uncertainty to the next. Is this what drives the insanity of the Machine Cult, of all the strange human faiths that came before it?

The black despair becomes a dull pain behind my eyes and they close. For a moment the world disappears and I see the tamed darkness within me stir, blossoming around the bars of its cage, excited at the scent of hopelessness.

Pain at a fingertip drags me from the reverie. I have bitten all the nails of one hand down to the quick. In search of distraction I turn to Hilda's bookshelf, and the bitten hand falls upon the middle row. Worn bindings bear titles in ancient scripts, so my fingers settle on something recognizably German. I suppose that must be where she is from, although I never asked, and the varied collection makes my conclusion far from certain. An imprint of patchy, golden gothic font declares my volume to be *The Book of Maccabees*.

The book seems to fall open at a page heavily annotated in barely legible pencil markings. As I begin to read, my voice echoes like a stranger's in the quiet room, but the sounds seem to soothe Levi. He rolls onto his side and the moans fade, then stop. After a few minutes, the muscles in his back and shoulders loosen and he starts to look more asleep than immobile. The story is hard to make out; there are so many words I don't recognize. There's something about a great king, Saul, who disobeys the prophet Samuel and consorts with a witch called Endor. As far as I can tell, he loses a battle as a result of his blasphemy and the victors take his body, or perhaps just his head, to the temple of their deity, Dagon. Dagon, a god of the deeps, is greatly pleased with the sacrifice of a king, and lends his strength to the Philistines' warriors, rendering them invincible in battle. The great temple in Jerusalem is desecrated and a darkness falls upon the land. The passage ends with the words: *And when the beloved of Dagon speak his name, he shall rise from the seas.*

Before I came here, I read what I could of the history of this land. It was hard to tell where the myths ended and the factual record began; so much of it was based on religious texts, so much more lost in the data wars. From the little I know, this book seems to touch upon the real history of the fall of Jerusalem's First Temple, but it's so wrapped in culturally specific allegory it's hard to know what any of it means. I think the story is expressed in something that might have been poetry in the original Hebrew, but any trace of metre or rhyme has been lost in the German translation. Still, it does not seem to matter to Levi. By the time the story ends, he's breathing steadily enough to risk leaving him for a drink.

In the kitchen, Hilda is half hidden behind an open cupboard door. She closes it at the sound of my entry and smiles tiredly.

'How is he?' She twists the knob of the tap and water gushes noisily into the spout of a hemispherical kettle. She places it carefully in the wireless power stream, and a clouded light on the side glows blue.

'He looks better. Looks like he's actually sleeping now instead of lying still after getting hit in the head with a brick.'

She smiles at that. 'Well done. It's amazing what simply having someone at the bedside can do. It's one of those little miracles that makes faith easier.'

'All I did was read to him.'

Her smile cracks for a moment before reappearing. 'You should be careful with those old books, Clementine, some of them are falling apart.' She spoons dark granules of Zanzibar coffee into mugs still stained by their previous contents. They dissolve with a faint hiss.

'Yes, of course, I'll try to be. Did you lose many in the fire?'

Something like suspicion clouds her eyes then vanishes before she speaks. 'We lost some we were storing in the roof-space, but the most precious volumes are all in my room. The collection is the work of decades, so I like to have them close.' A breath out dispels the steam rising from the mug before she takes a hesitant sip, grimacing at the heat.

'I still don't understand why they're important, not really.'

'I know our religions are strange to you, Clementine, after everything you've been through, but these stories are rooted in our most ancient memories. They are part of what makes us human, but so many of the stories are lost, and the knowledge of what we were, what we are, is gone.'

'Then why are you the only ones preserving them? How could such precious things be lost?'

'The wars, partly, but mostly through human arrogance, although you could argue they're the same thing. The holy texts we have now – the Bible, the Talmud – are just a fraction of what was written. There are the books we know as the Apocrypha, still preserved by a few minor sects, but there were dozens more discarded by the compilers of the Talmud and the Bible for ideological reasons. Some they condemned outright as heresy.'

The black coffee is bitter on my tongue. 'Heresy': it is one of those strange, all-too human words I can define but never truly understand. Hilda's utterance of it conveys at once both the excitement and toxicity, but even her emotion cannot render it anything more than an abstract to me. Perhaps it will come in time. I can hope.

She stares down and swirls coffee around the now half-full mug, catching semi-dissolved granules stuck to the side. 'Be patient, Clementine. This is all new to you, and there's a lot competing for your attention. In time you can draw your own conclusions about what all of this means. That's what we all have to do, and it never feels like you've got the information you need to make the decision.' She nods towards the door. 'Come on now. Show me your patient.'

We have to cross a patch of open space to get back to the chapel and Hilda's room. The sun setting over these dry hills bathes the dust at our feet in blood. Even the green circles of the farms on the valley floor are tinged purple in this red light. I stop for a moment. In the twilit figures of the workers still labouring in the fields, I see the ghosts of my brothers and sisters from the factory labs. Most of them will have met their fates months ago, never thinking to ask the questions that plague me now, comfortable in their ignorance until death. A sudden breath of cold wind catches me by surprise. The day has disappeared into my bedside vigil for Levi.

Hilda waits for me by the chapel door and ushers me in. As we walk between benches empty of worshippers, I smooth away the goosebumps raised by the chill outside. She holds open the door of brown smoked glass and waits for me to go in first.

My eyes go straight to the bed.

Levi isn't there.

Behind me, Hilda gasps and I drag my gaze to where she's looking. Levi is on the floor staring at us, or maybe through us to somewhere beyond. His eyes are wide open but dark, as though the pupil has expanded impossibly to swallow light; his body . . .

He is naked apart from a T-shirt. There are streaks and spots of blood on the floor. It dribbles from small, messy gashes on his fingertips which he wields like a paintbrush of gore, arms twitching in a frenzy of movement as he marks out a broken pattern on the floor.

In a low crouch, he lurches around the edges of a half-formed circle as if addressing the points of a compass or the Stations of the Cross. At the edge facing the bookcase he stops and leans back, his spine describing an impossible curve. Without thought, my mind delivers the equation, as if the solution was already within me. Suddenly I understand. His body is not him. It is geometry. It is a mathematical abomination, an expression of numbers conveying meaning no human can understand. Or survive.

33.

Silas

I am surrounded the moment I set foot outside the door. Unusually, I have chosen to leave the city museum by its front entrance, but the imminence of the police raid on the Mission has forced me to bring forward the official announcement of my candidacy for the Justice Ministry. Of course, it was already an open secret, but for the sake of appearances the small scrum of press lining the steps has the look of a spontaneous gathering, dedicated newshounds reacting to the pulse of the city. The older ones know they're having their strings pulled, but the young ones do so enjoy the fantasy of independence. Even the veterans don't want their faces rubbed in the somewhat sordid truth, so we all dance the dance, knowing the public won't see past the smiles.

Somewhere among the pack are my two tame reporters, but I shouldn't need them. On occasions like this they are a useful backup if one of the hacks is feeling unusually brave and starts asking difficult questions, but it's important not to be too obvious about these things. My mother used to say, 'When performing a quickstep, it doesn't do to look at one's feet, because people will see that you are trying, and there is nothing so repulsive as naked effort.'

A thickset, stubbled man barks a question at me. 'Doesn't the recent loss of one of the most precious antiquities from the city's collection cast a shadow over your re-election campaign?'

'Yes, I'm afraid it does. Some of you will be aware that this is not the first of our city's precious artefacts to go missing . . .' The pack silences itself. As little as twenty-four hours ago, a public attempt to link me to missing antiquities would have been career ending. '. . . although it is perhaps the most famous, the most tragic loss to date. I am sorry to say these thefts are the result of corruption that permeates our city.' Now, the only sound is the dull roar of evening commuter traffic in the distance as they listen, rapt at the prospect of something more enticing than what they came for. 'I have come to the reluctant decision that this is an issue I cannot address adequately in my current capacity as Minister of Antiquities. Therefore I will be standing for election as Justice Minister, on a pledge to root out corruption and restore the law in our city.'

The silence survives the end of my little speech. That last bit was Sybil's idea: a little mawkish for my tastes but it is the sort of thing people expect on occasions like this, and it plays well in small doses. The unshaven man is the first to recover his wits.

'How do you respond to allegations that you, personally, are connected to the disappearances of several of these items?'

'Forgive me, I don't believe we're acquainted. You are?'

He ignores my invitation to identify himself, instead leaving a silence for me to fill with an answer. For some reason I am unable to place this slightly repulsive gentleman. This kind of aggression cannot be allowed to go unchecked. Still, the mark of a skilled dancer is the ability to improvise. I manufacture a laugh.

'I don't respond to allegations I haven't heard: allegations no one, to my knowledge, has made apart from you. In the absence of any tangible evidence, or even a concrete accusation, I can only assume this is some kind of smear.'

From there the questions rapidly descend to the platitudinous and the predictable. I field a few for the sake of appearances before passing the baton to Sybil, who takes the floor with the barely restrained eagerness of the apprentice wielding the master enchanter's wand. Her appearance elicits soft howls of derision from the pack, who rapidly disperse, save a few who remain out of politeness, or perhaps a canny instinct for where the wind is blowing. Two minutes invested in Sybil now is a small price to pay for the potential returns after my office changes hands.

It is only a short walk through the museum's manicured gardens to where my car awaits. The soft leather embraces me with a muted squeak of contact. Unfortunately for us all, Sybil's advancement is dependent upon my own, which still hangs in the balance. Amos remains a formidable obstacle simply through his continued presence and undeniable competence. This new imperative of his to take an active role in investigations, in defiance of a century's tradition, is potentially disturbing. I have invested a substantial portion of my earnings from the Antikythera project with a cartel of Lebanon-based hackers to nudge the polls, but, as they take great pains to point out, the greater the influence, the greater the risk of detection. So, I must exercise tiresome restraint and persist with other schemes to ensure the desired outcome.

As the car hums into movement, the data terminal chimes with an incoming call. I count to fifteen before answering. The cultural attaché for the Sino-Soviet Republic of Humanity can wait a little.

'Silas. Big day. Are you sure you want this?' He knows. Vasily usually knows, and there's no reason to think today would be an exception.

'Ha! It's a little late for questions like that, don't you think?'

His voice softens, becomes contemplative, a touch emollient. 'Perhaps. For someone of your gifts, perhaps not. From a purely professional standpoint, I hold you in the highest regard, but the Law? There is a certain unavoidable accountability. These are difficult things. Not pleasant things. They have a way of getting to a man.'

Trust a Russian to get philosophical when business is pressing. 'I'm touched by the compliment, Vasily, but I have no idea what you're talking about.'

'Do you know how many languages I speak, Silas?'

'Please, flabbergast me.'

'Eight; seven if you discount old Ukrainian. Every single one has a phrase that translates as "Be careful what you wish for".'

And I thought I'd left the platitudes on the museum steps. 'Umm, Vasily, please don't think me ungrateful for your pearls of wisdom, but I really wanted to talk about our arrangement.'

'The terms are unchanged.' His words are stone now, delivered direct from the Urals.

'Yes, that's understood. What I wanted to discuss was turnaround time. The polls are very nearly upon us, and I'm going to need documented evidence of Glassberg's colourful past pretty quick for it to have time to sink in with the electorate. If I get you what you want, how quickly can you produce it?'

There's a faint sound that might be a whispered laugh, or perhaps just interference on the line. 'Silas, Silas, I had the documents made and couriered from the state archives the same day you first mentioned the idea. They are in the safe in my office. They "prove" conclusively that Amos Glassberg was recruited as an FSB asset during his time as a student in Moscow. We've added a little colour about how he wanted to stay and become a citizen, but was ordered to go home, where he could become more useful. The authenticity is unquestionable. And if you try to steal them, I'll have the thief shot and nailed to the city museum's front door with a little note explaining how he got there. Is that businesslike enough for you?'

The subtext is unmistakeable. *Silas Mizrachi, you are a big fish in the small, dirty pond that is Jerusalem. I am the representative of one of the world's great powers. If you start asking favours of us, it is on our terms.* Of course, if his masters become too demanding, they will discover precisely how toxic Jerusalem can be to empires, but for now it suits me to play along.

'OK, Vasily. You made your point. I'll get you your knick-knack within forty-eight hours. At some point, I do hope you'll tell me what you plan to do with the wretched thing.'

My attempt at levity receives only a grunted acknowledgement before he ends the call. The car's data terminal chimes the instant my back makes contact with the seat leather. Sybil's face appears in an arc of light. She's still wearing make-up from the speech. The effect is disconcerting.

'I thought you were wowing the press.'

'There's not much to say, is there? Not yet, anyway. Something came through. I thought it was urgent.'

'Everything is urgent today. What is it now?'

'Your expensive Korean data miner has finally done something to earn his money. He's worked out how Peres pulled off the Antikythera theft.'

'Interesting, but isn't that rather redundant information now? We're going to take collection of the artefact in a matter of hours, after all.'

'If your man is right about what he's found, the raid could pick up something more valuable than the Antikythera Mechanism.'

'More valuable? What are you talking about?'

'He says he's identified an intrusion into the warehouse network. Despite extensive counters, it left a unique data signature. It's a human-AI hybrid.'

'A what?'

'Organic artificial consciousnesses implanted in human bodies – only a few known to exist. Most of them are failed experiments. They go mad. Loneliness, apparently.'

'Loneliness?'

'They have no common experience with true AIs, and they get freaked out by real people – too strange and demanding – so sooner or later they always find a way to end themselves.'

'Why the fuck should we care whether these monstrosities get lonely? I still don't get why you're bringing this up now. We have other fish to fry, Sybil.'

Her jaw tightens in irritation, and then relaxes. For a moment Sybil seems almost to stare through me from the screen.

'How much do you think Vasily Tchernikov would pay to get his hands on a tame Machine?'

34.

Clementine

Levi's head turns in a twitching motion. A joint pops as his body attempts to describe a sine curve, then wobbles upright, one bloodied hand on the bookcase. Red eyes do not see us.

'What did you read to him?' Hilda's voice drags me from the horror.

'Read? What's that got to do with anything?' One of the hands comes away from the bookcase, and the Levi thing takes a staggering step. 'I don't know –some old bit of the Bible.'

'Clementine, I need you to trust me that this is important. *Which bit?*'

I see the dark-bound volume with the flaked gold lettering on a shelf behind his head. 'That one, *The Book of Maccabees.* Something about a witch and a battle and a sacrifice. I'm not sure, it was like some kind of weird poetry, but it seemed to calm Levi when he heard it.'

Hilda's nodding in comprehension while I speak. Before I finish talking, she kneels down and starts rooting in the detritus underneath her desk. She emerges from the chaos of papers and books with the green plastic unit containing the defibrillator kit she used to revive me. Wordlessly, she flicks a black switch and twists a dial adjusting the current.

'What are you doing? That could kill him!'

Her fingers grip the handles of the defibrillator paddles and she speaks without looking at me. 'If I'm right about what's happened to him, he's dying in front of us. I don't know how long we've got. We might already be too late.'

An electric whine fills the air. Ionizing molecules pop as the defibrillator's charge builds. Even as the eyes stare into nothing, something within Levi senses threat. His lips part, showing teeth stained crimson from worrying at his own fingertips. The half-naked body jerks upright in a sickening limbo motion.

Hilda rubs the paddles' faces against each other in a slow circular motion, making sounds of sliding metal, eyeing Levi like a primeval hunter facing a sabre-tooth ready to pounce.

'What are you doing? He's just standing in front of the bookcase. There's no reason to shock him.'

'The thing standing in front of the bookcase isn't Levi, not any more.' She speaks low and fast, not taking her eyes off him.

'What do you mean? What's happening?' Her words are a jumble of impossibilities, but the fear they strike into me is real. Levi is a corporeal human, his psychic self inextricably linked to his body since birth. The technology to override the link does not exist, not even in the Machine sanctums. What can he be if not Levi?

'That passage you read ends with a summoning rite for Dagon. Something inside Levi responded.' She takes a half-step towards him.

'That's insane.'

She turns her head to draw my attention to where the defibrillator box lies on the floor behind her feet. 'Move it forward. The leads aren't long enough for me to get to him from here.'

The whine from the defibrillator becomes high-pitched. I shake my head to deny the reality of what's happening, but the sound pours in from either side. In spite of myself, I pick my way through the mess on the floor and shove the plastic case forward with my foot, creating some slack in the curled cables tethering Hilda. She takes a step towards Levi. The air around the edges of the paddles hums and crackles.

Levi moves almost too quick to see. His palsied left arm slashes into a blur of motion. Blood trails from the gashed fingertips as it smashes the defibrillator from Hilda's grip in one backhand blow. The sub-routines in my cortical enhancement modules recognize the dynamics of a threat situation before the paddles hit the floor. They land in the corner with an audible pop as the current discharges and my body assumes a combat stance, chin tucked low, forearms and elbows guarding my head, with no conscious thought. I stand still like that, twitching and nauseous with the sudden dump of adrenaline, watching Levi ignore me as he bulls past Hilda's prone form to grab the straps of the canvas bag containing the Antikythera Mechanism.

'STOP HIM OR HE'S GONE FOREVER!'

Her voice booms out, and my body twists to obey. The lead foot pivots at the ball, generating momentum which travels up the length of my body to my shoulder, amplified by the muscles of the hips and core. All the hand has to do is form a fist and allow itself to be whipped around by the force the arm transmits. The resulting punch lands flush with the centre knuckle on Levi's temple. He blinks and turns to face me. The force of throwing the blow coils my core like a spring. I expend the momentum with a high, spearing knee into the solar plexus that forces air from his lungs, and follow it with an upward elbow.

His nose explodes with a wet crack. He should be unconscious. The punch was a clean knockout. The knee should have overloaded his nervous system. The pain from his nose should be excruciating. None of it's working. I'm going to have to break bones if I want to stop him.

He shoves through me and I pivot aside on my left foot, allowing him to take two steps towards the door, but setting my bodyweight for a low kick that will wreck his knee joint. His bloody hand spasms onto the door handle and jerks it inward and open, but a robed figure fills the doorway, blocking his path. Suddenly, Levi's body starts to twitch and I hear a buzzing and a clicking. I pull the kick back just in time to prevent my shinbone connecting with his kneecap. Levi falls back anyway, trailing two wires from his chest. They connect to something that looks like a shaving tool. I have to blink before I recognize the hand holding it as Ludmila's. Her thumb stays pressed against a red button in the centre of the tool and Levi's body keeps twitching in its palsied dance, saliva pouring from the corners of his mouth. I feel Hilda's bulk behind me and turn to see her coming to her feet, the paddles of the defibrillator gripped firmly once more.

'No! Can't you see he's had enough?' Statistics conjure themselves into my forebrain unbidden – percentage risks of heart failure, clinical outcomes from system shock, symptoms of brain damage, all of it useless. I have no data for what is happening to Levi.

Hilda shakes her head grimly and advances. 'This is how we brought you back. Don't you think we tried everything else first? If we don't do this, he's not coming back.'

I turn my head away but I can still hear the tremble of his limbs against the floor. I don't want him to die; I've only just learned to know him. Without Levi, these strange disciples of a nonsensical faith are my only link to humanity. I will be lost.

The crash kit emits its high whine as the charge builds again and Hilda shouts . . .

'CLEAR!'

I step aside and she bustles past, paddles rubbing with that sound of sliding metal. The thump of current discharging into Levi's chest fills my ears.

35.

Levi

Somebody burned holes in my favourite T-shirt and threw it on the floor. Whoever it was also left me naked in a room that smells like singed hair. My fingers are covered in dried blood and it hurts to touch anything. I haven't tried to move yet but the warning signs are all there; it's not going to be fun, so I skip it. My head falls back on a single thin pillow and the ceiling speaks to me, faces in the whorled wood of the beams mouthing insults. They're right; Levi Peres is a fucking idiot.

At least I know where I am. The cheap pale pine and the absence of anything fun tells me I've got to be in one of the Mission's empty accommodation huts. I would like to know how I got here. I would also like to know what day it is – the way my body has buried itself into this bed tells me I've been here a long time.

Or maybe not.

Maybe it's just because I'm fucked up, but I swear there is something going on in my head, like I'm watching myself thinking. A part of me thinks I only just got here, and all these thoughts are stupid and meaningless, the buzzing of a fly crashing into a windowpane. It's like sometimes when I have a hangover, I hate myself for at least six hours, but this is worse, like someone else is doing the hating.

The realization that the burnt smell is coming from me flashes a memory of pain and light through my skull. What's left of my chest hair snaps between fingertips and the touch screams on my skin.

Shit.

I was on my way to the Gethsemane bunkers. I can remember a glimpse of the Old City silhouetted in the twilight before I entered the tunnels. I remember the dark but I don't remember going in – no journey, no transition. There's other stuff, memories too jagged to touch: the image of a tattooed man with a gun holding his finger to his lips; a girl with metal hair – I see her moving but at the same time I see her lying in the water on the tunnel floor. The pictures are true but jumbled. I don't know what they mean. Did I ever? There's a shadow in my head and it boils when I try to think.

Just lie here.

My body sighs as it hits the mattress. The bed feels good but a part of me, the part of me that's still me, knows it's not right. I can't just lie here; that's giving up. My brain throbs with the urge to flee; my limbs twitch, uncertain. How can I run from thoughts?

The muscles of my spine howl in protest as I lever myself up to sitting. My left arm spasms under the strain of lifting, and my hand slips on the cheap sheet covering the mattress, pitching me onto my side. My elbow catches on the bedframe. The jolt of pain is lightning in my skull. In its flash I see the shadow recoil like it's alive. What am I even looking at? I've never seen pictures of the inside of my head – no, my mind (what's the difference?) – before. This isn't imagination. This is something I don't understand.

The weight of my legs swinging to the floor drags my torso to an approximation of upright. The door frame slants diagonally across my eyeline. There's something wrong with my vision? Balance? I'm still going through the possible permutations of neck muscle and spinal adjustments when the skewed door opens and a rectangle of faint daylight frames a diagonal Clementine.

The sight of her makes me cry. I look at her face and for a moment I see my mother, a snapshot from my earliest memories, before I knew about the bruises she hid with her hair. But Clementine isn't my mother. She's a strange, beautiful child that I dragged into all of this. She glides over like a ghost and kneels in front of me, looking up. Those weird, deep eyes: I know what they are now – they're where she's been marked, remade into something different, but they don't stop her being beautiful.

'Levi, you're weak, you shouldn't move. We're safe here. Rest.'

She's wrong. I'm not safe. Nobody's safe. My jaw shivers. A weak sound leaks from my lungs. Why can't I say that? Clem puts her fingertips on my chest and pushes like a breeze. I fall back into the bed flailing like a drowning man, shaking my head frantically, except I can see in her face that I'm not. The command to perform the action of head-shaking echoes pointlessly around my head, blocked by the shadow.

'Help.' The word rises to my lips with no conscious effort, a cry of animal instinct to survive – that's how it escaped. Clem's eyes defocus and her body stiffens. In an instant she transforms subtly from nurse to predator. Her fingers dig painfully into my shoulders but the sensation nails me into presence – I am here, now, in this body. It is mine. She stares through me at the presence within. Her lips draw back in a snarl, and then the sun explodes in my head.

'Clem . . .' I can talk.

'Levi, I'm sorry, I didn't realize it would still be there. I thought, I hoped, we'd killed it.'

'Killed it? What are you talking about, Clem? What the hell's happened to me?'

Her fingers unclench from my shoulders but stay touching, the pressure a gentle reassurance – for me, or for her?

'Something inside the Antikythera Mechanism attacked you, infected you. It attacked me first when I touched it but my vital signs started dropping through the floor. My heart stopped, so

Hilda zapped me with the defibrillator. It seems this thing plugs into the human nervous system and overrides commands from the brain, so that makes it at least temporarily vulnerable to sensory overloads. The shock from the defibrillator gave me a chance to take back control of my body. I wanted to warn you, but you'd already gone by the time I could talk.'

'So that's what happened to the other people in the tunnels with me?'

'We think so.'

'I don't understand any of this.'

She shakes her head, apologetic. 'None of us do. Hilda calls it a demon. Whatever you want to call it, the thing from inside the Mechanism is old. It spreads like a computer virus. It takes control of anything it touches.'

'But you can beat it? With your stuff . . . you just blasted it out of my head. I can't feel it any more.'

'The things that seized control of you and me were bursts of tailored code, fragments of its essence designed to make us receptive to the commands of the creator. I have remade myself more than once – as soon as Hilda gave me a chance, it wasn't hard for me to exorcize a bad program. I can't do that inside your head. The biological functions of your brain are messy and imprecise – I can interact with the code, but not you, not internally.'

My hands move uselessly to the sides of my head. 'It's still in here?'

Clementine nods slowly, eyes not meeting mine. 'You have a headache. It's a neurological after-effect of the arithmetical wrestling match we fought for dominance of your head-space. It lasted micro-seconds – you probably experienced the struggle as an instant of blinding pain, but the code is still reliving it. I trapped it in a data loop, except I tweaked the ending so it won. If we're lucky it could stay transfixed forever, or at least until some contradictory data intrudes. I've bought you time, Levi. I hope it's enough.'

Time. I want to ask how much, but I know she doesn't know. I want to scream. I want to dash my head against the wall until the thing inside comes out. I do none of these things.

'So what do we do? Destroy the Antikythera thing? At least that way it doesn't get anyone else. Maybe that's enough to fuck up this piece of shit code in my head too.'

Clem's hand squeezes gently, but she still won't look at me. 'I'm not sure we can.'

'What are you talking about? Antique bronze meets sledge-hammer, or laser cutter, or acid bath – whatever, it's all good.'

'The thing inside . . .'

'The demon.'

'. . . the thing inside the Antikythera device isn't the same thing as the device itself. I think the device is a containment mechanism.'

'Like a prison.'

She tilts her head, weighing the word for its suitability. 'I suppose so.'

'So you're saying we shouldn't break it?'

'I don't know, Levi. I'm guessing about all of this stuff.' She points to herself with a thumb and looks goofy. 'You really want to get your advice on fighting monsters from a six-year-old?'

'Are you kidding? If you want to know about fighting monsters, a six-year-old is exactly who you ask. Seriously, nobody else understands this like you do. I don't think anyone in Jerusalem could see it even if it was staring them in the face.'

Fear shadows Clem's face as the truth sinks in. It's us who have to deal with this thing, which means her. 'Maybe Hilda . . .'

We both know the thought is wrong, but she doesn't get to finish it before the door creaks open. It's Ludmila, looking different again, any trace of the showgirl vanished with the coat. She pauses a moment to take in the sight of us, then utters a single word.

'Hide.'

I feel Clem flinch. 'Levi's still too weak, he can't move yet.'

'What's happening?' My voice comes out as a croak. I shift my bodyweight in the bed to see if anything's changed since I woke up. Clem's hand pins me in place so easily, I'm not sure she's even trying. Ludmila's face darkens.

'The police are coming. We just saw vans on the camera next to the main road. The track gets too narrow for them pretty fast, so they'll have to get out and walk. You've got maybe ten minutes before they're on you.'

Ludmila's impatience breaks her stillness. She bends at the waist and starts gathering my stuff from the floor into a bundle. Clem shakes her head, gives me a look like she's apologizing, and then hoists me out of the bed in one movement. Before I know it, I'm staring at the floor, draped across her shoulders in a fireman's carry. The burns on my chest howl harder, and every muscle in my body joins in, but Clem moves smoothly, pivoting so I fit lengthwise through the door. As soon as we're outside, she turns to Ludmila for direction. 'Where?'

The tall nun points to one of the greenhouses with her free hand, clutching my clothes to her chest with the other, and Clem sets off at a steady run, eating up the metres as if she didn't have a full-grown man on her back. Ludmila matches her stride for stride, even though she's got to be maybe twenty years older. In two minutes, Clem's bending to ease me through the heavy plastic curtain that serves as the greenhouse door. She's not even out of breath.

For a second I feel like I'm drowning as the humidity swallows us. The air's so thick I can't see the sides of the polytunnel through the greenery, even though it's only a few metres away. My ears fill with the hisses of water under pressure and the snicker of sprinklers. Everything in here drips.

'What's going on, Clem?'

Ludmila's voice answers from behind us. 'Someone must have traced us from the precinct house when we got you.'

Clem opens her mouth like she's about to say something, but looks away, guilty. The conversation stops as we pass through another heavy plastic curtain.

We stop next to a massive pile of compost. I swear I can see it steaming, even in here. I can sure as hell smell it. She lays me out on it and lies next to me, curled into a ball; then Ludmila drops the clothes on us and covers us with what looks like a tinfoil blanket. 'We can't rule out the possibility they can detect Clementine's EM signature. This should block the obvious wavelengths.' I'm still trying to work out what the hell that means when the first forkful of manure lands on my face.

'Are you sure this is a good idea?' I spit out some stinking rotten straw that strayed into my mouth.

'It gives you a chance if they bring sniffer dogs.'

'That's not what I mean. Most people in the city already think you guys are pretty weird, maybe even dangerous. If you start aiding and abetting felons – it could all blow up in your face.'

She pauses a moment with the fork in her hand. A look passes between her and Clem. 'It's too late for us to back out of this now.' She resumes forking the dirt.

'Seriously, you need to think about this . . .'

'Close your mouth or I'll fill it with dung. I've got maybe two minutes before the cops show up. The Mission exists to help the helpless. We don't stop whenever it gets inconvenient.'

Another clod of manure on my face cuts off what I was about to say. I breathe through my nose. The dirt around me muffles the sound of heavy feet running outside.

36.

Clementine

I see it when I sleep; the darkness bleeds through the bars of its cage and expands through my mind like ink in water. When I wake, the memory lingers, the mark of a dead god on my consciousness. The code lies dormant during the day. It is harder for Levi. Last time I saw him, his eyes were a battleground of two wills locked in mortal struggle. That was a few hours ago. I cannot know how much he has left to give.

They keep us all in separate cells. I think Hilda is somewhere close, but Levi is in the main block with the other male prisoners. The police ransacking of the farmstead was brutal, an act of war by a city seeking revenge. They found everything. Levi was turfed, stinking, from the dung pit. The bomb squad used metal detectors to find where we'd buried the Antikythera in the corner of a field of freshly fertilized zucchini, and they took it away in a different metal box. We were all put in a high-sided armoured van with tiny windows at the top and handcuffed to a metal rail on the wall.

I cried when Hilda told me the van was taking us to prison. All I knew was stories from films I'd seen in the tanks growing up – morality tales where harsh incarceration exacts retribution on deviants who flout the law. It's really not that bad. As 'a special-risk prisoner' I am alone in my cell, which is a blessing not conferred upon those deemed less threatening. In some ways this place is not so different from the Mission, although mould darkens cracks in the whitewashed concrete here. Around me I dimly sense the swirls and eddies of all the jail's data, but caution prevents me exploring. I have to assume I am being observed across the spectra. Deploying my antennae would tip my hand. I will only get one chance to play it.

A lawyer has visited me twice. He is young, older than me in strict chronology, but occasional moments of wide-eyed incredulity betray his nervousness. Before we were separated, Hilda warned me to say nothing about the device. She placed no other strictures on what I reveal, leaving it to my judgement which of our many secrets might offer some hope of reprieve or mitigation, but his reactions to the few morsels I offered convinced me Hilda's course is best, though it fills me with fear.

A brief hum followed by a clatter announces the extinction of the lights on our level. My bunk folds down from the wall and locks into position, held up by a chain at one corner. My body moulds itself to the hard wipe-clean surface, but sleep doesn't come. For two hundred heartbeats I stare into the shadows of the ceiling. Is this cell, or another like it, where my journey ends? In most ways it's no worse than the vats where my nameless, genderless siblings and I lived our ersatz childhoods, growing on a diet of synthesized nutrients and hormones, our minds shaped by propaganda. In here, the absence of stimulation is more than offset by the knowledge that every experience, every trivial itch or breath, is real. It's not so bad, but I'd hoped for more.

Soft footsteps from the walkway outside rouse me from my thoughts.

'Hilda?'

No response. I prop myself up with both elbows. The faint light from a guard post at the end of the corridor outlines the figure of a man standing still and silent outside the door to my cell. My eyes itch with the urge to engage my low-light image-enhancement module, but for now I must remain base-human.

'Who's there?'

'Not sleeping, Clementine?' The voice that issues from the figure is an old man's, but smooth and confident, like a singer's.

'Who are you?'

'You haven't guessed? Or used any of your marvellous tricks to find out?'

'I don't know what you're talking about.' Something like a flush of embarrassment courses through the scars along my spine.

'Oh, it took us a while to find out what happened in the museum storage facility, I'll admit that. We are a technological backwater compared to the white heat of your European war factories, but I like to think what we lack in sophistication, we make up for in persistence. Beautiful work, by the way. I was fully expecting Peres, or one of his fleabag associates, to shinny up the drainpipe, or something equally crude. I'd temporarily disabled the security systems to permit something of the kind to happen, but instead your tele-presence ghosts in, switches labels on two packages, and we deliver the Antikythera Mechanism to you. The theft would have gone unnoticed for months if it weren't for all this political nonsense, but here we are.'

The dark figure falls silent, leaving a gap I don't want to fill, but the thought of what's in Levi, of what's inside me, forces me to speak. 'Give me the device and let me out of here, or you will die.'

'Is that a threat?' Light glints off metal on his wrist: an antique timepiece. I remember it from Levi's descriptions of Silas. This must be the man he was so frightened of.

'I'm in no position to threaten. It is merely a probable outcome of the situation as it stands.'

He laughs. 'Why? Is it supposed to be sacred in a way a heathen like me couldn't possibly understand? You're a Machine; why do you care about an archaeological curiosity?'

The question takes me off guard. I expected to be dismissed out of hand. This man, for all his calculated evil, is open to learning in a way I have learned most humans are not. Perhaps there is hope. 'The Mechanism is dangerous. It is killing Levi. It will kill anyone it touches.'

'Hmm . . . Peres did look a little off-colour when I stopped by his cell. What did it do to him?'

My pulse quickens. How do I communicate a threat this man is unequipped to grasp? Hilda perceives it through faith – a distorted understanding, but one that conveys the necessary menace. The language for this does not exist. 'It's . . . difficult to explain in terms a human would understand. There is an intelligence in the Antikythera Mechanism, and it has colonized Levi. It is alive in him now.'

'Like a parasite?' His brows crease. He does, at least, look interested.

'Yes, like a parasite with the capacity to reproduce and spread infinitely. He will die soon. So will anyone else who's exposed.'

'I see. Well, we'll certainly take precautions.' He shrugs. His voice is dismissive. He can see the device only as a technological problem, to which a solution must be available. I have failed. 'Listen, Clementine – that's a lovely name by the way, did you choose it for yourself? Please don't think I'm not touched by your concern, but I actually came here to talk about something far more exciting. I realize you might feel things are at a low ebb, but this could all work out rather well for you, if you're willing to be pragmatic.'

A guard's flat feet slap the concrete of the corridor below. Nothing matters now.

'I wanted you to know, you don't have to share the fate of your fellow terrorists. We don't have anything like you in this part of the world. That makes you valuable. If you want it, there's a job for you with me, in the new administration. You don't have to decide now. At any point in the coming proceedings, whether you're in the courtroom or in your cell, you can ask to speak to a guard. They'll get a message to me, and then all of this will become a memory: one you can partition away until it's gone.'

Fear sours my mouth. Is this where my journey leads? I was born with my destiny set – to die on a radiation-soaked battlefield in the Ural foothills. They grow us in batches of a thousand, a nice round number to process. Statistically one or two of my genderless twins might still be alive. I became something else; I witnessed my own remaking on the operating table. In my new form I endured the squalor of Marseille and the desperation of the crossing to Ceuta, finally sneaking through the barriers around the harbour's edge to reach the camps. All the way through the desert, my actions were links in a chain of self-preservation. The first glimpse I had of another life was a dirigible shining in the skies above the glowing mosques of Tripoli. It was a promise of Jerusalem. I don't want to believe it ends like this, in another servitude.

'No.'

'Hmmm? Like I said, you don't have to answer now. However, there is another factor you ought to consider. If you won't accept my generous offer of employment, then the city of Jerusalem has no interest in keeping you fed and watered for the duration of your imprisonment. The Republic of Humanity will pay a handsome price for you, and I'd imagine your creators would also have a lively interest in seeing what's become of their escaped creation. Some sort of rendition would seem like the obvious best outcome for all parties, except you of course. But then, you're already well acquainted with the ins and outs of the vivisection process, so perhaps that holds no terrors for you?'

My last physical destruction was painless, my consciousness already distilled into an electronic medium. To the insurrectionist scientists dissecting it, the muscled, vat-grown form on the oper-ating table was a source of data, intelligence for their doomed war; to me, watching through cameras linked to the mainframe where

I was stored, it was nothing more than an abstraction. The prospect of this body's destruction is altogether different. For all the flawed decisions in its creation, because of them, because of the journey it has taken, it is me. Even if I could somehow survive it, I would not want to.

The soft footsteps slip away.

37.

Silas

The white lead-lined box mocks me with its silence. From what I can gather, the threat it poses is through physical contact, although the scientists I consulted were frustratingly opaque when it came to describing the mechanisms by which the device wreaks its destruction on the human psyche. Too afraid to say they don't know. I remember touching it once before, laughing at the thin white rubber gloves the curators insisted upon. In hindsight, perhaps they should have been lead.

'Sybil.'

My soon to be ex-assistant takes only seconds to fill my doorway in response to the summons. Her round face betrays no sign of the impatience she must surely feel as her elevation draws near. Once I have the Justice Ministry, some of the city's invisible strings will pass from my hands into hers, but for these final, chafing moments, she must still attend to my whims.

'Why do they want it?'

'Who, sir?'

'It's the unknown, isn't it? It's a blank that people fill with dreams of what might be possible.'

'It has killed at least four people to our knowledge, and inflicted

252

severe damage on two more. The obvious conclusion is that it's a weapon; the Russians, the Machines – that's why they want it. Seems straightforward.'

Her expression is a silent calculation of the value of the thing. To the outside world, she hides behind that housewife's face, but when we are alone together she makes no effort to conceal the steel in her gaze. Dear, dedicated Sybil, this is where you fall short, for all your mastery of data and your fearsome efficiency. There are things at play here that cannot be captured by your grim calculation. There is an art to ruling.

'We have weapons enough in this world. Whatever this is, it promises something more.'

'How could anyone know that? It's spent a century in a glass case and two thousand years before that at the bottom of the Mediterranean.'

'I don't know how they could know, but somehow they do know. Myth perhaps? Legends?'

Her head tilts to one side and her expression hardens. 'You're telling me you want to hold onto this thing because someone made up a story about it?'

'No . . .' My hand comes up in a conciliatory gesture. 'But other people do, and thus its story acquires a kind of truth. That you have to accept, even if you don't believe in it.'

'With all due respect, sir, it sounds like bullshit.'

'Potent bullshit, Sybil. Bullshit powerful enough for the Russians to go to the effort of bringing down our tinpot government for us, remember that.'

'So?' Her gaze drops to where the thing rests. Many of the accretions from its millennia on the seabed have fallen away, and the bronze gleams in patches where the verdigris has worn to bare metal. This newly acquired lustre wholly defies all the curators' prognostications of doom for the ancient artefact. When news of its theft reached them, they balefully assured me the precious thing would disintegrate at the merest hint of rough handling, and yet here it is, looking, if anything, newer than when it was put into storage.

'For the moment it is ours. I do not want to bid it adieu, only to find out I've missed the opportunity of a lifetime once it is gone. If Vasily calls, stall him, but don't give another deadline. That was silly of me; leave the ultimatums to him, I want to see what cards he has to play. I'm going to find out why everybody wants this thing before I let it go.'

'You've always told me buyers of antiquities are fools duped into unrequited love affairs with the past.' I have to admit, that does sound like me. Sybil's memory can be a curse. 'I don't understand why we can't just give the Russians the wretched thing, leak the evidence against Glassberg, and watch the election results roll in. It's a good plan, we should stick to it.' A catch in Sybil's voice betrays a trace of desperation. She's too close now to accept even the spectre of an obstacle to her ambition. *Tough.*

'No, I want to know. Get whoever's in charge of the Machine Cult – is it still that idiot Barnes, or have they axed him already? Bring him down to the museum basement for a private chat. Those useless fucks were after it – there must be a reason.' In a perfect world I'd bring in a tame Russian, but the collateral would be too heavy if we made a mess, whereas Cultists are expendable. Barnes's masters are most likely unaware even of his existence. 'I'm going to the pre-trial hearing; have him here when I get back. If you can avoid inflicting any damage, so much the better, but don't trouble yourself unduly.'

The visual clamour of the news feeds fills the dark space in the ministerial limousine bearing me to court. The news is, on the whole, positive – depending on your perspective of course. Without my lifting a finger, demonstrations against the Christian outrages have erupted in four separate neighbourhoods. A wall of angry bodies has sealed off the Mission's squalid little outpost in the Old

City. Their rancid customers will have to find some other source of succour. At least they don't vote.

As the car pulls into the parking lot of the city's Hall of Justice, a comfortable sense of ownership suffuses me, the lord returning home to the manor. The mob surrounding it perform my bidding without awareness – Christian, Jew, Muslim, and Machine Cult alike – all too wrapped in their own agendas to glimpse the bigger game being played out around them. Anger radiates from the building like heat. Even outside you can feel it, seeping through the sagging concrete, a malign presence darkening the mock-classical pillars of the portico. Idiot rage flows through the crowd gathered outside, all the way in to the lucky few who've gained seats in the galleries. Inside, the anger of the defendants, inwardly raging against the falsity of their accusations, is a more delicate aroma. Amos Glassberg's quiet, dignified horror is the perfect garnish to it all.

38.

Clementine

I am a terrorist, a thief, an accessory to murder. A fierce man in a headdress and a knee-length skirt strides forcefully as he enumerates my crimes. My guilt is a given, carved into the faces of the watchers lining the galleries for the preliminary hearing. This room is a vast jumble of anachronisms, nods to history, layers of meaning I cannot hope to comprehend. The scuffed panelling of Lebanon cedar that lines the walls is shrivelled and odourless from years of desiccation by air conditioning. It stops abruptly a third of the way up, yielding to a dull layer of faux marble reaching all the way to the ceiling. Murderous fans chop the air and scatter the smells of people.

We are packaged together, the aiders and abettors, Hilda, Ludmila, Levi, and I, arranged in a row on a bench inside a copper cage facing the crowd, armed guards at either side verifying the fiction that we are dangerous. My former self would have raged against this injustice, but the rage built into that warrior body was burnt with my redundant flesh. In its place this body harbours only despair. There is no evil intent in what is being perpetrated upon us: no intent at all, just a series of instinctive responses to ancient fears, the herd turning upon a perceived predator.

The witnesses arrayed against us are policemen, officials, carefully selected pillars of state. It is not we who are on trial, so much as the Mission itself. The prosecutor poses them binary questions, carefully constructed and ordered to build a narrative of our anarchy and rebellion. Some of them are complicit in the storytelling; others have the answers dragged out of them, attempts at qualification ruthlessly quashed by the bewigged prosecutor.

When he is done with a witness, one of the bailiffs opens our copper cage and Ludmila steps out to take her turn at cross-examination. The holy sister plays the part of our lawyer. She still wears her dull robes, but she has become something different. She is relentless, picking apart the stitches in the story so carefully woven by the prosecutor, underlining every inconsistency, switching angles to provide alternative interpretations, cutting his clean, straight line of narrative into meaningless fragments of data.

For all her brilliance, it is clear to me we are the victims of a flawed process. The humans watching from the galleries cannot unmake the story they themselves have created. The logical fallacies are glaring, but the proceedings permit no interruptions. Amos Glassberg watches from the judge's chair like a statue, stirring only to remonstrate with the prosecutor when he veers into hyperbole. He, at least, is aware. Beside me Levi slumps insensate on the bench, silently locked in a life-or-death struggle invisible to the crowds who gawp between the bars of our cage. He barely stirs as the judge hammers to announce a recess. The bailiffs prod us towards our holding cell with wooden clubs held at arm's length, as if fearful of catching Levi's nameless contagion. His shoulders feel thin and brittle in my hands.

'Levi,' I whisper through the side of my mouth. He doesn't move. 'Levi.' Louder. He stirs, tilting his head slightly to indicate he is listening. Dark circles hide his eyes. 'I think I can stop all of this.'

Levi sits heavily on one of the holding cell's hard plastic chairs. He sniffs hard before talking. 'How? You going to bust us out? We're guilty, remember? We stole the Antikythera Mechanism; we did it, we're going to jail.' His eyes close and he turns away from me. All I can see is the sallow, slack skin of one cheek.

'I don't mean us. It's all the other stuff – the assassination attempt, the Mission plotting anarchy and rebellion. They're innocent.'

'Are they, Clem? Do you know that? Do you really know those people? Who do they work for? Why do they do what they do?'

'They helped me when I had no one, after you turned me away.'

'Maybe they are good people, but good people get used. You ever think of that?'

I shake my head but the words ignite an ember of terrible uncertainty. Doubts about my benefactors are a luxury I have been unable to afford since coming to this city, but the questions have always been there, my brain always unable to provide the other half of the equation for the Mission's generosity. I still know so little. These first few relationships are the foundations of my constructed humanity. If you take even one of those away, what is left? If I'm merely a tool to be used by stronger wills, I should submit to Silas. That is the position of pure logic, but other impulses war within me now. I cannot know Hilda's motivations for offering me refuge, or whether the Mission serves some ulterior purpose; the data humans yield is never unequivocal, but I can make a choice about what to believe, and in the end it is choice that defines me.

'I choose to believe in them, Levi. I don't know if it's right, but it's how I feel. They don't deserve any of this.'

'Maybe, maybe not.' His eyes half close, shutters drawn to exclude the pain of light from his internal struggle.

'I've got an idea.'

He shifts uncomfortably, closer to upright. 'Go on.'

'It's like you say; we're the guilty ones, we should take the fall. Say everything was part of our plan – we used the Mission as cover.'

'What?' For a moment, panic banishes the fatigue from his face and he is the Levi I remember from when we met. 'Right now we're

looking at ten years in jail, maybe fifteen tops. Conspiracy to over-
throw the government could put us in the execution chamber.'

'Yes.'

'Are you insane?'

'Perhaps.'

He stares at me now. The dark in his eyes is the yawning maw
of the thing eating him from within. 'What if you're wrong? What
if all the stuff about feeding the homeless is just an act . . . if they've
been playing you . . . us, all along?'

'Would it matter all that much, Levi? Now that we are where we
are? We have very few choices left to us. If I choose the path of
self-preservation, I am nothing more than the Machine my creators
made me to be. Even if it is the end of me, even if I am wrong, I
wish to be something more.'

'To err is human . . .' Levi's voice is soft.

'What's that?'

'It's something one of my teachers used to say at school, to make
kids feel better when they fucked up. I guess it didn't mean what
I thought it meant.'

'You don't have to do this, Levi. I can say it was just me.'

His mouth creases in a peaceful smile, the first I've seen since
he was infected. 'I'm tired, Clem.' He shrugs and points at his head.
'I'm losing this fight. How long do you think I've got before it takes
over?'

'It could be months, maybe even longer. I can't say – there are
too many variables.'

'But it's only going to go one way, right? If I was going to beat
it, I'd have done it by now.'

'I think so.' A cooling of the skin by the corners of my eyes is
tears drying as they form.

'Easy choice, then.'

A bell rings somewhere outside, and muffled sounds of movement filter through the door as the court fills. Two guards usher

us through with their sticks. As the judge hammers for order, the crowd quiets itself. In a moment of calm, Levi stands up. The chains holding him to the bench rattle noisily before pulling taut.

'Everyone! Listen to me! I want to confess . . .' His voice echoes around the sudden silence in the courtroom. '. . . to everything.'

Ludmila pivots from where she is standing ready to begin a cross-examination and regards Levi through narrowed eyes before switching her gaze to me. Hilda smiles beatifically and looks up to heaven in prayer; then the clamour of four hundred voices smashes the silence.

39.

Silas

The demi-human's head bends away from its neck at a fatal angle, leaving the body sprawled like a store dummy stuffed into the interrogation chair. Its metal appurtenances shimmer with reflections of the museum basement's stuttering neon strips, heedless of their wearer's death. The metal makes it hard to tell whether it ever had a gender. They would have you believe they pass beyond such human trivialities early on the journey towards Mechanical apotheosis, but the truth is they're all cowards, scared of sex. I don't blame them really. Loss of control is a dangerous thing; that's why I keep it transactional. Anyway, this poor bugger, whatever it was, didn't know the Antikythera's secrets, and now it has paid the price of my dissatisfaction with today's outcome in court.

It's not that the hearing went against me. Materially, I can still claim a victory. The anarchist plot I concocted will be vindicated by two convictions in court, and Amos Glassberg, Minister of Justice, man of principle, will be forced to deliver a verdict he knows to be false, one that also exonerates me of any possible wrongdoing. And yet, his face at the end of it all – he was not beaten. The judgements he delivered on the two thieves were forced exaggerations, uncomfortable for him no doubt, but convicting those innocent Missionaries as terrorists would have broken him. He would have done it, I think, in the misguided belief that bending to the popular will would put him ahead of me in the polls, thereby safeguarding the city from the threat I present. He would have sacrificed his integrity, and then lost anyway, and it would have been delicious. Instead, I have this.

Sybil ushers in two men in grey overalls who lift the red-robed body and deposit it in a wheelbarrow with an unbecoming clank. The arms splay out at the corners and the legs point almost vertically into the air. Her face shows no record of our recent contretemps, but the memory will linger, even if she chooses not to show it. The stakes are too high. She is too close.

'Do they always use a wheelbarrow?'

Her head tilts in contemplation. 'I think so. It would make sense to have something more bespoke, wouldn't it?'

'Yes. See to it, would you?'

'Hmm, OK.' She watches the body roll away, wincing slightly as one of the hands catches on a door frame.

'What's wrong, Sybil? You seem distracted.'

She waits until the corpse has trundled awkwardly out of sight. 'I don't know what we're doing any more.'

'I thought I'd made it pretty clear. I want to know what it does.'

Her gaze flicks away from the doorway to settle on my face, soft cow eyes narrowed into harsh focus. 'Why?'

'Does it matter?'

'It matters to me; I've worked for you for seven years.'

'I'll take your word on that.'

'I have done unspeakable things.' Her eyes close, shutting down unwanted memory.

'And? It's a little late for regrets, don't you think?'

A snort of laughter escapes her. There is no mirth in it. 'Whatever we've done, I've never had cause to doubt your judgement until now. You've become obsessed. You've forgotten why we needed the

Antikythera Mechanism. It was only ever supposed to be the means to an end.'

'Sybil, I can see how it might look like that, but there is a bigger picture here. If this thing merits even a fraction of the effort the great powers have employed to obtain it, it could be game-changing in our little regional squabbles. With sufficient power, elections are an unnecessary sideshow. The Greater Levant Co-Prosperity Sphere could become a reality in a matter of weeks instead of years. This could herald the end of Jerusalem's dark age.'

Silence. Pinched lips press tight against her teeth. For a moment I watch as the pressure of exasperation building inside her threatens to crack the veneer of control. 'How? Explain it to me. Make me understand and I will make it happen for you. I can't do that if I can't see the endgame.'

'You can, and you will. At this stage in proceedings, your obedience is all I require.'

Her face goes hard and lean, jaw tight. 'I—'

'You wanted clarity. I believe I have supplied it.'

A muscle in her jaw twitches, then her cheek goes slack and she speaks in the dull monotone of resignation. 'Well, you'll have to deal with Vasily. He's stopped being polite. He knows you're stalling. He says if you don't fucking deliver he can have an airborne brigade here in forty-eight hours and he'll take it.'

'Don't you see? Doesn't that prove to you what we have here? The threat is transparently bullshit – Vasily must be getting desperate even to think of making it. If it was that easy, Sov shock infantry would already be goose-stepping through the Lion Gate, but every soldier they have is tied up on the Ural Front. If Vasily is going heavy, it's not going to be on behalf of some Politburo fag with a yen for antiquities. The great powers are prepared to go to war for the Antikythera device; I would be mad to give it away.'

Sybil takes a deep breath and frowns. 'How can you say that when we don't even know what it does.'

'If they can find out, so can we. It's ours, for fuck's sake. Get me the nun.'

'Which one?'

'The one in charge – the fat one. The other one looks like a handful.'

Her frown deepens. 'That won't be straightforward. They're being released from custody.'

My hand drags from the dry skin of my forehead down the side of my face. 'Do I look like I fucking care?'

Thankfully, the day's disappointments have not diminished Sybil's efficiency, and I have only a short wait for the rotund nun's arrival. She smiles the deranged smile of the holy, but, needless to say, I am not taken in. I had Sybil look at the organization's accounts – that farm complex out in the hills is turning a massive profit, and donations to the Mission's city shelter far outstrip the meagre expenses of food and staffing. It's a business, and a good one. I was going take it for myself if Levi Peres hadn't been overcome by that bizarre messianic urge and let this frump off the hook. We'll see; it might still work out.

'Have a seat please, Mother Hilda.' I gesture to the chair so recently vacated by her deceased opposite number in the Machine Cult. For a moment, she looks at it as if the body was still there, then the stupid smile reasserts itself and she gazes directly at me.

'I cannot help you, Silas Mizrachi.'

'No need for introductions then? Good, that'll save us some time. What is it you think I want?'

'Love.'

'Oh, please fuck off! If we can't make this an intelligent conver-sation, then I'll have to end it painfully, and I don't mean that metaphorically.'

'By "intelligent", you mean "limited in scope". Very well. Despite what you think, I am no martyr; I fear pain like anyone else.'

'Well, we'll see about that. Tell me about the Antikythera Mechanism. What is it? What does it do?'

'I can tell you what I know, but you will not like my answers.'

My hand twitches with the urge to strike, but after the last interview's somewhat abrupt end, our reserve of relevant clerics is limited. 'Why don't we just try? And then I can decide for myself whether I like it.'

The smile subsides and the middle-aged woman stares at me with something like sympathy. Her eyes are green. For a moment I see the face of someone younger, a girl with golden hair and soft, pale skin. It feels like a memory of loss; then it's gone.

'The thing within the Antikythera Mechanism is a false god.'

The fatuousness of the answer breaks the spell of the moment. Sybil looks at me as if to say 'You were warned'. It's obvious I'm going to have to play the game to get anything out of this one.

'How do you know it's not a real one?'

'God does not reside in machines, even if mankind chooses to see her there.'

A tortured breath escapes me. 'Fine, let's say you're right. It's a false god – whatever. What does that mean? What does it *do*?'

'What false gods have always done – it warps the minds of men, bends them to its will, ultimately reducing them to mere extensions of its consciousness.'

'Like mind control?'

'Call it that if you will, but do not make the mistake of thinking this is some technological bauble you can use for your schemes, Silas Mizrachi. It is ancient and powerful beyond human understanding.'

I suddenly find myself mirroring her stupid, holy smile. It is, of course, the same Bronze Age bullshit priests have been peddling in this town for four thousand years. Obviously, she cannot perceive this object except from within her own paradigm, but there must be some reality underpinning the voodoo, or the Sino-Sovs wouldn't give a shiny shit about an antique.

'How do you know all of this, Mother Hilda?'

'It awoke in Clementine's presence, and then it rose in response to a reading from *The Book of Maccabees* – a ritual of summoning for Dagon.'

'Dagon?'

'A Sumerian deity, a false god of the Philistines that placed itself as a rival to Jehovah. The consciousness within the Antikythera device might once have been known by that name, or others, but that is speculation.'

'And can you conduct the ritual?'

'No, the Lord has not blessed me with those gifts. Novice Clementine is the only one of us able to commune with it.'

The day's disappointments vanish in an instant. The synthetic! Her Machine-built co-processors must be capable of interfacing with it. It's not as if I needed proof the Antikythera Mechanism was nothing more than a hot piece of tech, but that clinches it. Somehow the Machines and the Soviets found out about this thing while it was under our noses in the city museum, or maybe Vasily's telling the truth – his lot only want it to stop the other guys getting it. None of that matters now; the important thing is, the device might just be worth the hassle after all.

'Sybil, I think young Clementine should show us what our new toy can do. Have one of the "guest rooms" prepared for her in the annex. You'll need tech support, but keep the bodies to a minimum – people you can trust – and don't tell them what it's about. The device's value halves with every person who knows what it can do.'

The smile I direct at the seated nun is entirely genuine. 'Thank you, Mother Hilda, you've been most helpful. You can go now. Sorry to have taken up your time.'

She stands up; her expression suddenly sombre. At the door, she hesitates. 'It's not what you think it is, Silas Mizrachi. No good can come from worshipping false gods.'

'Thank you for your concern, but really, there's no need to worry on our behalf. We can handle everything from here.'

Sybil watches the woman walk away, then turns her gaze to me. 'You let her go?'

'I did, didn't I?'

'I didn't think that was the plan.'

'It wasn't.'

'Shall I . . .?' Sybil's implication is unmistakeable. Mother Hilda is a loose end. All I need to do is nod, and she will make a call and the fat woman will die peacefully in her sleep, to be discovered by her mournful congregation when she fails to turn up for morning prayers. It would be the simplest thing, and yet something prevents me: a memory of loss, a soft, pale face crowned with golden hair.

40.

Clementine

His face is predatory triangles, scalene cheekbones gleaming in the yellow light from the ceiling, isosceles nose; the rest of him is shadows. Silas stands silent at the centre of the cell while a guard secures the door behind me and handcuffs one of my wrists to the bars. The air is dry and still, with a faint scent of pine. Whatever this place is, it's cleaner than the city jail, but empty. I saw no other prisoners on the way in, only one corridor of three vacant cells before we reached this one.

The metal is cold on my wrist. I blink three times and the low-light filters descend invisibly over my eyes, cutting through the contrast that blinds the human optic nerve. In the darkness along one wall I see Levi's skinny form huddled on the fold-down bench. He looks lost in the fabric of an outsize orange prisoner's uniform and he doesn't move.

'We haven't done anything to him, before you ask.' A glint of white in Silas's grin briefly overloads my image intensifiers and the rest of the room plunges into darkness as they overcompensate. When my vision returns, it is striped in cautious shades of grey. 'We had a perfectly civilized conversation with young Levi Peres, and he was very forthcoming. If you cooperate too, I foresee no need for the unpleasantness I'd feared.'

He takes small steps in a semi-circle around the point where I am chained, his gaze dissecting me, trying to perceive the juncture at which my illusion of humanity fails.

'What do you want? We've confessed. We've made no attempt to implicate you. We're going to die. You're going to win your rigged election. Isn't that enough?'

'No.'

'No?' My voice is an idiot echo bouncing from the bare walls of the cell.

'I want you to show me how to use the Antikythera device.'

'Use it?'

'After I spoke to your Mother Superior, my scientists were finally able to put the pieces together. We know what it is now: a mind-control device; it emits signals at the same EM frequencies as synaptic transmissions. We can turn humans into puppets. With something like that, there's really no limit to what I could achieve.'

'Like what?' The words are thin and high, a little girl's.

'Oh, I don't know . . . Make something out of this wretched city – a proper country perhaps? A device like that could make diplomacy a great deal simpler and more rewarding.'

'I don't think it's something that can be used. Hilda called it a demon.'

'Or a false god. I know.' There is laughter in his voice.

'It's dangerous. It hurts people.'

'Yes, you said as much, but we have an understanding of how it works now. With your help we can make sure it never hurts anyone ever again.'

'My help? Please, listen to me – I don't think you understand. I don't know what your scientists have told you, but I have only brushed against this thing twice, and I think the only reason I survived those encounters was because it was newly woken from a dormant state – even the thing killing Levi is just a sub-routine it reeled off without thought, an ancient preservation reflex, and I couldn't save him. It has had days now to assimilate data and establish parameters. If it gets a foothold in another consciousness, it could spread through humanity. There is no limit to the harm it could inflict. For all we know, this thing could be responsible for any number of the disasters in humanity's past. You know what I am. Believe me when I say it is beyond me. It is beyond any human technology. It's not a god; it's something far worse.'

He gives a bland smile. 'Honestly, you're as bad as the nun. We're not the mindless primitives you take us for, you know, and contrary to what you may believe, I am not incapable of taking advice. I accept that there may be risks involved. I am not proposing that you should commune directly with the intelligence.' He gestures to a white metal box beneath Levi's bench that shows pale grey in my vision. 'You can start by showing me how to control the code within Peres; that should suffice until we're ready to move on to grander things. This cell has been fitted with a suite of sensors so we can record whatever's happening in the electromagnetic spectra, study it, and reproduce it at our leisure. In the event of any mishaps, the entire cell is sheathed in copper and silver mesh to prevent trans-missions outside. If this thing does pose a risk as you claim, it is only to us.'

A silence hangs between us.

'Why would I help you? We're going to die anyway. Me in the execution chamber, Levi probably sooner when he's wiped clean.'

'Because there is a chance, Clementine, that I might let you live if you prove yourself useful, and what are you if not a creature of logic?' Another look assesses my worth, measures it against possible risk. I am a limited variable within this man's calculus. 'Surely even a glimmer of hope is preferable to the certainty of death?'

Adrenaline shivers through my body. It is the base animal response

– fight or flight. Levi was terrified of this man – he ran and ran and it didn't work. Two options; one is proven ineffective. What am I, if not a creature of logic? What choice do I have? Everything that has happened to us happened because of him. It must end.

'You have *The Book of Maccabees*?'

'That curious Talmudic apocrypha with the ritual in it? Yes, the nun mentioned it. Is it really necessary?'

'Any intelligence needs an identity, even your warehouse watchdogs. The being within the Antikythera device could have many names. We know it responds to Dagon.'

'A name is one thing, but why do we need the scripture? It seems pointlessly elaborate.'

'It's code. I don't know how it works – the data almost certainly isn't the words themselves – it could be intonation, rhythm, specific combinations of sounds or even concepts. I can only guess.'

'Fine, do what you have to, but keep the theatrics to a minimum. I don't want any distractions.'

'All I have to do is read, although you might want to step back. If Dagon rises and seizes control of Levi, he could start moving unpredictably. If it goes wrong, so could I. For your own good, stand clear of us both.'

My words elicit a frown, but Silas Mizrachi retreats, pressing against the cell door to maximize the distance between us. With my free hand, I rest the battered old book on my knees. It opens in a waft of mildew and dust. The words of the ritual are black in a precisely printed neo-gothic script.

'I will need to touch Levi.' I rattle the chain of my handcuffs against the bars to prove his unconscious form is beyond my reach where it lies on the bench. Silas eyes me suspiciously, then looks around for the lackey who has already absented himself. 'There will be danger, but I think not yet. I was reading to Levi for hours before Dagon rose.'

'Do you have to call it that?' With visible distaste he shoves Levi along the bench until his bare ankle is within my grasp, before retreating hurriedly to the cell door, where he presses himself back against the bars and watches.

The harsh German sounds of the words bring with them the memory of reading to Levi as he lay helpless in Hilda's bed. I remember that time it seemed to bring him peace. The pulse in Levi's calf quickens beneath my fingers as the words flow. It's happening faster now. The pain along my spine is my antennae extending, an animal's instinct, a wolf's ear twitching at sound.

In this cell, I am in a dead space, a caged hole in the electromagnetic world. Silas is a blank, stripped of any devices that could render him vulnerable to infiltration – he's cautious. The box containing the Antikythera device is another emptiness, the thing's transmissions trapped within by layers of alloyed metals. The only activity is the code animate within Levi, which barks and growls unintelligibly through the VLF and microwave bands. It senses me, but does not attack instinctively as it did before. The defeated fraction of its essence caged within my consciousness functions as a kind of inoculation – I am marked with its scent.

The wet biology of Levi's brain is a barrier insurmountable to my perception, but as I read the text from the battered tome, Dagon's excitement is palpable across the spectra. It is a dog in a cage, slavering and yelping as its keeper approaches, promising liberation.

Levi's leg stirs beneath my touch, then jerks away. Dagon has woken. My touch is redundant. I close the book and set it down on the floor. The avatar of the false god stands up wearing Levi's flesh. Silas's face is a rictus of fascination and terror.

'I didn't believe . . . I mean, I wasn't sure. I couldn't know.'

The Levi thing sways on its feet and stares around blindly, reacquainting itself with unfamiliar sensory inputs. Silas reaches into a silk-lined jacket pocket and produces a large black pistol which he waves alternately between me and Levi's head. The darkness at the end of the barrel is a promise of oblivion.

'Control him. Get him to sit down on the bench.' Even as Silas issues his commands, gesturing with the gun, he cringes back against the bars of the cell door. The widening of his eyes tells me he is beginning to understand what he has unleashed.

My finger brushes Levi's face. It is burning hot, and sweat flows from his pores. The fragment of code within him is struggling to manage the complexities of operating a human body, but the touch permits me a clouded sense of what's happening within. Freed of the burden of struggle with Levi's consciousness, it writhes and reconfigures for the task at hand, tailoring code to execute the tasks of moving fingers, processing smells, interfacing with the dominant exterior consciousness it mistakenly believes to be me. Dimly, I perceive what remains of Levi huddled into itself like a man freezing to death while the darkness rages like a storm of black snow.

I try sending some data, routing it through the part of Dagon's consciousness caged within me. Levi's eyes briefly flick up at mine as its counterpart within him establishes protocols. For all its ferocity, it is relatively simple – it cannot conceive of commands coming from an illegitimate source. To its still limited perception I am indistinguishable from its creator within the Antikythera device.

Levi's body twitches beneath my touch. It is beyond exhaustion. As the thing responds to my instructions, I feel it pass through me, a dose of ancient data borne on a jolt of current. The nerve-endings of my fingertips sense the brief surge of voltage through the imperfect electrolyte of Levi's sweat. Too fast to regret, it passes into me, and then out through the metal handcuffs binding me to the bars of the cell. It is a crude circuit with its terminus at the sweating hand of Silas Mizrachi.

By accident, or unconscious response to the invisible spark of creation, his hand comes away from the cell bars. He's still talking, but I tune the words out as I extend my senses searching for any remaining spark of Levi; the damp matter of his brain is like a blinding fog. Suddenly, the chatter stops.

'What have you done?' The voice from the corner of the room is a gasp. Silas's eyes stare at the gun in his hand like a Neanderthal seeing fire for the first time. The fingers twitch as Dagon's proxy establishes itself in its new home.

'I made it a better offer.'

'Offer?' His voice trails off, no longer his own. Does what remains of his consciousness still connect to his senses? My conversation might, in any meaningful sense, already be over, but the human urge to respond drives me on.

'I can no more control this thing than I can control the tides, Silas. But I can inform it that its host is exhausted and point out that its existence will end when he expires. All I had to provide was a route into its new home.' Something like hatred glitters in his eyes. 'If there's anything left of you to hear this, I want you to think about what you've done. Think about what this intelligence could do if someone unleashed it into the wider world. I cannot know what decisions took you to this point, but it's possible you still have one left to you.' Silas stands paralysed, locked in his own silent battle, still staring at the pistol. 'I've watched that fragment of its consciousness tear Levi to pieces. If there is anyone or anything in this world you care about, I'd recommend the gun.'

Cartilage pops audibly as I narrow my wrist and hand to slide from the cuffs. The discomfort barely registers amidst the storm of data and emotion battering my senses. Have I murdered a human? Or merely facilitated a course of self-destruction he set in motion? Even posing the question feels like a sickening sophistry as I watch Silas Mizrachi end.

There is no resistance to my fingers rifling through his silk-lined pockets, retrieving a mix of access cards and physical keys. One of them opens the cell door. Metal tumblers clash noisily within the lock, a crude barrier impervious to any hacker, but the key does not care who wields it.

I scoop Levi from the bench like a forklift. His body, always skinny, is insubstantial now, as if whatever gave it substance has departed. Or perhaps that is merely perception? His body folds in the middle, a weighty, barely animate blanket around my right shoulder, my right hand gripping a bony shin to keep the load in place.

The burden unbalances me as I turn, and my gaze falls upon the white metal box beneath the cell bench. Humanly, I want not to see it, deny its existence, retroactively edit the thing from my own history, but a small, stubborn part of me knows I cannot. Once, it would have been the cold, hard logic of the Machine driving me to confront the threat, but now it is something else, harder to define, that guides my hand to the smooth moulded plastic handle. It is Hilda's gaze as she gave me shelter; it is Levi's arm when he discovered I was a child; it is all the love I still hope to know. None of that can exist if this thing is let loose.

The metal corners cut into my calf as I walk lopsided between my two burdens along the dark corridor of cells, willing myself to the rectangle of light at its end.

Suddenly the brightness expands, filling my vision with blinding intensity; then it dims, obscured by a small silhouette that stops in front of me. As my eyes adjust, it resolves into the figure of a woman, young but with strands of premature grey amidst mousy hair tied back in a tight bun. She looks at me, questions shining in soft, intelligent eyes. Her gaze stops at the metal box hanging uncertainly from the fingers of my left hand, then raises up to examine my face. If she has any kind of weapon, or merely raises the alarm, my life will be measured in minutes. I am helpless beneath my burdens, but more than anything, my taste of murder has robbed me of the will to fight. I would rather die, and the thought brings calm. A hesitant voice breaks the strange silence between us.

'Is he dead?' For a moment I think she's talking about Levi, but her eyes look past us.

'No, but it's a matter of time.'

She nods to herself for a few seconds, as if weighing some decision, then flattens her body against the side of the corridor and steps around me, walking into the darkness in the direction of the cell. I take a step forward and close my eyes to shield them against the light beyond the doorway. From behind me comes the dead echo of the gun.

He is a shell. There is breath, a heartbeat, and little else. I can dimly sense the code coursing through synapses, bundles of data borne on neurotransmitters. With each passing moment, it evolves to become something new, a more effective operating system for the body it has possessed, and Levi sinks deeper. His face glows green in the light from the screens behind the bar. Yusuf's massive hands clench around a rag. It sweeps the dented metal beside the outstretched body, searching for dirt that isn't there. His eyes beg me for hope.

'How long has he got?'

'I don't know. The thing inside him – it's becoming him. Soon I won't be able to see it at all.'

A warmth on my shoulder is Hilda's hand. Tears prickle in my eyes as if released by the contact. 'It's for the best, Clementine. Seeing his suffering will not diminish it, and it could harm you. You are not free of the taint.'

'I wanted to talk to him.' The grief shudders through me.

'You still can. Saying the words can be healing.'

'He won't hear them. I'd be talking to myself. It's not enough.' My words tumble out, poisonous with anger, but Hilda only smiles.

'It never is. Letting go is perhaps the hardest thing for humans to do.'

'I'm not sure I can. I feel like I might break.'

'It will pass.'

I look away, unable to bear the kindness in her gaze. Everything she says would be true if I was human, but I'm not, and it isn't.

To the self I was born as, Levi's death would be a data point, a net resource loss that could be remedied by a replacement. A human who loved him would be consumed by grief, but they would draw upon the love of others to rebuild themselves. I have been truly known only by two people. I'm not ready to let go.

'I can reach him.'

Hilda looks up and her hood falls away. Tears glisten in her eyes, mirrors to my own. 'What do you mean?'

'Levi is still there, he's just locked in, denied access to sensory input and motor function.' Thoughts tumble into place, almost lagging behind the words voicing them. This is human intuition. It feels more true than any calculation, but it is fallible – reason tainted with emotion. 'When the intelligence took hold of me, I had a refuge, a sense of self to anchor me. It was the memories of my creation – the knowledge of what and who I was that kept me alive. What is Levi? Where does he go to survive?'

The sounds of sport drone from the vid screens. Yusuf's face is a sickly green in their light. For a moment he looks lost, like a man listening to a language he doesn't understand, but then he stands straight, and the rag drops from his hand.

'He's at the beach.' His voice rises from a whisper. 'You know Levi. He doesn't like to talk, but when he gets drunk, it's always the beach – complaining about sand and bad food. He says he hated going there with his family, but . . . well, that's Levi, isn't it?'

'Then that's where we go.'

Confusion banishes the fear from Hilda's face. 'You mean physically taking him somewhere else? What difference will that make?'

'If the code is functioning anything like a human mind, or even a rudimentary AI, it will seek comparison and context for any sense data coming from the body. If we subject the body to beach stimuli – sand, sea air, sunlight reflected from water – it will search until it finds them in Levi's memory. It will create a path to him for me.'

'You expose yourself to it again.'

'Yes.'

Another silence fills the space between us; then she smiles, beaten. 'And what if the last of Levi dies while you are within him? What happens then?'

'I don't know.'

'Go with God, my child.'

Her hand is warm on my face before she turns away.

The streets are almost empty in the grey light before dawn. Jerusalem is monochrome until the sun bathes the ancient stone in blood. The last of the Old City's cobbles sends shudders through Yusuf's van as we pass the ruins of the Jaffa Gate. We make quick progress along the Ben Gurion Way, through the deserted government sector, heading northwest, towards the sea. Levi's dying body lies beneath a blanket in the back, but the few police we see are looking for a different kind of trouble.

A duet of two plucked lutes trickles from the radio; the singer's high tenor infects me with its sweet melancholy as the sun rises behind us, casting long shadows across the road. Yusuf sings the words without thought, too quickly, too inflected for me to pick out syllables.

'What does it mean?'

He looks away from the road and shrugs. 'It is a famous song; everybody knows this. It is a boy who loves a girl, but she has died and gone up to heaven. He is singing about how it will be when they are together again. It is sad, but the sadness is truth.'

'And it makes you feel less sad?'

His head moves side to side while he weighs the question. 'Only a little bit. Would you like a different song?' His hand hovers over the dash.

'No, I don't think I'm in the mood for anything. Can you get the news?'

He shrugs and taps the screen. The display glitches, then lights up with the live visuals for the news feed. A small, mousy woman stands behind a lectern on the steps of the city museum. She looks the same as she did in the prison, but for a change of clothes. These ones are expensive.

'Today, we all mourn the loss of a dedicated public servant. However, it is my sad duty to report that the handover operation has uncovered irregularities in the ministerial records, and possible evidence of links to organized crime. As acting minister, I will be launching a full investigation into my predecessor's activities, with the goal of rooting out the corruption that has so long plagued our great city.'

Yusuf makes a noise of disgust and taps the feed to switch it off. 'She is the same. They are always the same.' Minutes pass in silence until he finds music again. The gentle sound of the *oud* battles against engine noise as we accelerate to join the highway. The road opens up before us, heading west towards the sea.

41.

Levi

I see the sea, but it's numbers, bright breakers dissolving into ones and zeroes. Code. Representation. Simulation. Or just a different way of seeing? I am not me; I am something else, non-Levi.

Suddenly the noise is all around me. Waves crashing drag me into light. I'm on a beach, my feet are half buried in damp sand and the ocean trickles away through my fingers. Clementine is sitting next to me, looking up at where the sun should be in a grey sky. Even though we're on the beach, she's still wearing those weird tight clothes, which is funny, but I don't care because I'm happy to see her.

'Is this real, Clem? Are we really here?'

She smiles at that. She looks like she's relieved about something. 'Yes, Levi. We're really here.'

'I remember being in the cell with Silas. I thought I was going to die.'

Her smile breaks, and she looks away. 'You did, Levi.'

I should feel sad, or heartbroken, or something meaningful. Instead, all I feel is cheated. 'But you said this was real.'

'Oh, this is all real.' She scoops up a handful of watery sand and lets it pour through her fingers. 'But you're not. You're a memory of Levi.'

I look down at my wet feet – the water wicking away in the wind is cold, the hems of my trousers are damp and stiff with salt. It all feels so real. 'I don't understand.'

'You lost your battle. I used the code within you to infect Silas. I thought that might give you a chance – that it might work differently within a human brain, maybe it would flee from your dying body into his and leave you clear.'

'But it didn't . . .'

'No, it replicated itself.' She says it like an apology for something she should have known, but we didn't know anything. All of us were just reacting to that thing, even Silas.

'You said I'm a memory of Levi, but that's all any of us ever are, isn't it?' For the whole of my short life I'd have considered it a stupid question, but now in death, or whatever this is, it seems to be the only thing that matters.

'You're something new, or perhaps something very old. The code has control of your higher functions, but without input from the intelligence in the Antikythera Mechanism it has no agenda other than basic self-preservation. It's running on autopilot, physical memory, and right now, what this body remembers is being Levi Peres on a beach.'

'I feel like I'm watching myself, but that self isn't me. Is this what it's like being you?'

Her lips narrow in concentration, then crease in a sad smile. 'That's the one question we can never answer, isn't it? Even if I could perceive the electrical activity of every thought within your brain, I wouldn't know how it felt to be you.'

'How long do I have like this?'

'Your body will die some time in the next day or so. The nervous system is faltering – the war between Levi and the code has destroyed it. Some parts of you have already shut down. When the paralysis reaches your heart or your lungs, it will be over; even this memory of Levi will be gone.'

'If I'm just a memory, what am I doing here?'

'It's me being selfish. I wanted to talk to you, to spend some time just being, but after we came out of the prison, it looked like you were already gone. Yusuf thought of it. He said you always complained about going to the beach when you were a kid.'

'I see the sea . . .' The words escape in a whisper of memory. I came here with my family, before we fought, before everything fell apart. I remember my father sitting fully clothed in a deckchair, bare feet his only concession to the beach. I think my mother must have stayed in the car. 'I can't see her . . .'

'She's not here, Levi. It's just us. I brought you here so your body would remember who it was.'

'It remembers enough. I didn't get much right, did I, Clem?'

'No, you were an idiot.' She laughs like music.

'You know, sometimes, when I was alive, I'd feel like I was just acting in a play someone else wrote. I thought that would change when I left my family and started working for myself in the Old City, but it never did. Did you ever feel like that?'

'Yes, and no. I think that must be part of being human. I am a product of conscious decision, first a scientist's, then my own. In a sense I am less free, but the constraints of logic are transparent. It's more complicated now. I make choices, I believe I have agency, but it could be an illusion. I could be moved by external forces I cannot perceive – without being able to gauge my decisions by the criteria of hard logic I would not know.'

'What changed you?'

She looks down at herself. Sunlight through a cheap plastic visor colours her nose and cheeks green. 'It's this body, I think. It is an artificial creation, and at first I could only see it as a temporary home, but the interplay of a brain and its nervous system with the flesh is a strange seduction. I am wedded to it now; it is me, and with it come all of the strange human urges, the desire for love and meaning, and now, yes, I am moved by forces beyond the rational.'

'What forces? Where do they come from? Why do we feel like this?'

Clem gives me that funny look, like a technician diagnosing a fault. If you didn't know her, you'd think it was hostile, but it's the face of someone trying to understand. 'I don't know. I assumed they were just there – part of the package of being human.'

'But why is that?'

'Who's to say there should be a "why"?'

'There's always a "why".'

'For humans, yes. Not for the universe.'

'I don't care about the universe, Clem, I just want to know why I'm dead. I can't help feeling it's not random, like it's part of a bigger plan. Like, did it ever occur to you to ask why everybody seemed to want that Antikythera thing?'

Her head tilts in surprise at the question. 'Technology, power – the usual reasons humans want anything.'

'The Machine Cult thought it was their god . . .'

'They're deluded idiots who cut off their own limbs so they can pretend to be Machines; I could have told them that was a mistake.'

'But what is God? Isn't it like a plan, a will that orders everything? There's code in my head, Clem, and it's part of me. I think I understand now. I think the Antikythera Mechanism wanted to be stolen. I think it wanted all of this to happen.'

She laughs in a way that would have annoyed me when I was alive, but now I just think it's beautiful.

'No, it was dormant until I connected with it. All of this is my fault. That's why I brought you here – to say sorry.'

'Don't . . .'

'Why not? It's true, isn't it? I only know two people in the world, and I killed one of them. Without me sticking my nose in, that thing stays sleeping in a glass case until doomsday.' Her body shakes softly and tears flow into sparkling crescents on her cheeks.

'We don't know that though, do we? We don't know anything about it before the moment we took it out of the station locker.'

The technician look screws up her tear-streaked face for a moment, and then she relaxes, staring at the empty sky. 'How funny.'

'What?'

'You're suggesting I've committed the essential human error. I imagined myself to be central to everything, that I was driving events, but perhaps I was just a passenger.'

'Maybe, maybe not. I don't know whether it's the machine in my head, or whether being dead just forces a healthy re-evaluation of your own importance, but I'm starting to think you're the only thing in all of this that's not part of the plan.'

'What do you mean?'

'Think about it: if you were an ordinary schmuck like me, you'd already be dead or a vegetable, or a puppet, and so would anyone else who came near that thing – like a computer virus, but for people. Two thousand years ago, no one would have known what's going on, so it really is a god – Dagon, Jehovah, whatever. But you show up – you see it, Clem, and it doesn't want to be seen or known. You're where the plan breaks down.'

'I saw God?' Her confusion looks like pain.

'In the Talmud, seeing the Almighty is a death sentence – if you're lucky you might be left blind and crazy. Bottom line is, we never know what it is those people see, but there's nobody like you in the stories, Clem. You fucked everything up.'

'Well, I certainly did that.'

'In a good way, Clementine. In a good way.' Suddenly my head's too heavy for my neck and it falls forward. All I can see is the tide ebbing away to expose the sparkling sand between my knees. 'I can't move, can I?'

There's movement at the edge of my vision and Clementine appears in front of me, lifting my chin to look at her, blocking my view of the sea. She has her collar pulled up high, and that cheap visor shields her eyes from the sun and unwanted attention. Even on a grey day at the beach, she's hiding. That was what she wanted – to disappear, but I couldn't give her that. I can't give her anything now.

42.

Clementine

Levi's eyes close without conscious thought. He is gone. The ghost of him might still remain in some buried recess of animal brain, but that will expire when his breathing stops, which can only be hours away. His body is already stiff and unyielding in my grip as I carry him to the van where Yusuf waits, solicitous but scared.

'Did it work? Did he say anything?'

'It worked for a while. We didn't get the chance to say much. He said he was an idiot, which I think is as close to "sorry" as Levi Peres gets, even in death.'

Yusuf surrenders to a laugh, but then his jaw clenches, stopping a tremble before it can begin. 'So, what are we going to do with him now?' He looks around as if nervous of being spotted, but no one sane comes near Acre beach – still too full of mines from the wars.

'To the docks. Can you get me a boat?'

'I'll need to wave money at the owner if they start asking questions.'

'It's OK. Silas is paying.'

The van jerks to a stop on a cracked stone dock that looks old enough to have seen Phoenician trade. A confusion of orange and blue nets prevents us driving all the way to an Arab-style dhow. Black solar panels gleam darkly where its ancestors carried sail. Yusuf confines me to the van while he engages in noisy negotiation with the owner, an unenthusiastic fisherman who has some kind of business connection to the city's smugglers. I catch enough of the coarse street-Arabic to understand Yusuf's buying passage 'for Levi and a friend', which is true in a sense.

The chatter stops and two booming slaps on the van's side summon me into the light. The fisherman's face when he sees the state of Levi suggests little appreciation for the cleverness of Yusuf's semantics. He regards me with the mix of contempt and lust I've learned to ignore. I brace myself for the leering comment or the ungentle hand, but I am left alone. Either Yusuf's presence is a deterrent, or he senses something of the danger I present. The welling sickness of grief within me begs the catharsis of physical violence. At least, that's how it feels.

The dhow separates from the worn tyres lining the dockside like a parting kiss and edges noiselessly into the harbour's empty waters. The real fishermen have all been at sea for hours and will not return until dusk. As we pass the ancient breakwater and the ruins of Acre fall behind us, I become aware of the growing silence. The little port was quiet compared to the electromagnetic cacophony of Jerusalem, but the absence of noise in this empty sea is something new, the solitude restful yet terrifying. The flow of current from the solar sail to the dhow's batteries is a gentle murmur that fades to nothing in the sound of waves slapping against the hull.

'Where do you want to go?' The skipper addresses the question pointedly to Yusuf, who turns to me.

'Tell him to take us where the currents out to sea are strongest.'

The man's sun-beaten face wrinkles an acknowledgement without seeking male confirmation. No point arguing with an easy payday. Levi lies against me on the foredeck as if sunbathing. His breath comes softly as his body gives its last. Yusuf watches from the dhow's railing murmuring the Surah Ya-Sin, a prayer for the dying. He rests a casual arm on the white metal box containing our burden. I have told him of the danger it poses, but even with the evidence of Levi in front of us, it is a difficult threat for humans to comprehend.

Wailing gulls circle above us. A grey bird with a cruel beak, red-tipped as if dipped in blood, settles near the prow, eyes fixed patiently on Levi. Acre is beyond the horizon by the time our skipper cuts the engine and emerges from the dhow's little wheel-house.

'From here a four-knot current runs northwest to Cyprus, and then west to Crete. The sharks and the crabs will be done with him long before anyone gets close.'

Yusuf pales at the image of Levi's consumption, and grief surges like bile within me, but there is nowhere for it to go, so it settles, choking, in my chest and throat.

'Give it to me.' My words come out harsher than I intended but Yusuf either doesn't notice, or doesn't care. He stands and grips the box by its plastic handle, stepping cautiously across the deck as the dhow rolls gently in the waves. 'Hold him.' He kneels down to support Levi's slumped form and I take the box from his hand.

Even for me, the Antikythera Mechanism is heavy within its confining cage. My thumbs hesitate on the catches. Am I doing the right thing? Will this put the device beyond the reach of man? Or will it still exert some malign influence from the seabed, using frequencies I can't perceive? Would it not be better for me to destroy it? To smash it into a thousand pieces?

The truth is, I cannot know these answers; the workings of the device are still a mystery to me. I cannot know where in the ancient metal the will that binds it resides. Ultimately, the being within the Mechanism is as unknowable as any human. All I can do is trust to history. The sea protected mankind from the device for two thousand years before the series of astonishing coincidences which led to its recovery. To the sea it must return.

The catches click and the lid opens. Eight points of pain along my spine are the sharp tips of antennae emerging reflexively in response to the riot of transmissions pouring from the device. The wrath of a caged god is an assault of sensation, tainted data choking me with its brimstone reek. In sudden dreams I see buildings crumble and bodies reduced to desiccated husks. I see temples and sacrifice and the devotion of terrified peoples. I see no love.

My antennae quiver minutely in the hellish rainbow of frequencies pouring from the thing, heedless of my desperate urgings to withdraw. Panic flashes through me. I had thought myself inoculated against the Mechanism's influence through previous exposure, but it has effortlessly suborned my mechanical elements, my eyes, my augmented neural processor. Nothing except base human flesh responds to my will.

Blind, I reach into the box and grasp the device. Sharp edges of worn bronze and ancient submarine accretions bite the flesh of my palms as if it were a living, moving thing. No, it's false data, inputted through its spinal access to my nervous system. I'm fine.

I'm fine.

I stand up slowly, eyes still closed or useless, cautious of my traitorous sense of balance. My arm pulls back and extends in an arc that releases the weight of bronze from my fingers. The splash as it lands in the sea restores my sight. I am free of it. Some instinct drives me to the dhow's railing to watch it sink, but the Antikythera Mechanism is already gone, and all I see is the blue.

Acknowledgements

If you're reading this, you've more likely than not reached the end of my peculiar book. Thank you, whoever you are. Every writer's ambition is to share their stories, and you've helped to fulfil mine. Acknowledgements rarely make for gripping reading, but they are nonetheless a necessity. That one brief page represents an author's best opportunity to correct a lie perpetuated on every book cover – that the book is their work alone. So, I must list the most prominent of my co-conspirators.

I'd like to thank my wife, Bea, for giving me the space and time to write while we juggled work and children, and my kids, Lucas and Charlotte, for being patient while their father stared into space dreaming of imaginary worlds. My editor, Jack Renninson, has worked unbelievably hard on this book, and done an incredible job of shaping my strangeness into something ordinary humans can digest. My agent, Will Francis, has been the best guide any author could wish for as I navigated the uncharted (for me) waters of publication. This book only exists because he had a vision for it.

I also owe a debt to my fellow students at Curtis Brown Creative and the Faber Academy, who helped me grow as a writer. When I started this book, it didn't make an awful lot of sense, and I was reasonably convinced people would think I was mad (they still might). My tutors, Charlotte Mendelson and Helen Francis, helped me believe I might really have something to offer.

Finally, I must offer an apology of sorts. I have twisted all sorts of facts to shape my narrative, and those facts had to come from somewhere. I suspect Simon Sebag Montefiore might not approve of the use to which I put knowledge gained from his fabulous *Jerusalem: The Biography* but I still must acknowledge the debt. To the scholars of the Antikythera Mechanism whose work inspired the book, I can offer only the sincere hope that my flawed fiction might bring well-deserved attention to the fascinating science surrounding a genuine mystery.

Of course, no list of this nature can ever be comprehensive, but I am grateful to everyone who played a part in bringing this story to the page.

Greg Chivers
London, December 2018